Margie's Revenge

JAY TROTT

"These assurances of faith and endless Love,
The one all-consuming power, —
Will you make them with all your heart as well?"

TRUE NORTH

ACKNOWLEDGMENTS

Many thanks to Beth Trott and Linda Trott for their
invaluable assistance with preparing the manuscript.

*The story and characters depicted in this book
are fictitious. Any resemblance to real persons, living or
dead, is purely coincidental.*

IN THE MASTER'S CELL

HENRY DIDN'T REALIZE it was the devil because she looked so cute. She was little in a fetching way, pretty and petite, & she came to him with those dark dewy eyes, and it was all about "Poor Alicia" and what they were doing to Alicia was just awful and Alicia was one of the best they had ever seen and it was just jealousy and sexism and she and everyone looked up to him and couldn't he help her?—etc.

But it wasn't really about Alicia. He realized this later on. It was about her.

As far as Alicia goes, it was just your usual case of bare-knuckled university politics. There was this Great Big Thing going on in the department, this background noise you wouldn't know about unless you were in the middle of it and had been for some time, perhaps not even then; a titanic struggle between the forces of "professionalism"—the Credentialists, as Henry liked to call them—who wanted everyone to have a Ph.D. like themselves, and those who just wanted the students to be exposed to the best teaching and the best music and didn't really care about degrees or think they were important.

Henry Larson was definitely in the latter group. He was a world-class violinist and leader of the renowned chamber group Forum. He believed passionately in the art and the love of music, the Magical Moment which he and his fellow travelers were seeking, playing together with one intent, one spirit, one soul. Yes, Henry was all about the music and the love, which is why he didn't

1

usually allow himself to get dragged into departmental politics. He was also practical. Like most of his fellow professors, he needed the job. Chamber musicians aren't generally known for getting rich and they accrue a lot of expenses that other professors don't even have to think about.

In thirty-plus years on the faculty Henry had managed to arrange things so as not to get drawn into a single political battle. He would sit through faculty meetings with a pleasant smile on his face as if he were in tune with what was going on when in fact he wasn't listening at all—his mind was a thousand miles away—caught up in the *Trout* quintet or whatever; that was the real reason why he was smiling. In front of students he was hot; with his chamber group he was on fire, playing Brahms or Beethoven; but with his colleagues he was as bland as vanilla pudding, keeping a neutral expression while clinging tenaciously to the thought of the little remuneration that appeared in his bank account every month and not allowing his passions to be stirred by the Lilliputian machinations of his coworkers.

The thing was he knew his own danger. He knew how passionate he could be, underneath all the apparent calm and nonchalance and cultured polish, a threat to his own well-being. He had learned this lesson the hard way in his first teaching position at another school many years ago where he became outraged on behalf of some now-forgotten cause and reaped the whirlwind. So now he was careful to bury his passion. He would sit there trying to daydream, and they looked at him and didn't know quite what to think because they didn't know what he was thinking—which was the whole point.

To tell the truth they were a little afraid of him. Not many of them were performance artists—what one normally thinks of when one hears the word "musician"—and none of them had achieved his degree of notoriety. Okay, we'll just say it; they were jealous. Some almost hated him when he wasn't there and it was announced he was in Prague or Paris for yet another concert tour or workshop. They hated him because they were stuck in New York, and not even the good New York but up in the sticks, and no one would ever invite them to Prague or Paris—and they knew it.

Anyway, Henry buried all that passion and sat there all those years because the job was the thing that enabled him to do what he loved to do. He didn't have to go the commercial route as so many of his friends from Julliard had done. He didn't have to try to sell himself to dilettantes who wouldn't know good music if it came and knocked them on the head and who got their opinions from clueless newspaper reviews and program notes written by semi-desperate publicity agents.

The job was good to him. It was a bargain a lover could make with reality. He knew his stuff and had tenure. They let him try out new pieces on campus with his ensemble and gave him a reasonable schedule with some appreciation and theory in addition to his string students and workshops. Let's face it; he had a pretty good life there. He thought about old friends who were killing themselves to play in the five-thousandth performance of *Phantom* or whatever and grabbing any gig they could lay their hands on just to make ends meet, and he felt pretty fortunate. He had a nice little house. He and Gabrielle were comfortable, at least as far as the living space was concerned. He was content.

They were perhaps not perfectly content with each other, but that was a different story. That was a long story and a complicated story and it began when they were at Julliard and their mentors decided they needed to be matched up for the sake of their careers. They were matched, but they were not necessarily happy. They both had careers—separately—and they lived together—also separately. They did not quarrel. They never really quarreled. It wasn't that kind of relationship. Actually they had become pretty good friends down through the years. But first and foremost their marriage was a business arrangement, self-consciously made, and they approached it in a businesslike manner.

So all right, maybe that's partly why poor Henry was a little more susceptible to Margie's charms than he might otherwise have been. Margie was—well—hot. No, really. She didn't look like a professor at all. Her male colleagues all agreed she was hot, when they were out of earshot of the harpies, and Henry could not disagree. He did not agree either—he did not indulge in that kind of classless talk—but he would just sit there and smile when one of the boys went off on, you know, a tangent.

He was quite flattered when she bundled into his office on that bright but frozen February day. It had never happened before, the pretty little Margie coming into his lair. He was sitting at his desk looking over abysmal student papers and there was a timid knock on the door and then there she was, walking in all by herself, and he had to pinch himself because to tell the truth there were times when he had imagined such a thing happening, idly as it were, even though he was a world-famous classical musician and honored professor who was often seen wearing tails and looking very sophisticated, for things are not always what they seem. Anyway, she had come to get his help—would he help her please? She looked up to him so much—everybody did—he was such a great musician and such a Presence in the department and an institution at the school. She hated to bother him with mundane things, but there was Alicia and what "they" were doing to her, and it was just awful.

Let's get one thing straight right now: it *was* awful. He knew what was going on. He didn't have to be told. They were trying to get rid of her—the hardasses, the little people with big titles and big honors and important committee responsibilities and impressive but meaningless CVs. They had let her into their little club because she had a stellar background in orchestra circles and they figured why not take a chance? Besides, she was a woman, and Hispanic to boot. But the thing was she was a mere M.A. Okay, so it was from a good school, but it still wasn't the *sine qua non*, the Ph.D. It wasn't "where the department wanted to go" as it sought to establish its credentials for the university establishment. So the Credentialists got together and they stirred each other up and they got hot. They didn't realize the situation when they hired her—she was whisked in when they weren't paying attention—they had to get her out of there—she made them look bad.

Boy, did she ever! Somehow she got her grasping little hands on the orchestra when one of the trolls wasn't looking and did a concert at the end of October that would knock your socks off. It was challenging music—Bach and Schubert and Brahms—not the kind of pabulum Malcolm Faust, the regular orchestra conductor, normally did—and there was precision and true pianissimos and fortissimos and changes in tempi and an unusual grasp of the gestures of the music and sheer magic coming out of her wand. In twenty-five years it was the first time Henry had heard the orchestra sound like they were making music; except when he was conducting—but he was too modest to count that. Under Alicia they took on a challenge and delivered at a high level of artistry.

This was her second, fatal mistake: showing up the grandees who sat on Reputation and churned out the same warmed-over spit year after year. The hall was electric that night and some people knew it and the fraternity of the mediocre died inside; and then they came back stronger and more dangerous than ever, like Lord Voldemort, like the vampires they really were, just in time for Halloween, looking for some warm blood to suck. They themselves did not have warm blood; perhaps that was why they were bloodsuckers. Their blood was cold and their music was cold and this distaff upstart was not to be tolerated—"Not on my watch!"

Oh, they couched it in the best intentions. They always did. Maybe they even believed this stuff themselves. Who knows? Self-preservation is a funny thing. What set off the inquisition was a couple of whippersnappers from the viola section whining that Ms. Baptiste was a "slave driver." Apparently she earned this encomium by requiring them to be disciplined and show up knowing the music, unlike Malcolm, who believed in letting kids be kids. Also it was whispered that her bedside manner left something to be desired. She could be a bit brisk with them when they didn't perform to her standards. "Mean," even.

The Fraternity took up this whining and carried it on their shoulders to the city gates. Something was seriously wrong with the newest member of the adjunct faculty. She was expecting too much. She did not understand what kind of pressure these poor students were under. She was acerbic, not nurturing. She was treating them like professionals. She was Changing the Way Things Were Done, and why? To what end? To make tuition-paying students miserable? To show how tough she was? This storyline almost made Henry gag the first time he heard it. The poor suffering aggrieved students! What a joke.

First of all, if they gave back just twenty percent of the time they spent partying and hanging out and playing hearts they could probably memorize the entire chamber oeuvre of Schubert in one semester. Second, they were music majors, for God's sake! They were *supposed* to work hard on the music and get it right. Also they needed to get over themselves. These were people of modest talent and no appreciable accomplishment who had been coddled their entire lives and told how great they were and moved along from level to level as if they were actually moving along and had not leveled out long ago, probably somewhere back in tenth grade. Not a single one of them could get into Julliard. They should consider themselves lucky they were even getting a music degree from a recognized university.

Then the second wave of kvetching began. It was about the credentials, of course. They held back on this one all semester, keeping their powder dry, but now they could not help themselves. Alicia was incompetent to teach at the university level because she didn't have enough training. The faculty should have stuck to their guns and insisted on a doctorate, as they had agreed to do. Instead they had let another substandard specimen creep in, and now she was Causing Problems.

Who was it coming from? Malcolm and his gang, of course. Malcolm was not a very good conductor, by Henry's lights. He was not even a musician. He could not play an instrument credibly, as if he knew what he was doing; Alicia played several. His performances were pedestrian, uninspired. The tempos never changed. Largo, andante, allegro, presto—it didn't seem to matter. It all came out sounding the same. But somehow—Henry was not quite sure how—Malcolm had cast a spell over the campus and the entire community. Malcolm was the one winning the prestigious university awards. Malcolm was the one the local papers came to when they needed someone from the university to help them look artsy. Malcolm was the one whom the students supposedly loved.

To Henry he was the emperor with no clothes. He was a good-looking guy, tall, blonde, always dressed to kill, glib, extremely personable when he wanted to be, very good with words, very good at making people think he knew things he didn't really know. Because he didn't really know them, not in Henry's view. He knew the buzzwords but he didn't know Music. It was all a show. And this was why he had to put poor Alicia in her place. She showed what a truly gifted conductor could do with the orchestra—and there was poor Malcolm, naked, his preposterous pretensions exposed. Only they weren't exposed, were they? Henry and his friends saw it—it was blindingly obvious to them—but who else? The truth was most people didn't know the difference between real music-making and Malcolm's kind of empty show. And that included most of the administration and even some of the music faculty.

Malcolm would get up there on the podium in his beautiful tails looking quite beautiful and he would swoop and he would look expressive waving his arms and he would smile at his charges and they smiled back in a knowing way right in the middle of the performance because they were Sharing a Moment and wasn't it so charming? This relationship they had? The middle-aged women would swoon and say "Isn't he just like Toscanini?" And to tell the truth some of the men would swoon, too. This was why Alicia had to be crushed. She threatened to break the spell of this glorious illusion. She was unpretentious and not even much to look at and eschewed theatricality and barely moved her hands on the podium, like Jochum, but she made real music. People like Henry knew the difference, people who were respected, and they were talking about it. All the time. And for this unforgivable sin she had to be punished.

Now Malcolm may or may not have been a real musician, but like a good child of Oz he did have something Henry didn't have: a doctorate. He had been using this impressive degree as leverage against Henry ever since he arrived at the school fifteen years ago—subtly of course, never openly. But now he was using it openly against Alicia in order to protect himself from wagging tongues. If they wanted to be a great music department, they had to have standards, and in a university the Ph.D. *was* the standard. They had let Alicia in without one, and now they could clearly see where it led.

Henry just had to laugh when he heard this kind of talk. They were supposed to be a music school, dedicated to the art of music. Having a doctorate didn't have anything to do with that. People with doctorates weren't necessarily any smarter or more gifted or musical than people without them. It simply meant they had stayed in school longer. It meant having the fortitude to endure insufferable graduate courses with insufferable droning on and on by pseudo-intellectuals who often do not know what they are talking about. And it usually meant going to some big state school where they pass out Ph.D.'s like candy. Processing centers, Henry called them, though not when anybody from the school was listening.

It went to the very source of his frustration, the witch hunt they were perpetrating against Alicia. He had been there for over thirty years basically going nowhere and not being paid attention to, keeping his mouth shut and smiling thinly during faculty meetings, being passed over, by and around in the department hierarchy—

and he was the only one in the whole mad bunch of them who was an actual musician! He was the only one who had earned the exalted designation of artist; who knew and understood music; who had a national and international reputation; who had played in all the best halls and with many of the most famous classical musicians in the world.

He alone in the dreary stonefaced department of the dreary stonefaced state university had these credentials—and yet to the Credentialists it was almost like he was invisible! The irony was not lost on him. It couldn't be when so many of his friends insisted on pointing it out. Every now and then the department potentates would lose their rudder and let him conduct the orchestra, usually when Malcolm had better things to do or was on sabbatical, and that was always a big mistake because he was a passionate conductor, invested and skilled, who inspired the students to heights they did not know they could achieve; and when they played Tchaikovsky or Grieg under him it was more like a revolution than a concert, an event, and there were screams and whistles from the audience, even between movements, and people sensed Something Happening.

Of course they wouldn't ask him again for years afterward. Not until they forgot or got careless again. They wanted to push him aside, push him down. Not consciously, perhaps, but in actuality. He suspected he made them uncomfortable. After all, they were supposed to be music professors, but he was an actual musician. He knew what they were pretending to know. He didn't try to make them uncomfortable, by the way. Far from it. He was a loving guy by nature, a magnanimous guy and very supportive of others. But they were not supportive. That was not the word he would have used to describe the slugpit of jealousy and nitpicking that constituted his workplace. Angry, perhaps. Depressed.

It didn't matter how supportive he was, it didn't matter how generous he was with his time or his praise or his attentiveness to people who didn't really deserve it; this positivity was never or rarely reflected back to him. For years and decades it had gone on like this, Henry pouring out his life-force for them every day while they sent iron in return. And then it was less and less every day because he began to feel worn out by it all. There were too many hurts and too many people he didn't really want to see. He began to look for ways to avoid being there. Funny thing, they resented that too. The same people who resented him when he was around also resented him when he was not around. They decided he was a "snob." He was a prima donna. He wasn't a team player.

All these years he had gone all around the world and he had played the great halls to glowing reviews and made critically acclaimed CDs—and in his own department it was like none of it ever happened. It didn't seem to matter how much he did or accomplished; they could never be impressed. They whispered about him behind his back. Even people he counted among his friends couldn't always resist the temptation to use their devious little muscle in an attempt to cut him down to size. There were betrayals. There was damage and awful things that could not be taken back or forgotten, no matter how hard he tried. He believed in the rule of seventy times seven, but sometimes it was too much for him. He was only human, after all. He was not a man of steel.

And don't you know they had taken it out of him over the years, piece by piece, his patience and his sunshine, piece by piece they tore it out of him and left him feeling older and less sanguine but not wiser—because he still let them get to him; he still allowed himself to be hurt. Picture him pock-marked in your mind. Picture him sitting in his beloved rocker in his office with pieces of his face gone missing, and pieces of his soul, and you will be inside his head, because that is just how he felt from time to time. Especially on cold and desolate and sunless February afternoons in the depths of winter. He'd even had a dream about it once. He reached up to touch his face and a chunk of it fell away on his fingertips. It took him several minutes of waking-up horror to convince himself this was just a dream.

Anyway, Margie came in and she sat down and she smiled and he wondered what this was all about, because she had barely spoken to him in the past, certainly not alone like this, only at faculty gatherings, and then only fleetingly; so it must be something important. But she came in and she sat on the edge of the chair and she seemed a little edgy, and he was all attention. He was hers.

"You're probably wondering what I'm doing here," she said with a nervous laugh.

"I thought maybe you came to say hello," he said with his well-polished charm, giving nothing away, putting on his Wise Old Man face, wise old veteran of the department and sage and confidante—and careful! Little did he know he was playing right into her hands.

"Well, to tell you the truth this is hard for me."

"Hard? Why?"

"To come in here like this. I mean, you're practically a legend."

"Oh, come on."

"No—really. This is like the Inner Sanctum. Look at me—I'm shaking. I'm so nervous."

"There's absolutely no reason to be nervous. I don't bite," he replied laughing, although he kind of wanted to.

"That's the effect you have on people. You don't realize it, but you do. Anyway, I had to come talk to you. I'm kind of upset about something. And you may be the only one who can understand."

Hmm, this was interesting. "I'm flattered."

"So you know what they're trying to do to Alicia, right?"

"Not really."

"You don't know? You haven't heard?"

"Well, I guess I've heard some rumblings," he confessed. "To tell you the truth, I've been focusing on our concert at Alice Tully next week, so I haven't been playing too much attention to what's going on in the department." (Okay, so he let himself indulge in a little name-dropping with this pretty girl.)

"You heard about the famous complaint from the students?"

"I understand some of the little dears were unhappy about having to know the music."

"Right. Well, now they're trying to get rid of her. Malcolm and Jeff and the rest of them."

"Seriously? Get rid of her?"

"Yes! They were talking about it at the last department meeting, which you didn't go to."

"I was doing a workshop."

"Yes, I know. They knew, too. Which is why it was on the agenda. They knew you wouldn't be there."

"Probably true," Henry said with a sigh. "So what are they saying?"

"Oh, it's the usual nonsense. First of all they're saying she's too hard on the kids. She's trying to turn us into Eastman and we're just a teachers' school."

"The usual. So we should aspire to be mediocre."

"Well, *they* are mediocre, so maybe that's why it's so important to them."

Henry looked at her in surprise. This was their first real conversation and already she was making a good deal of sense. It was gratifying to have others in the department who felt the same way he did about these things, especially about Malcolm, who had become his arch-enemy. It made him feel less isolated. He who usually played things close to the vest with people he didn't know very well surprised himself by agreeing with her.

"That's exactly why. They don't want anyone in the department to excel because they are incapable of excelling themselves. But is that all they're saying? Because I don't think you can't get rid of someone just because she hurt your feelings by doing a good job."

"No, they went into the whole degree thing, too. You know, 'she only has an M.A.' and all that. Although an M.A. where she went to school is like a Ph.D. for them. They really have an obsession with it. Strange, though, there seem to be certain exceptions to the rule—like Randy."

"Sure. If you're one of the boys you get a pass. Or if you're cool and you teach jazz percussion. So what else? Is that it?"

"I guess so. It's funny—saying it to you here, it doesn't sound like much. But they really are talking about getting rid of her."

"And where is Bertram on all this?"

"He didn't say a word. He just listened."

"That's what they call 'leadership.' I'm very disappointed in him. I thought he would do better."

"Well, I can't tell if he actually agrees with them. He doesn't run things with a heavy hand, like Malcolm did when he was the chair. But he kind of agrees with them just by not saying anything—if you know what I mean."

"Yes, because no one else spoke up."

"Right," she said, and he thought she blushed, but he forgave her. "The truth is, people are afraid to speak up. If you don't have tenure you're not going to speak up against them, not unless you're crazy or suicidal, and if you do have tenure it's just not worth it, because you know Malcolm's going to go running to the dean."

"'Running.' That's a good way of putting it. They have the entire department cowed with this professionalism garbage. It's the never-ending putsch that seems to keep reviving itself, no matter who the chairman is."

"I think you should be the chair."

"Oh sure," he scoffed. "Like my master's degree is any more impressive than Alicia's. Besides, who needs that kind of misery?"

"But you agree it isn't fair?"

"Of course it isn't fair. It's ridiculous. She did one of the best concerts I have ever heard here in all my thirty years. She obviously knows what she's doing. But that's the problem. She's too good for them. She probably would have been better off doing poorly, as strange as that sounds."

"They're just jealous. Malcolm doesn't like her getting all the attention and good feedback. He's afraid she's going to take his job away."

"No, that's not what he's afraid of. He's afraid of her taking his shine. He's built up this thing here—I don't know how—where everybody puts him on a pedestal and they give him the 'Teacher of the Year' awards and he goes into the Distinguished Conductors program and gets sent all over the state to spread his poison to unsuspecting high-school students. Of course he doesn't want another conductor to do well. It exposes him."

Margie's mission was successful, far beyond her wildest dreams. The burr had been set and it wouldn't let go. She walked out of his office smiling and then Bertram walked by and Henry saw the quizzical look on his face. He shook his head because he knew what was coming next. It would go around the whole department. Margie had been alone with him in his office.

WHETHER TO TAKE ARMS

WHEN SHE WAS GONE Henry tried to collect himself. Was he in pieces? Well, yes he was, in a manner of speaking. He was astonished at what had just happened. Not the news Margie delivered—he had been afraid of something like this from rumblings he'd overheard—but his reaction to it. Normally Henry kept himself buttoned down. He rarely gave much away, never to strangers. He might perchance engage in blunt talk with Richie, his only close friend in the department, the only one he fully trusted, or with Matt from the philosophy department, or with his ensemble or friends outside of school. He was not above venting his frustrations and longsuffering at the hands of the politicians in the department.

But with someone he didn't know? Really? He shocked himself. He rehashed some of the things he said to Margie and was shocked by them. There was something about her that seemed to draw it out of him, the angst he was normally so successful at concealing; this pretty, soft-spoken, adorable girl sitting there in her blue dress and smiling at him. But it was more than that. He was flattered by the attention from Margie, but that wasn't the only reason why he felt his heart pounding. It was the story itself, the outrageous assault on Alicia. And maybe it was the place he was at.

Later on, looking back, he could see it was the perfect storm. First of all there were the health problems he'd been having lately, especially this strange fluttering in his heart, which he blamed on stress. He'd never had health problems before. Then there was the frozen February weather, no end in sight to a bruising long winter. There were the ongoing slights and iniquities from his colleagues, the drip drip drip of living in a world sick with emulation. There was Margie, who was pretty and flattering and basically too much for him. There was his age and a certain existential anxiety he had felt coming on for some time. But most of all there was the thing they were doing to Alicia, smiling Malcolm and his friends; so unfair, so petty, and worst of all right in his face.

It burned him up every time he thought of it, which is why he had been trying not to think of it at all. He wasn't Alicia's friend— hardly even knew her—but it burned him up that they were unable or unwilling to acknowledge how good she was, how musical, what a miracle she had pulled off with a bunch of students who were basically clueless and thirsty for what she could offer them, whether they realized it or not; the best thing that had happened to them and to the department in many years. She was a little like him, Henry thought, a natural musician who could not help stirring up envy when all she was trying to do was to make music. To be condemned for being too musical! In a music department, of all places! It was infuriating.

And then there was the thing about her only having an M.A. This was galling because it was personal. It was like they were using her to attack him, so unfair to them both. No, he didn't have a doctorate, and he had no desire to obtain one. Was this really such a crime for a musician? Would it make him more of an artist to have one? Help him to play his violin? Could a doctorate save him when he was sitting up in front of fifteen hundred people and had to lead Forum through some devilishly difficult pieces and stay on point for a ninety-minute concert? Would it make him a better teacher, more knowledgeable about his instrument or the orchestra or the history of music? He already knew more about these things than the Ph.D.'s in the department. He had lived them his whole life. They knew them only from books.

Yes, he had been trying very hard not to think about Alicia. Every time he did he became enraged—and he didn't know if he could afford to be enraged. They were so blatant about it, openly criticizing her for no reason, making cracks about her in the lounge and everywhere else, people who could not begin to do what she could do. It was obvious that they wanted her out of there, and they would probably get away with it too. Alicia was just an adjunct and nobody stood up for them. Malcolm was a smooth talker. He would tell his lies and twist the facts like he always did and the administration would believe him, not necessarily because they were evil people, but because there was nothing in it for them. It was far easier to take his lying and manipulation at face value than to try to stir the surface and see what lay underneath. After all, they were there for their careers, not for truth and justice.

In the past Henry would have absorbed Margie's news about Alicia, no matter how painful; he would have ingested it into a special reducing area he had created in a corner of his mind where he ground up hard emotions to get rid of them. He was an old hand at grinding up bad news and making it go away, even if it meant acid reflux and indigestion, even if it meant a fluttering heart and sleepless nights. But something was different this time. A week went by and then two weeks but he could not grind up this upsetting news. Life went on as usual. He taught his classes; he tutored his violin students; he rehearsed with Forum; he practiced and worked as hard as always. But inside a storm was brewing. He tried to blow it off course but it kept on coming.

He would see the conspirators in the hallway, smirking as usual, and he would burn inside. He was tired of their supercilious smirking. He wanted to smack them. He made his hands into fists when they walked by. They were not musicians, by his lights. He even wondered if they could teach. Malcolm was popular with students and won awards, but that was mostly for pandering, as far as Henry could tell. The students had no way of grading him objectively because they did not know what or how they should be taught. They were lazy and liked teachers who let them be lazy and didn't challenge them; or better yet, who had circus tricks for making them feel like they were being challenged when actually they were not.

They were dilettantes. And there were an awful lot of them in the university setting. It was entirely possible, for example, to be a world-famous Shakespeare professor at an Ivy League school, a historian who knows all the obscure references in the plays and everything there is to know about the social and political history of the time, and still be woefully ignorant of Shakespeare. The essence of him, the spirit. And the same was true of music. Malcolm would dazzle his young charges with theory and ornate descriptions of the chord progressions in the *Eroica*, for instance, as if such knowledge gave him a deep understanding of the music or even occult power. But Henry knew Beethoven didn't give a damn about theory. The great composers did not use theory to compose. The theory was based on them; not they on the theory. To give the impression that they were theorists was sheer hubris or wishful thinking.

Still, these were the kinds of people who were running things now. Music to them was a set of Standards and Practices. You had to do this with the bow or articulation or you had to sing the vowel this way or do the lift that way. They used these standards and practices in an attempt to make themselves seem like legitimate academics and masters of music; to put themselves in an elite club and keep others out; to give themselves high grades and mark down those of whom they did not approve. As far as Henry was concerned, it was all garbage. They didn't seem to understand that the standards and practices had come after the fact and were nothing more than a means to an end. True artists knew who other artists were and didn't need any rules to tell them. By the time they managed to become artists they were a rule unto themselves.

For Henry, great music was not about rules. It was about love and generosity of spirit. And for this strange belief they crucified him. They themselves were neither generous nor loving, as they showed when they talked about him behind his back and called him a freak, an anomaly, an anachronism. In the future there wouldn't be any more like him. There would be real professionals who were disciplined and who honored Academic Standards and didn't go around spouting pseudo-spiritual nonsense about love or vague generalities about "art." Henry had to laugh when he heard things like this. Disciplined! They had no idea what it meant to be disciplined, to prepare a Brahms Piano Quintet for a concert or to be on tour and play ten dates in fifteen days.

But if Henry was such a non-entity in the department, such a pariah, then why did Margie come to him? He thought he knew why. He was the only one who could help her friend. He was an outsider in some ways, but in other ways he was the ultimate insider. He was the most powerless person in the department and yet at the same time the most powerful. He rarely spoke up in faculty meetings—but everyone was wondering what he was thinking. He made no attempt to play politics—but other staff members looked up to him instinctively, especially the quiet ones, the timid ones. Henry had won far more battles than could have been expected over the years just by being who he was.

Margie had come to him! Not to anyone else. Her confidence in him was flattering. She saw him as her champion and protector. He ran into her now and then in the hallway or lounge and she always gave him a knowing look. It was a sign of the bond between them. But what about Gabrielle? Why didn't he talk to her about the situation with Alicia? He saw her every night and every morning. They slept in the same bed and ate at the same table. She taught at a university. She knew all about the politics and always had good advice for him. But for some reason he was loath to talk to Gabrielle about Alicia and her tale of woe—or most of all about the dark-haired Margie.

Perhaps we should pause and say a word about Henry and Gabrielle and the unusual relationship they had. They did not marry in the traditional Western way, for love. There was no real spark between them, as far as Henry could discern, except maybe a musical spark. In school they had been in ad-hoc chamber groups together and orchestra. Gabrielle's brother Karl was the cellist in the ensemble Henry was even then coalescing, the innovative flex group that eventually became Forum Chamber Ensemble and then just "Forum" as it went on to international fame. For these and so many other excellent reasons, their mentors seemed intent on pushing Henry and Gabrielle together. They respected the elders, the gurus, so they allowed themselves to be pushed. They did not push back.

The elders meant well, but they underestimated Henry's passion. They thought, because he was such an accomplished player at an early age, so poised and mature, that he was singled out for Apollo and not for Eros. They tried to turn him into a modern version of the castrati—desex him for the sake of art and music, as it were. This was not their conscious intention, but it was the net effect of their meddling. They found him a nice young woman to marry, a high-minded girl who did not have sex on her mind but was serious and proper and dedicated to making music. To their way of thinking, this was the best way to protect him from certain destabilizing forces in the world.

They thought they were doing him a favor, but he was not like them. The same fire that thrilled them in his playing and made them starry-eyed when they thought about his future also made him ill-suited to the type of marriage they had in mind. Sure, they were going to let him sleep with the girl. She wouldn't mind. After all, they were married, right? But other than that it was supposed to be all about the music. The marriage was mostly for convenience.

This arrangement seemed to work out just fine for Gabrielle. She really did seem to be turning into the music nun they wanted her to be and even took to wearing gray as a sign of it. But Henry was no nun. The result of a loveless marriage was entirely too predictable for him, and probably for almost any male: he dried up in the marriage bed without really drying up. Yes, there was lovemaking, as prescribed, but it was not of the passionate kind. Over the years it dwindled and then it pretty much stopped. Henry was embarrassed by his desires. It was like touching a shrine, reaching out tentatively to touch her back in a question that was never answered, since she seemed to want *him* to answer it; and what she really wanted, he suspected, was for him to leave her alone.

As he became more widely known, albeit in somewhat rarefied circles, he was surprised to notice that women seemed quite attracted to him. All kinds of women, in sundry places, after sundry concerts and even at university receptions. Had he suddenly become more handsome? If so, his mirror didn't tell the story. These women were not like Gabrielle. Their attraction seemed much more elemental, warm. To tell the truth he'd been tempted to succumb sometimes as Gabrielle grew more distant sexually, but he used the discipline of hard work to stay honest even when he was touring the world with Forum. True, sometimes there had been nights of near madness alone in his bed in hotels in foreign capitals—but he had never broken his marriage vows.

These considerations complicated his desire to talk to Gabrielle about the situation with Alicia. On the very night Margie came to him he was standing in the kitchen with his wife of thirty-five years, shuffling through some papers for an upcoming concert program while she cut scallions for the sauce for their poached salmon.

"So how was your day?" she said in her somewhat flat way.

"Oh, fine," he lied. "Busy, but manageable. Yours?"

"My day wasn't bad, but I can't say as much for poor Karen. Hibbard is still on her case, still making life miserable for her. The whole choral department is in an uproar and nobody's doing anything about it. Nobody tries to stop him because they're all afraid of him. He's a strange man. You never know what's going to come out of his mouth."

"That's been going on for a long time."

"I don't know how she stands it. She's so good, she does so much for the students. For him to treat her like this, year in and year out—so abusive. I don't know how she can take it."

"She's strong."

"Not that strong. Not really. I know you've said that before, but it's mostly a façade. You don't understand—you're not a woman. She tries to look strong because she doesn't have a choice. She has to protect herself. But she is suffering all the time. She tells me. We talk about it. She would love to get out of there if she could, but she feels she's too old."

"That's probably why he's after her. She's not young anymore and he senses a weakness."

"Oh yes, that's exactly what it is. He's completely pitiless. He sees her as a victim, and that's why he goes after her. It's her very weakness that attracts him, like a vulture."

Gabrielle paused to take a sip of her wine and the conversation ended. Henry almost went on. He wanted to go on—the story with Malcolm and Alicia was similar in many ways. He was trying to decide whether or not to get involved, whether to do Margie's bidding. It was a difficult decision, and he trusted his wife to be objective. Gabrielle always gave good advice. She was protective of him and always had his best interests in mind. But he didn't say anything. The words were on his lips but something stopped him. Maybe he didn't want to trouble her with something so silly. Or he was afraid she would try to convince him to stay out of it—when he was hoping to do something for Margie.

A DECISION MUST BE MADE

S O THERE HE WAS WALKING THE HALLS of the music building and completely consciously looking for Margie now, for "chance" encounters with the dark-eyed charmer. He knew he was. He never went out of his office very much when he was at the school, usually he was there only to teach private students and do grading and lesson planning; but now he found himself going to the coffee machine or the copier or the bathroom or whatever—basically making up things to do that took him out into the highways and byways—always with an eye out for the wee wonder.

Why didn't he just go to her office and return the call? Come on, too blatant. He did not go to other people's offices unless he had official business to transact. It was not his style. He went to Richie's office from time to time, but that was different. Richie was his friend. And even then he rarely went—four or five times a semester, at most. Usually Richie came to him.

Margie did not return to him and he did not go to her, which left him—exactly where? He wasn't sure. There was a department meeting coming up at the end of the month, a chance to talk about Alicia. Should he try to defend her? It seemed like the right thing to do, the gallant thing, that much was certain. Over the years there had been many ridiculous things and many personal things, many outrages and many things that were dull and pointless; but to Henry's mind this was the first case in a long time where the politics and the meanness were so blatant. Could he let it stand? Should he?

He decided to drop in on Richie for a temperature check.

"So I guess you know about this thing with Alicia and the Nazis," Henry said in a joshing tone that was completely fake. "Nazis" was the term applied loosely to those in the department who had totalitarian enthusiasms and a love of the concept of the well-oiled machine.

"Oh!—that whole thing is terrible, embarrassing. How can they get away with that? If anybody should be invited back, it's her."

"So your information is the same as mine. They are trying to get rid of her."

"Of course! What else? We can't have somebody who's good on staff; that would upset the equilibrium. Now supposedly there were 'problems' with her concert. Malcolm's running around saying there was too much contrast and too much vibrato in the Bach and something or other about a portamento in the Brahms. I didn't realize he was such a big fan of the Authentic Performance crowd."

"Oh please, he doesn't know the first thing about that. He doesn't know what Harnoncourt and the others had in mind. I know Nick Harnoncourt personally. I've talked to him about this. He was in a completely different place from where they are."

"Not interested in the 'rules' per se."

"No, he never was. But that's what these people hear. It's another way for them to get their little hands around the throat of the music and hold onto their power."

"Cover up their deficiencies, you mean. It's too bad, but they do seem determined to go through with it. Apparently Malcolm has been canvassing people pretty hard to make sure they have the votes. That's what I'm told, anyway. He didn't talk to me."

"No, of course not. He's too much of a coward. But are people actually listening to this crap?"

"Can't say. He must have some of them on his side or he wouldn't have taken it this far. He's not the kind of guy who goes out on a limb. The thing is this could get her blackballed. That's what worries me. If word gets around that her stint here was somehow subpar, it could cause a lot of trouble down the road."

"But that's just it," Henry said in frustration. "That concert wasn't subpar. There was nothing subpar about it, not even remotely. Believe me, I know. I've conducted that orchestra. I know what she did and how hard it is to do it."

"You know that, and I know that, but apparently Malcolm doesn't know it. Or if he does, he's not telling. And people listen to him. I know it seems ridiculous, but they do. He's the 'orchestra guy,' and according to him she's not making the grade, so now this is the hot buzz around the department."

"I'd like to grade him—with a grader," Henry fumed. "I hear he's bringing up the stupid M.A. thing again. These people really need to get over themselves. Mozart didn't go to college."

"Mozart had talent. We have a bunch of Salieris."

This conversation served its purpose. It confirmed Margie's claim that the inner circle was determined to get Alicia out of there. He found out what their excuse was, and it was infuriating. There was absolutely nothing wrong with Alicia's concert. It made his blood boil that they were claiming otherwise. And Richie brought up something he had not even contemplated—the potential impact on her career. He was right; it was a black mark that could not be wiped out. It might even drive her out of the profession. Henry had seen it happen to other talented people. This he could not tolerate. He would not allow them to ruin her. He decided to break his iron rule and defend her against these ridiculous charges.

Henry was fired up—but the meeting was still two weeks away! He wanted to do something now, before he saw Claudius on his knees and lost his resolve. But what? There didn't seem to be any point in going to Bertram; he was on their side. Then he had a brilliant idea. He would go see Camilla DiCaprio, the new dean. He had never gone to see the dean before. Maybe it was time he did. After all, someone's career was hanging in the balance.

He called her office and was given an appointment right away, which seemed like a good omen. And he was very warmly received.

"Dr. Larson! So nice to see you," Camilla said, rising quickly from her desk and offering her hand with a smile as he walked in.

Henry blanched at the "doctor" part but didn't bother to correct her. "Yes, I thought it was about time I dropped by for a visit, now that you're settled in."

"Settled in! It's been almost a year."

He blinked. "Has it been that long? Time flies."

"It does indeed. But I'm so glad to see you. I'm a big fan of yours. Heard your concert last month at Cornell and was blown away by it."

"Oh—that was a good night," Henry said modestly. "We have sort of a following up there because of Michel, you know, the violist. He teaches there."

"I have family in Ithaca. That's how I wound up going. Anyway, it was a great concert. But what can I do for you?"

"Well, I was thinking more of something you can do for yourself. We have an interesting situation in the department. Or maybe I should call it an opportunity. It's one of the adjuncts."

"So many of them. Which one did you have in mind?"

"There's a gifted young lady by the name of Alicia Baptiste. Very talented, intuitive. Would be a great asset to the department, no question about it. I know. I've seen a lot of these people come and go over the years, and she's one of the special ones. She gave a wonderful concert last fall—Bach and Brahms. Brought down the house. Perhaps you heard about it."

"No, I don't believe I did," she replied, keeping up the same bright smile that had greeted his appearance. "Tell me."

"Well, what can one say? It was superb. When someone makes music like that, words become meaningless. I was impressed, especially for someone so young. It was like a breeze of fresh air had blown through the department, a new way of looking at things and a new enthusiasm."

"Were we in need of a fresh breeze?"

"It doesn't hurt to have one," he replied a little more cautiously. "Alicia's different, brings a different perspective from what the students are used to. But it's good to be exposed to something new, don't you think? Good for them to be challenged."

"Yes, I agree. And I'm glad you think so highly of her. That says a great deal. But I don't think you came here to tell me this. Or did you?"

"Well—no. I didn't come to praise Alicia. I came to make the case for keeping her. I think she brings a new dynamic to the department. She enriches us and our point of view. You understand what I mean. We are both proponents of diversity and its power to make us stronger."

This was the understatement of the century, sort of like saying Ford was a proponent of cars. Camilla had been relentless on the subject of diversity ever since she arrived on campus.

She just smiled. "Diversity is important to me. I'm glad to hear it is to you, too."

"Now of course I'm not just talking about the fact that she's a woman, although that's important. There aren't many women conductors, so it's definitely a new frontier to be conquered. But there are many different kinds of diversity. There are the diversities of race and gender, to which we have all been rightly attentive in recent years; but there are also diversities of point of view and technique. My experience is that music students learn and grow best when they are exposed to different approaches. It isn't just one path for everyone. They need to see different ways of doing things so they can find their own way. And it would be wonderful to be able to offer that here. It would be a great draw for the more promising kids and help to elevate the entire program."

"Which I assume is where Alicia comes in."

"Yes, diversity in method—and also of course also in gender. She comes from a first-rate school. There is nothing wrong with her training. Some of her methods might seem a little unorthodox, a little demanding to students who aren't used to having a lot expected of them. But in my opinion they're very effective. She is a boon to the students and a gift to all of us."

"High praise indeed," she replied, although the smile maybe did not seem quite so bright. "I will have to meet this Alicia. But I still have the feeling there's something else you want to tell me."

He could not avoid it any longer. "You're right. I don't want to lose her. To make a long story short, it seems she has been under attack from some quarters for being a little too strict with the students."

"Oh dear, how did that happen?"

"Apparently she required them to learn the music beforehand. A couple of them complained—you know, the usual thing."

"But she wasn't being unreasonable, from your point of view."

"Not at all! High school orchestras are required to learn their music; I don't think it's unreasonable to expect at least as much in college. Anyway, there seems to be a movement now to get rid of her. Some people are saying she's not right for us, not a good fit. And I can understand having different points of view on a subject like this. I just want to make sure the whole story is told."

"When you say 'get rid of her,' you mean right now? In the middle of the semester?"

"No, I mean not renewing her contract, not bringing her back next year like they do with almost all of the other adjuncts."

She sat back and looked at him. "Maybe they don't feel they need her next year, or can't afford her."

"Well, it's not really that simple. I wish it were. No, I think there's a subtle form of discrimination going on here, which they might not even be aware of. Let's just say Alicia does things a little differently from how they've been done in the past. Some people may find that a little unnerving. It goes against certain notions they have about good pedagogy. But it shouldn't. As I said, her results are excellent. I just think she should be evaluated on her results—on substance, not style."

"So you feel she's being discriminated against because of her gender. That's what makes her approach seem so unorthodox."

"Yes, maybe that's it. I don't know if this is conscious gender bias, but it may amount to it in the end. In any case I think we should encourage the broadest possible experience for our students. They should be exposed to excellence in all of its many manifestations."

Camilla seemed a little puzzled. "What you're saying certainly makes sense to me. Students should be exposed to different ideas. But is there something you want me to do?"

"Well, that's an interesting question," he said with an uneasy laugh. "I know you're busy. I don't want to make things worse for you. In fact this is the very first time I've come to the dean's office in all my years here. But I did want to make you aware of the situation. It would be a tragedy to let this one get away. She would be a great asset to the university."

"Is this really your first time? I'm flattered. And yes, I am very busy. But if you say she would be a great asset here, I'll just have to believe you. I'll tell you what. Why don't you let me make a few phone calls and see what I can find out. Sound like a good idea?"

Henry just nodded. He was starting to feel rather sheepish. He did not realize, until he was actually sitting across from the somewhat imposing Camilla, just how thin his case really was—not until he heard it coming from his own lips. His opinion of Alicia's merits was heartfelt and sincere but of course entirely subjective. True, he was Henry Larson—he could see from the way she responded to him that his opinion carried some weight—but what if someone else had a different opinion? What if Camilla called Malcolm, as the presumed expert on orchestra conducting, and he told her there was a performance faux pas in the Bach or some other idiotic thing? How would she know the difference?

And again, Alicia was just an adjunct. Camilla picked up on this. She seemed a little surprised when she realized why he was there. "Maybe they don't feel they need her." Basically this said it all. The conversation started out well but he was not sure it had ended well. In fact the whole situation with Alicia was starting to seem a little overblown. It was certainly not the worst injustice he had ever witnessed in the department. Terrible things happened all the time to actual tenured faculty, including friends of his. In fact there had been some unsavory goings-on just before Christmas, and he had not lifted a finger. Why now? Why for Alicia, a mere adjunct, someone he did not even know?

He knew why. It was Margie and her dark eyes. Without that, he never would have gone to the dean. Not that he was wrong to have done it, to have spoken up for Alicia. The little game Malcolm was playing was sadistic and disgusting. But he felt he had used up an awful lot of political capital on her behalf. It would be different if Camilla had jumped right in. He would not be having second thoughts now if she had taken up his cause and become as outraged at Alicia's predicament as he and his friends were. But this was not the case. He did not feel he had connected with her—he who was an expert on connecting with audiences. And this troubled him.

Besides, people in management positions do not want you bringing them problems—not unless you have a solution to offer. Henry knew this perfectly well, being the lifelong leader of a chamber group. But he did not have a solution to Alicia's problem. There was no way to stop Malcolm and his friends from doing what they seemed determined to do. So then why had he gone to her at all? Was he just agitating for the sake of agitation? It was not a good way to endear oneself to the dean.

The moment Henry walked out of Camilla's office he lost all desire to wage war. He was allowing himself to be drawn into the very trap he had so studiously avoided all these years—into department politics in all their pettiness and spite and sheer stupidity. Did he really want to throw away his carefully cultivated impartiality for what seemed like a hopeless cause? Yes, even as he sat there talking to Camilla he knew the cause was hopeless. He could not prove discrimination or malign intent. They were going to get rid of her. He was tilting at windmills.

THE RECKONING

ENRY RETREATED BACK INTO HIS CELL and closed the door behind him. What had he just done? Had he lost his mind? He never went to the dean. He never expressed personal feelings or opinions at school, and there was an excellent reason why. Work was not supposed to be personal. It was not a crusade. It was work, a way to make a living. And it was a good way. He liked to think he was playing a positive role in the lives of the students he taught, broadening their experience, exposing them to art and culture, keeping the flame of classical music alive. On the whole, he liked his work.

Henry took his responsibilities seriously. He poured himself into being a good teacher, constantly looking for innovative ways to make the past come alive in the iPad dullness of the present, nurturing his string students like an affectionate father to help them become true musicians. But as to the business of education—all of the things that went on outside the classroom—there he cultivated a perfect indifference. Oh, he used to care, when he first started. There was an individual, a talented composer and conductor, someone with the true soul of music, with whom he had formed a bond. He watched this person suffer over the years. He watched what they did to him, how they ignored him, mistreated him, made fun of him; how he died at fifty-eight from a ruined liver, bitter and alone. After that, Henry simply steeled himself to the everyday drama of university politics.

Were there good people in the department? Of course! Many good people who loved music and were just trying to be good teachers. Did he hurt for them and the indignities they had to endure? Of course! He ached for them in his soul—but he knew he could not help them. He may be Henry Larson, but he could not solve their problems for them. He was not their savior; it was not why he was there. He had taken a role many times over the years in good causes, to alleviate suffering, right a wrong, but always behind the scenes, with an invisible hand, managing by influence. There were times when he had helped someone save face or prevented a co-worker from being crushed by the administration. Once he had been able to save tenure for someone who was worthy.

But now he seemed to have given up his usual circumspection. He had gone on the offensive, fired off a missile without knowing exactly where it would land. In short, he spooked himself. For the rest of the week he walked around in the corner of his eyes, wondering what people were thinking and saying behind his back, wondering if they knew he had gone to the dean. They would know soon enough. She said she would make calls. Word would get around that he was opposing Malcolm and the triumvirate over Alicia, and there would be a firestorm. He was almost tempted to call Camilla and tell her to forget the whole thing—but how, after he had made such a show of support for Alicia?

The day for the department meeting was coming up. Henry did not know what was going on with Camilla and her investigation—if anything—but he made a solemn pact with himself to remain silent and not get drawn in any further. If Camilla actually did something with the information he had given her, fine. He would not be surprised if she didn't, but in any case it seemed to him he had done his part. There was no point in overdoing it. On the way into the meeting he ran into Margie. He looked at her and she looked up at him with that smile and for a moment he was moved. He was singled out by that smile and was almost back on his charger again, ready to do battle. Almost. Not quite. The moment passed and he was on his way to his seat by the window and to making his reverie.

The meeting went by with all the usual bureaucratic tediousness and Henry was just starting to feel safe again when disaster struck.

"So I guess we can move on to an item that is not on the agenda but probably needs to be addressed," he heard Bertram saying out of his state of abstraction. "I'm sorry I didn't list it, but it just came up. It seems we have some issue with one of our adjuncts. [Here Henry began to wake up.] As you know, this is the time of year when we generally start talking about what our needs are for next year and thinking about posting for part-time help. But we have kind of an unusual situation this year with one of our adjuncts and some difficulties apparently foreseen by one of our esteemed colleagues. I'm talking about Alicia Baptiste—you may remember she was discussed briefly last time. Henry, would you care to enlighten us? I understand you've been talking to Dean DiCaprio."

Henry froze. He looked around at the other faces, a little dazed, and realized they were all looking back at him. He roused himself to reply. "Well, Alicia is, in my view, a very valuable addition to the department. I appreciate her musicality and the dedication and focus she brings to the process of education and performance, the integrity she obviously possesses. I simply expressed my hope to the dean that she could be retained for another year, as in my view she is a real credit to the university."

"That's funny—that's not what she told me," Bertram replied in an even tone. "She said you seemed to feel there was some discrimination or even mistreatment of the person involved."

"I didn't say anything about mistreatment," Henry replied defensively. "What I said was it is important to value diversity of all kinds in a truly diverse university. In this case, what we have, in my view, is a diverse approach to pedagogy. It's different from some of the standard approaches encountered in colleges and our own department—I'm well-aware of that. But obviously it is effective. It gets results. I think we should encourage it instead of being dismissive."

"So this is a polite way of saying we're trying to get rid of Alicia because we disagree with her," Malcolm scoffed.

"Or not so polite," Jeff added.

Henry was getting hot. "I'm saying there can be more than one approach to music. We should watch out for getting too set in our ways, no matter how good they might be, and make sure we stay open at all times to other points of view. Alicia is a good conductor and a good teacher. You can hear it in her music. And yes, we should honor that. For our own good we should honor it, if we want to make the department as attractive as possible."

"But that's not what this is about," Bertram said, his head in his hands. "Believe me, nobody's running Alicia out of the department. The state is cutting back, and that means we have to cut as well. The dean already told us we have limited funds for adjuncts next year. Alicia was one of the last ones hired, which is why her name came up. Not for any other reason."

All of the color drained out of Henry's face. He had not heard about this directive from the dean, nor had she mentioned it. Was it a ruse? Should he retreat?

Before he had a chance to do either, Malcolm chimed in. "Also, I really don't think it's necessary to cast aspersions on our fellow department members. That doesn't strike me as very good team-building behavior. We're trying to make serious decisions here. Nobody likes it, but it's not like we have a choice in the matter. Some positions have to go. That's just the way it is. There's no need to go over anyone's head just because some of us may not like what the department decides."

Henry lost it. "Right, and I suppose you didn't sit here last time in my absence talking about the fact that she only has a master's degree. Read the job description that we ourselves posted on the Internet. It clearly says 'M.A. required.'"

"Yes, and it also clearly says 'Ph.D. preferred,'" Malcolm rebutted coolly. "There's a reason for that, which you would know if you paid attention. It's hard to find Ph.D.'s to serve as adjuncts for a lot of these positions, so to open up the field a little bit we include M.A.'s. But the Ph.D. is preferred. It's the standard we all agreed we should have for the sake of professionalism."

"It shouldn't be preferred," Henry said, getting hot. "It's meaningless. Having a doctorate doesn't make you a conductor any more than it makes you a doctor. We are a music department. What we should be looking for here is people who are musicians and know how to teach the art of music, not just people who have certain academic credentials."

"I believe we're all musicians here, aren't we? Besides, I think you're getting a little too personal about the M.A. thing. This isn't about you. You're a special case, everybody understands that. It's about what kind of department we want to be and where we have to go in the future if we want to make ourselves a vital part of the university. There's a new standard here and new expectations. Everybody has to step up to the plate. And that includes our sleepy little department. We can't just go on doing things the way we've always done them. That won't cut it anymore."

Henry burned, burned, burned at the patent dishonesty of this declamation but did not reply. He looked around to see if anyone else was going to say something. He looked at Richie; his friend looked glum and was keeping his eyes on the floor. He looked at Margie—she was encouraging him with her smile but he could not go on. He knew he had already lost. There were some who were sympathetic to his point of view, who despised Malcolm and everything he stood for just as much as he did, who were just as outraged about Alicia as he was, but they could not afford to speak up. The lines had been drawn. It was not just Malcolm and Jeff; it was Bertram too. And the usual suspects would support them.

Right after the meeting Richie came to his office. "Wow, what happened in there?"

"I lost it," Henry admitted. "Completely lost it."

"No, I mean the ambush. You notice how he waited till the end to bring it up? The whole thing was a set-up. He was trying to lull you into a false sense of complacency."

"Or maybe he was just putting it off because he really didn't want to talk about it. I wish I'd done the same. I wouldn't have made such a fool of myself. Bringing up the M.A. thing was a huge blunder."

"It's kind of hard not to when that's their main complaint against her. Besides, he egged you into it."

"Doesn't matter. I let him paint me into a corner. Anything I say from now on will be automatically discredited. Not that I'm planning on saying anything. I've said too much already."

"But it's such a lie, pretending it doesn't have anything to do with her personally. I wish you'd been at the last meeting. You would have not have believed what Malcolm said about her."

"Are you trying to put me in the hospital now? Look at this— I'm shaking. I can play in front of a thousand people at Carnegie Hall and not shake, but look at these hands. Look, we both know what's going on here. We both know why Malcolm's so eager to get rid of her. But there is no way to prove it. That's the thing. There are some people around here who think he's the greatest conductor on the face of the earth. They're clearly delusional, in my mind, but there's nothing we can do about it."

"We can fight back. We can try."

"'We'? I didn't notice too much 'we' going on in there."

"I know—I'm sorry. I wanted to say something, but the whole thing took me by surprise."

"No, you were smart not to say anything. There's an ironclad rule in politics—never speak from a position of weakness. I forgot it and have no one to blame but myself."

"What 'weakness'?" Richie scoffed. "You're the only one who gives this department any kind of national validity—never mind the international reputation they keep talking about. Is there anyone here who has an international reputation except you?"

"Doesn't seem to matter," Henry said with a laugh. "Never really mattered in all the years I've been here. If anything it's a hindrance. It makes them want to distort everything I say."

The conversation was not helpful. Richie wanted him to lead an insurgency, but this was something Henry could not do. He was too old. He was too tired. He went off to teach a theory class, and by the time he came back he had managed to calm down a bit—until another visitor arrived. It was Margie.

"I've been hanging around just to thank you," she said, her dark eyes shining. "I mean, just the fact that you spoke up for her—it was amazing."

"But ineffectual, unfortunately," Henry replied, letting down his guard again to this almost-stranger. "I broke my policy of keeping my thoughts to myself, and you can see where it got me."

"Ineffectual! Not at all! It was the best thing anyone's ever said in one of those stupid meetings. Everything you said was so true. They all know it was."

"I wouldn't go that far. I think some may know. A lot of the others are probably clueless."

"But how can they not see it? She's obviously better than he is, just like you said. I don't see how anybody could think otherwise."

"Did I say that? Oh my. I didn't mean to. Malcolm has his supporters. He's a smooth operator, and it's very dangerous to oppose him. Take it from me, my dear, don't even try. I know Alicia's your friend, but he will roll right over you. I've seen it happen before—not pleasant."

"He's not going to roll over me," she replied with a strange smile. "And anyway, there's no way he can roll over you. You're way above him."

Henry sighed. "Malcolm is very good at being Malcolm. What more can I say? It's the way of the world. Is he a musician? No; not in my opinion anyway. Is he a good teacher? I don't know, and I don't think anybody knows. But he certainly looks good. He sounds good. He's clever with words. I can tell you one thing—he has a lot of people convinced he's the most valuable person in this department. And not just Bertram. People in high places."

"But how? He's such a phony, with those knock off suits and everything. He just—yechh."

"Yes he is. I agree. You're a very astute young woman. But he's giving them what they want, which is the appearance of professionalism, academic excellence."

"That's exactly what I'm talking about! There's nothing 'professional' about him."

"I said *appearance*. Listen very carefully now. I've seen musicians praised to the skies who did not have an ounce of depth in their being, but they were very good at appearances. They understood the game and dressed the right way and had the right connections and credentials and knew how to project what they needed to project. It's an art, this appearances thing—and Malcolm is the great artist. All anybody in the administration knows is his reputation and what he projects, which of course is very grand. But think about it. They would have to be very close to the situation to see it any differently. And they don't want to get that close. They don't want to see what really goes on."

"But we're talking about his own colleagues. Why can't they see it?"

"Some do. There are plenty of people who aren't crazy about Malcolm or the direction he's taking the department. But there are other people who seem to be wholeheartedly in his camp. Why, I don't know—but there are. All you have to do is look at Jeff."

"But the way he treats women! How can they keep pretending that nothing ever happened and he's still the golden boy?"

"There are little mysteries in life. I've seen this phenomenon throughout my career and never could understand it. I think it's partly inertia. People can acclimate themselves to any situation, and do. I think it's partly common decency. No one wants to attack a colleague, just as no one wants to be attacked. And I think it's partly fear. Malcolm has support from above. This scares people."

"But you're not scared of him."

"No, I'm not scared. Why should I be? I'm not in the game anymore."

"Were you scared before—when you *were* in the game? Was that why you never said anything?"

Ouch! This stung. "I wouldn't say 'scared.' I would say respectful. Aware of the damage he can do. No, the reason I don't talk in those meetings is there's no point to it. If you had been here as long as I have and seen the things I've seen you would understand."

"Well, I love it when you speak up. Everybody does. I don't know if you know that. You have so much respect around here. People are afraid to say anything themselves, but when you say something it blows everybody away."

Henry looked at her, and she at him, and for a moment their eyes locked. They locked, just for a moment, they locked and he was pulled. He became bold.

"I'll tell you what. Why don't we get together over dinner some night and talk about it. Maybe there's something we can do for your friend after all. She certainly deserves it."

"Really?"

"Sure. Why not? I don't mind speaking up for her, if it really means so much to you. But we do have to be smart about it. We have to plan and know exactly what we're about. Because I guarantee you Malcolm and his friends are planning. Probably even as we speak."

"I'd love to have dinner with you! It would be fun."

"How about Thursday? I have a three o'clock class. We could go after that."

"Thursday's perfect. See you then!" she said and went tripping off.

Henry sat there staring at the empty doorway after she left. What had he just done? He did not want to be mixed up in the Alicia mess anymore. He'd made a fool of himself with the dean, and he'd made a fool of himself in front of the whole department. It was time for someone else to step up, for someone else to come to Alicia's defense. Both Richie and Margie wanted him to carry on, but did they have any idea what they were asking? What kind of peril he was putting himself in by crossing Malcolm? Or did they think there was no danger for him because of who he was? If so, they were very much mistaken.

At the same time, those eyes! They locked with his. He didn't know what it meant—if anything at all—but he found himself very much wanting to know if it meant something. Margie was very attractive. He felt her attractiveness deep in his being. It was a joy having her in his office. Also he was impressed with her. He liked her passion, her desire to obtain justice for her friend. They were in complete agreement in their views on Malcolm and what was going on in the department. Plus, to her he was a superstar. He could see it in her eyes. He did not see himself as a superstar, but he kind of liked the idea that she did. He was very reluctant to let her down.

A MODEST PROPOSAL

THURSDAY WAS A LONG WAY OFF—two days. Henry had no classes on Wednesday, so he kept occupied by practicing all day long and teaching a couple of private students.

Gabrielle left midday for a weekend workshop in Michigan. He was there alone and in his aloneness he was not thinking about Gabrielle. He was thinking about Margie. An infection had taken hold of his being, spreading out into the peripheral arteries and fingers and toes. He felt a glow when he thought about her and this was not good, he knew it. Moreover, he seemed to be thinking about her all the time, her pretty dark eyes, even in the midst of a difficult passage from Dvorak; and this also was not good. It was distracting. It was taking up too much of his time and energy.

What did she want? Was she possibly—interested in him? It wasn't impossible. A lot of women seemed interested in him. They told him he did not look even close to his age. He took good care of himself, walking at least a mile every day, eating right, not drinking or smoking. Then he laughed at himself. He was an old man of sixty-two, maybe twice her age. What was he thinking?

But then what *did* she want? Was it just about Alicia? Probably—but he found himself wishing it was more. She had come to his office twice now. She had smiled that beguiling smile of hers and looked right into his eyes in the way that is never done between the sexes except when—but then again, how would he know? He was no longer in touch with how things were done between the sexes. The whole concept of modesty seemed to him to have changed, or been lost. Women were different now, with the pill and liberation. The old signals didn't hold.

The one thing he knew for sure about Margie was she had a heart for Alicia and her absurd situation. Also she thought he could help. She had complete confidence in him and his invisible powers. Henry was not so sure. He wanted to be that person—he wanted to live up to her ideal—but he had seen too much in his thirty years. He had long since ceased to have any illusions about being a hero when it came to the department and its never-ending follies, having been beaten up and beaten down. In fact he felt more irrelevant than ever—because he was getting old. They did not see him as a threat to their ambitions. They had actually scoffed at him in a public meeting. Nor did he want to threaten anyone. Not at this stage of his life. He was content, more or less, to fade into non-entity status, as long as they left him alone.

But Margie was bringing him back from the dead. She would not let him go into the land of shadows. She did not see him the way he saw himself or know the weariness in his soul. And he kind of liked the quickening. Henry was enchanted by her attentions. She made him feel strong again and he liked feeling strong, he liked having someone look up to him and consider him important. She made him feel young again and he liked this most of all. The sweetness of it flowed into him like a shining stream. Something had changed. He was walking down the hallway and he could feel it. The legs did not seem so faded anymore. There was a different picture of him in his mind.

Then on Wednesday he had a curious visit. Bea Marquez dropped by, long-time colleague and friend.

"That was quite the department meeting," she said leadingly.

"Wasn't it though? I don't think I've said that much in all my department meetings put together."

"I don't either. And I've been at all of them. I was kind of surprised when you spoke up for an adjunct. But of course you were right. The whole thing is ridiculous. They're both a couple of sexist pigs. It's a shame they get away with what they do."

"Yes, there seems to be a disconnect somewhere between university rhetoric and what actually happens on the ground. But how did you think it went, overall?"

"I don't know. I think everybody was in shock from you actually tangling with Malcolm. People just don't do that. Besides, I don't think they've ever seen you angry before."

"I know. I kind of lost it. Was it that bad?"

"It was…different. I don't know if I would say it was 'bad.'"

"To tell you the truth, I don't know what happened. I'm just as surprised as you are. I looked up at Malcolm's smug face and something just snapped."

"Well, that's enough to get anybody going. I think a lot of people probably enjoyed that part of it. They love to see Malcolm get put in his place. And you got in some good digs."

"I wish I could believe you. Richie has a theory that they had it all figured out in advance and were just waiting for me to say something."

"Oh, definitely. I thought the same thing. It all seemed a little too pat. And of course Bertram wouldn't do anything without consulting Malcolm. He acts like Malcolm's still the chairman."

"Yes, what's that all about? I talked to him about that. He doesn't have to defer to Malcolm. It's not like anyone's expecting him to."

"In any case it was nice to see someone stand up for Alicia. She's not capable of doing it herself."

"Because she's an adjunct."

"No—because she's so awkward! Kind of sad, really. She tries too hard and it just comes off being embarrassing. I think that's about ninety percent of her problem."

"To tell you the truth I don't know anything about her—except for what I saw at the concert. She wasn't even on my radar until someone told me what was going on."

"Are you by any chance talking about Margie?"

"Well, yes. How did you know that?"

"How much do you know about her?" Bea said, ignoring his question.

"Nothing! I don't think I ever said five words to her before. She just stopped by my office out of the blue one day and started talking about Alicia."

"I bet she did. I would stay away from her, if I were you."

"That's going to be kind of difficult," Henry said with a self-conscious laugh. "We're meeting for dinner tomorrow night."

"Dinner! Why?"

"She thinks I can help Alicia. She wants to talk to me about it."

"Alicia—right. Let me just give you some friendly advice. There's a lot going on with that girl. She's a bit of a train wreck. She's definitely not what she seems to be."

"Well, you can come along, if you like."

"No, thanks. I don't want to be a third wheel with you and Margie."

Henry hadn't meant to tell Bea about the appointment. Somehow it just slipped out. He could see why she might find the information a little disconcerting—a senior department member hobnobbing with one of the young untenured professors. It just wasn't done. But calling Margie a "train wreck"? That seemed a bit harsh. He could not imagine anyone who was less of a train wreck than Margie. It was just like Bea, however. She was not one to hold back when it came to the perceived shortcomings of others—while also being oblivious to her own. She seemed to have some sort of hidden animus toward Margie. Was it because she was so pretty? Was it because of the attention she received from men?

Henry had never seen Bea with a man. It was kind of hard to imagine such a thing. She was too brassy, too rough, too unshapen. She was not exactly masculine; it was more like being sexless. Was this by her own choice, or was she one of those women from the feminist generation who had pushed away men until it was too late to find one? He did not know. But he thought he knew why she was hostile to Margie, who was everything that Bea wasn't. Margie was not only pretty but also vivacious in the way that is highly attractive to men. Bea had nothing of this latter quality to make up for her lack of the former. The impression you always had of her was of someone bearing down, and not always in a pleasant way. She even walked like that, with her head down and her face frozen into a perpetual frown.

He thought about her claim that there was "a lot going on with Margie." This comment seemed unfair, in addition to being uncharitable. Of course there was a lot going on with Margie; she was popular. Bea was an introvert by her own admission. Not a lot goes on with introverts because they grow into themselves and push others away. It was hard for Henry to understand or sympathize with this personality trait, not being one himself. He could never have done what he had done if he had been an introvert, never had a public career in music. Unlike Bea, Margie had a lot going on for the simple reason that she was comfortable in company of others. She was open and approachable.

Henry wished he hadn't said anything about meeting Margie. That was stupid. He didn't think Bea would blab about it—she was very loyal to him—but he felt some embarrassment because he knew his motives were not perfectly pure. She did not give any sign of knowing this. She seemed willing to believe him when he said they were only getting together to talk about Alicia. But he knew better. He saw through his own excuses even if Bea couldn't—and was disappointed in himself. He did not want to be a fond, foolish old man chasing after sweet young things in his mind. He wanted his mind to be filled with nobler things, most of all noble music.

Henry was chastened by this conversation with Bea, not because he gave any credence to what she said about Margie but because his embarrassment made him mindful of his own foolishness. Still, he could not help looking forward to being alone with Margie, sitting across from her in the candlelight, feeding on her youth and beauty. The time in between was long. He could think of nothing else. Then suddenly they were meeting in the parking lot and getting into their cars and a little while later he found himself squiring her into a cozy little restaurant down by the lake, at the edge of town, far enough away to minimize the threat of any uncomfortable encounters with students and other faculty.

The restaurant was not crowded, but there were enough people to make Henry feel conspicuous. Fortunately Margie was chatty.

"It just galls me because everybody knows exactly what this is about," the adorable one was saying in her adorable way. "Everybody knows he's just jealous of her because she did such a great job with the orchestra. His orchestra. If it weren't for that, they wouldn't even be talking about getting rid of her. She'd be coming back for sure."

"That's what I thought, too. The only problem is it seems to be coming from Bertram, not Malcolm. They have to cut the budget, and this is what he wants the department to think about."

"That's just a smokescreen. He and Bertram and Jeff are thick as thieves. They're always over at Malcolm's house, watching his sixty-inch TV or listening to his ten-thousand dollar stereo system. Somebody told me they were there practically every weekend."

"I doubt that. Malcolm's wife wouldn't permit it. She's scarier than the three of them put together." But the point was well-taken.

They *were* thick as thieves. Bertram was more cautious than the other two but that was about it.

"I don't see how they can get away with it. Now that you said something."

"From the sound of it, they're going to try."

"But everybody was stunned by what you said. There are a lot of people that want to stop them from doing this. It's kind of the last straw."

"I'm sure that's what they're saying, but people are complicated and act in complicated ways. You'll notice that no one else spoke up. I was kind of left hanging there. It's going to take a full-scale uprising in order for anything to change at this point. And I just don't see that happening."

"You're saying they're lying?"

"No, they're not lying. People say things in the heat of the moment, and they really do mean them, but then they cool down and begin to see things a little differently. Self-interest takes over. They start thinking about the ramifications."

"I don't know, I kind of have to disagree with you there. I think the anger level toward Malcolm is so intense right now that everybody would rise up if they had someone to lead them. The stuff he pulled last fall with the contracts has the whole department up in arms. You're just not aware of it because you're never there."

"I'm not disagreeing with you. I do think people are up in arms. They should be, after some of the stuff he's pulled. But I also know they're too timid to do anything about it. And there's a good reason for that. They know how mean he is; they know what he can do if you get on his bad side."

"What could he do to you? You're Henry Larson. You're a world-class violinist. There's no comparison between you and Malcolm."

"Oh, I don't know about that," Henry replied with a modest wave of the hand.

"Are you kidding? Nobody puts you in the same league with him. Nobody! You're so far above him it's not even funny. Everybody in the entire department looks up to you, wishes they could be like you. Nobody looks up to him or wants to be like him. In fact most people can't stand him."

"It doesn't seem to matter. He's very good at managing up. We think he's a disaster, but the people above him don't see it and don't look at it that way. Certain people just seem to lead charmed lives, no matter how incompetent they are or how much misery they cause."

"Right—but that was before you said something. That's my point. Now everything has changed. You can see it in the way they reacted to you. They freaked out. Why? Because they're afraid of you. They know you can turn things around. You're not like them. You're in a league of your own."

Henry was trapped as he listened to her and looked at the softness of her features and her dark eyes. There was a part of him that could not accept her optimism. It had been a long time since he had allowed himself to feel any optimism about the department. Also he was not sure he agreed with her assessment of the political atmosphere. He did not sense the tidal change that she was describing. To him what had happened was much simpler. He made the mistake of speaking out and was thoroughly routed, as seen in the silence of his peers.

On the other hand there was nothing he wanted more than to invest himself in Margie's version of reality and be the potentate she considered him to be. She exuded a sweetness that came to him like perfume and filled his soul. He found himself putting his natural skepticism away for her sake. A part of him was starting to revive—a part he had allowed to die. He had never been one to speak up very much, for the reasons stated, but in the past decade or so he had stopped speaking up at all because resistance seemed futile, because they looked at him like an alien when he opened his mouth and talked about the way things ought to be, because his idealism ran into their world-weary pessimism and was tainted and spoiled by it and finally withdrew itself for the sake of self-preservation.

But the fresh-faced girl sitting across from him now knew nothing of all this. All she saw was a world-class violinist and leader of a famed chamber group. She did not see him as a worn-out old man, which was how he was sometimes felt. She saw him as a tower of strength who could make things better. Henry didn't think there was anyone who could resist Malcolm. He simply annihilated anyone who tried. But as he looked into Margie's trusting eyes he began to feel more confident in his powers. In all these years he had never openly opposed Malcolm or his increasingly outrageous schemes. Maybe it was time to try.

She clearly couldn't stand Malcolm, which endeared her to him greatly. In fact her strong dislike for Malcolm was perhaps the main thing that drew him to her. His young colleague had been grit in his eye for far too long. At first it was just disagreements over department policy, but then somehow it became personal. Henry began to feel that Malcolm was out to get him, actively conspiring to push him out of the department. But why? There was no reason for it. Henry had never done anything to him. In fact he had gone out of his way to support him. The only thing he could think of was jealousy. Malcolm hated him because he was an actual professional musician and because others showed him deference on that account. And it wasn't just Henry that felt this way. His friends all said the same thing.

It was gratifying to hear it fresh all over again from Margie, someone who was not in his immediate circle. They must have spent an hour going over Malcolm's character flaws and his pernicious influence on the department. It made Henry feel vindicated all over again. Was it wrong to feel this way? Wrong to feel confident in himself and his rightness when it came to Malcolm and his schemes? And it wasn't all about Malcolm. It wasn't all negative. They talked about some wonderful things, ways to make the orchestra more attractive to prospective students, ways to change the whole culture of the department. These were ideas he'd had for a long time. She agreed with virtually everything he said. It was exciting to talk about these things.

He felt himself completely absorbed by this girl. Was it love? What is love? He knew one thing—he had never felt this way about Gabrielle. It was sort of like being intoxicated, dizzy, warm all over. He admired Gabrielle; he thought of her as his friend. But passion was not part of the bargain. They married for the sake of their careers. They made a pact to help each other reach the goals for which they both had been working since they were young children. They had reached those goals—but why did he feel so empty? What was this unfulfilled longing he had?

No, he did not forget about Gabrielle while he was sitting there with Margie, but there had been a gaping hole in his life. He wanted love and had never had love. Was it so wrong to want it? All of the love songs people were constantly writing—was it wrong to want the same thing they wanted? He felt like he was on fire when he was with Margie. It was a precipice fire because he had no way of knowing whether these feelings were reciprocated—very much tended to doubt they could be—but it was fire nonetheless. Her delicate small hand was resting on the table between them, near the candle. It was honestly madness in his mind to see it there. He looked at it, knew he was staring, but couldn't stop himself. It was literally all he could do to keep from reaching over and touching it. Thank God she was chatty because otherwise he did not know what he would do.

As much as Henry admired Gabrielle, he still wanted love and tenderness. It had been a void in his life all these years. Many, many times he had regretted choosing a career over a family. He saw Richie with his family and he was terribly jealous. They seemed so normal, so grounded; they seemed to enjoy each other so much. The years went by and they had no children and then suddenly Gabrielle was too old for children. So nature decided for them in the end—nature closed the door—but this does not mean he was content. He was no different from anyone else. He had the same longings.

Henry left this little dinner conversation feeling quite shaken. He went into a world of unreality. The verities to which he had been clinging for most of his adult life were crumbling. No, they were still there, but they seemed to have lost their force. They were like shadows in the gauzy part of his consciousness. He was still aware of them—but now there were those dark eyes, and he saw them over and over again, and he wanted to be lost in them. He was tired of his reality. He saw himself in her eyes and he became a very different person. He was making a difference and changing things for the better.

But what was she thinking about *him*? Was she thinking the same sort of thoughts or anything like them? It just didn't seem possible. No girl her age, with her prospects and opportunities, would want to get entangled with a washed-up old man, not when there were plenty of young bucks to attach themselves to. It was not like she could be lacking in suitors. She was a very attractive young woman, making a good salary and desirable in every sense of the word. Was it possible she could be interested in someone like him? Reason and maybe something else said no, but another part of him wondered.

She had accepted his invitation to dinner. That was something, wasn't it? He had sat there across from her and they'd had a very friendly, even warm, conversation—but no more. There were no welcoming or encouraging gestures on her part. On the other hand, there was the sparkle in her eyes and the animation on her face when she talked about…well, him. There was admiration for his playing and what he had accomplished. She compared him to Malcolm and Malcolm was "nothing." Now Malcolm was twenty-five years younger than he, a very good-looking young man, always dressed impeccably and with winning manners; but Malcolm for all of his charms was nothing compared to him. She said so herself. She was quite emphatic.

What did it mean? He knew what he wanted it to mean. A strange compulsion took hold of him. He found himself redoubling his efforts at manufacturing chance encounters with the fair maiden. He was in the office every day of the week and out in the hallways as often as he dared on some pretended mission or other. People gave him strange looks. It was like the renaissance of Henry. And he did manage to see Margie a couple of times. The encounters were electrifying. Both times she smiled and waved. It was an adorable little wave, so much good humor and welcoming in it. Henry did not remember ever having felt this overpowering force of attraction before or being so utterly smitten.

But did she feel it? He had no idea. He kept hoping she would come to his office again, but this did not happen. A week went by and then two, and then he couldn't stand it any longer. He had to see her. He had to conjure up some way to bring them together. He could not go on like this, with hot coals in his heart, not knowing how she felt, dying to find out, even though part of him did not want to know; even though he wondered if he would be better off never seeing her again. One time he saw her coming into the building from his office window. She looked up and seemed to smile. He did not know what to think, except to think he was making a fool of himself.

Finally he gave in. He went to her office. He had planned the conversation down to the minutest detail, rehearsed it a hundred times in his mind, was more prepared for talking to Margie than for playing in front of New York critics, who could be as brutal as they were clueless. But the moment he opened his mouth he forgot all about it.

"Hi, there," he said, and now *he* was the critic, because he heard his words coming back to him. Were they natural? Was he as naked as he felt?

"Hello!" she said, looking up happily. "I didn't expect to see you standing there."

"Hope you're not disappointed."

"Never! You were just the person I wanted to see."

"Really? Tell me more."

"I was wondering if you'd had any time to think about—you know, what we talked about."

"Well, that's funny, because that's exactly why I'm here. I have been thinking about it—a lot. I have a plan. I was wondering if you might possibly be interested in getting together again so we can talk about it."

"Of course! I'd love to have dinner with you again."

"You would? I'm so glad. I don't know what your schedule looks like. I'm free tonight."

"Tonight would be great! Thursday nights are good for me."

Henry was thrilled. It seemed like a sign. After all, he could have just walked into her office right then and there and sat down and told her about this "plan" of his. They didn't have to go out to dinner. But she seemed to want to go out to dinner. Instead of calling him on his rather transparent ruse, she went right along with it. This could mean one of two things. Either she didn't realize it was a ruse—or she did and was willing to go along with it anyway. Henry was rather fond of the second scenario. It suggested some interest in him. It suggested she wanted to go out to dinner with him not just because of Alicia but possibly for some other, more delightful reason.

Then he started wondering what he could come up with as an excuse for a "plan." It was not really true that he had been thinking about a plan for the past two weeks. No, all he had been thinking about was Margie. Part of him was deeply pessimistic about saving Alicia. This was the part of him that was brown, produced through decades of mortifying himself for the sake of his position and his Little Stipend. He showered this pessimism on any potential crusades that happened to come his way in order to avoid disappointment and humiliation. Through these brown-colored glasses, Alicia was doomed. It was the same old nonsense. They had their agenda. It was not about the music; it was about power and position and politics. It was about keeping people like Alicia and himself in their place.

And the thing was they were good at it. They didn't want Alicia there because she made them look bad—but that wasn't how they were spinning it. Oh no, it was all about the budget cuts. It was about "professionalism" and saving the department from the philistines at the door. As far as Henry was concerned, factoring in all his experience on the faculty, as well as the manifold deficiencies of human nature, Alicia had already lost. Fate had decreed that she would be a sacrificial lamb. He felt sorry for her. She had come with the best intentions and the highest idealism and had stepped into a bad situation that could not have been avoided short of deliberately giving a mediocre concert.

But no, she had been like Henry and foolishly excelled. The difference was that Henry could get away with that sort of thing because he was already well-known by the time he arrived on the staff. They tolerated excellence in him, rightly calculating that mediocrity would prevail in the end by its own irresistible inertia. But they didn't have to tolerate it in Alicia. In no sense could she be deemed indispensable. They could push her aside with little or no danger to themselves. It was not as if someone from the administration was likely to be outraged over the sad fate of Alicia Baptiste. To them she was just another member of the faceless adjunct horde.

This is what Henry's brown side said, the dark shroud in which he had wrapped himself over the years to preserve his sanity and independence. But the shroud was unraveling in the face of the new joy that had entered his life. Something had changed, and that something was Margie. He had already trotted out the pessimistic side during their previous dinner engagement; now he had to move on to something new if he wanted to keep her interested. And in truth he was stirred by Alicia's cause. He agreed with Margie that what they were doing to her was terrible. It had been literally decades since he had taken a forceful stance on anything on in the department. Why not now?

The thing is Margie wanted him to confront them openly. This much was clear from their previous conversation. She thought he had the authority to stand up to Malcolm. She also thought they had momentum on their side and others were lining up in support of Alicia. Unfortunately Henry had no confidence in open warfare.

He was still stinging from his last encounter with the triumvirate. They were better debaters than he was, quicker on their feet. They were also more determined, since they had more at stake. Most of all, they were in a stronger position. His high opinion of Alicia was subjective while the budgets cuts were a matter of objective reality. It was easy for them to cast doubt on his position and impossible for him to budge them from theirs.

No, another frontal assault was not going to work. But he had promised Margie a plan. Finally he came up with something that he thought might satisfy her. He would go to the dean again. It had been a big step for him to go to Camilla the first time, potentially a dangerous step. It showed his devotion to Margie and her cause. But there was more to milk from that visit. Camilla had promised to make some calls and report back to him. Several weeks had gone by and he had not heard a thing. So the plan was to visit her a second time under the pretense of asking about the results of her investigation. Of course he already had his suspicions about the results. Apparently Camilla's idea of an investigation was to call Bertram. Still, it was something he could see himself doing for Margie. It was an excuse to see her again.

He and Margie went to the same restaurant as before in their separate cars, greeting each other a little awkwardly in the school parking lot in the fading afternoon light. The wine came and the food came and Henry began to relax; and then at just the right moment he revealed his great plan, in low stentorian tones. He told her about his first visit to the dean and explained how it left the door open for a second. Margie seemed excited by this news. He felt he had her in the palm of his hand as she sat there listening to him raptly and nodding and giving her assent and offering her undying gratitude.

Once again he was bewitched by the attractive young woman sitting there across from him in the muted light. Her hands were on the table in front of her just like the last time and they were so close to him he could almost taste them. He could feel them like a force field, only in this case the force was as gentle as a dove. He kept looking at those hands as he had a second glass of wine—which he rarely did, he rarely had even one—and then at one point he was talking and she was listening and he just couldn't help himself—he reached out and patted her hand. She did not react, she did not move or flinch. She kept right on smiling the same bright smile as he talked and patted her hand.

The moment passed and the conversation changed and his hand came back to himself and rested in his lap. But he was still patting her hand—in his mind. She was talking now and he was listening to what she was saying but he was not processing it. No, all he was thinking about was the touch of her hand. He was looking at her face but her hand was still on the table and he was really looking at the hand through his peripheral vision. His eyes were forward but his attention was focused entirely downward. She had not flinched! She had not drawn away! What did it mean? He couldn't tell. He knew what he wanted it to mean. He wanted her to be willing to have her hand touched by him. He wanted her to want him to touch her hand.

He did not try again. He thought it was better to leave well enough alone. He had gone farther than he had ever dared to go before. Besides, he was happy with just patting her hand. He could still feel its softness and warmth to his thin fingers. He wanted to devour that hand. It had been a perfect evening, far better than he could have hoped. They were completely in sync in everything. The talk was easy and it was good, there was the usual complaining about Malcolm and a lot of laughs, she seemed thrilled with his plan, and most of all he had touched her hand. Henry was in a glow as he left the restaurant, walking behind her, his eyes only on her. There was a brief friendly hug before she got into her car and drove away. He stood there watching fondly as she disappeared down the country road.

As he stated walking back to his car he noticed someone scurrying out of the restaurant in the dark, a woman with her head wrapped against the cold March wind. Something about her seemed familiar. He almost hailed her but she seemed to be in a hurry. He let it go.

THE BARTERER

DINNER WAS A SMASHING SUCCESS, as far as Henry was concerned. Back home he plopped himself on the couch in a state of exhilaration and went over it again and again in his mind, over and over the moments leading up to the point where he actually touched Margie's hand, until he could not go over it any more. Then he went over it one more time, laughing to himself, shaking his head and laughing and touching his hand to his cheek as if it were a foreign object—the same hand that touched her hand. He could not remember ever feeling this way before. Not even in his most sublime moments of music-making could he remember feeling this way.

Then Gabrielle came in and he put his laughing face away and went gray again—spoke in his usual modulated tones—"How was your day?"—"What did you think of Albert's paper?"—etc. Later, in bed, when his wife had already fallen asleep with her back to him, as she always did, the pleasant thoughts came back and the smile came back and he was happy, lying there in the dark and thinking about his happy evening. He drifted off to sleep and had pleasant dreams full of flowers and music and spring.

But then morning came with its sunrise glare and he woke up thinking about—not Margie but Camilla, with her executive veneer and her exquisite power wardrobe. He had promised he would go to her again to see if anything had been or could be done for Alicia, but now in the cold hard light of dawn he began to have misgivings about this hastily begotten plan. Was it really wise to be pushy with

50

someone like Camilla? He knew he wouldn't be pushing at all if there were no Margie. He would wait for Camilla to respond to him. It was a delicate balance. He had a certain status at the school on account of his successful career. In a sense he was on the same level as the administration just by virtue of being who he was—or above them. When he was with them they treated him with deference. But the key to staying on this level, he knew, was to stay above the fray, or seem to. To allow himself to be drawn into Alicia's troubles was to cease to be Henry Larson, international artist and leader of Forum, and become just another guy from the department with an agenda.

Besides, he remembered the look of surprise on Camilla's face when she found out they were talking about an adjunct. Nobody cared about the adjuncts, not really. They had way too much to worry about as it was—who was in, who was out, the latest outrage, their careers. It was odd for him to be stirring things up over someone who was rarely seen and rarely thought of and did not have a real presence in the department. He could almost hear what Camilla was thinking. With all the crap she had to deal with every day—and now this? Not that he agreed with her, but that was just the way things were in the university setting. People did not like it when you made their life more difficult. Especially on account of something as common and predictable as an adjunct not getting a fair shake.

No, he would never have gone back to Camilla of his own volition. It was very bad form. It was forcing her hand when she may have good reasons for not wanting to act, reasons he knew nothing about. Whether Camilla was a good person or a bad person, a good dean or a bad dean, was almost irrelevant. In any case she had a complicated job—and he was making it more complicated. She depended on people like him to understand and not be like the other needy children. That was why she was happy to see him the first time. She assumed he was not bringing her a problem. When she found out what his real mission was her happiness visibly diminished.

Henry wanted to see himself as one of the adults in the room. He wanted Camilla to feel she could depend on him to be self-reliant, but he had no choice but to go back to her if he was to be of service to Margie and her crusade. The alternative—open war with Malcolm—was unthinkable. So he forced himself to call the dean's office that very morning. As he did the thought occurred to him that he had not called the dean's office more than five times in the thirty years he had been there; and in every one of those instances it was about something he could do for the dean, not something he wanted done for himself. There was a huge difference. One was from power, the other from weakness.

Henry tried to sound confident and cheerful when the admin answered but wound up sounding too confident and maybe a little weird. She did not seem as warm and welcoming as before—but it might have been his imagination. He may have been reading his own misgivings into her tone. One thing that could not be mistaken, however, was the appointment he was given, a whole week out. This was a letdown from the open-armed reception he had received the first time. It suggested some slippage in his status in the dean's office. More than that, it was inconvenient. Henry did not want to have to wait a whole week to fulfill his mission for Margie. He did not want to have to be patient.

But then he had an idea. Why not use the delay as an excuse to see Margie again? Could he induce her to come out one more time and help him strategize about what to say to Camilla? He emailed her from his office and was delighted when the reply came back almost immediately: "I would LOVE to talk to you about that." He stared at the words. Then he stared at them again. He closed the email and kept going back to it again and again when he should have been preparing for class. Why the caps for the electric word "love"? He must have read that email a hundred times—and every time his eyes went right to the word love.

She accepted the invitation. He was jubilant. There was nothing in the world he wanted more than another chance to spend some time alone with her. Just to be in her presence was Elysium for Henry. And yet was this not madness? At his age, chasing after this pretty young woman? Living in some sort of fantasy world where they could be together? And was that even his fantasy? Or what exactly was he fantasizing about? He could not say. He did not have anything definite in mind. All he knew was he wanted to be alone with Margie at the restaurant. He wanted to sit there in the candlelight and look at her and talk to her. It made him happy.

It was a strange week leading up to his third meeting with Margie. In the past he had consciously, deliberately divorced himself and his emotions from the department so he could stay sane and focus on his students and his music—and now he found himself in the uncomfortable position of being dragged back into the same old stale mess; particularly into his conflict with Malcolm. Henry was not a hater, but he was close to hating Malcolm. He had seemed so promising when he first came, a breath of fresh air with all of his youthfulness and energy, but then something changed. His tone turned darker, more assertive. After a while he wasn't just the new kid in the department anymore but someone who had aspirations and liked to play games. Disturbing games that involved twisting the truth into something sinister.

And then he started to garner the accolades. Malcolm was getting all the praise and honor that Henry had never received himself. This shouldn't have bothered him—he had plenty of accolades of his own on the outside—but for some reason it did. For one thing it all seemed so fake to him. Malcolm was held up as one of the best teachers on campus, but to Henry he did not seem like a teacher at all. His idea of a teacher tended more toward the sages he had known at Julliard. They were not flashy and didn't try to be because teaching wasn't about winning awards. It was about something else, something deep. It was organic, like planting a garden. Malcolm's methods were not organic, not deeply rooted. They were all on the surface, as if he were trying to turn his charges into poseurs like himself.

Well, to be honest, these were just Henry's feelings. He had no way of really knowing how effective Malcolm was as a teacher. Still, it galled him to see his younger colleague winning all the awards and receiving all the praise. It seemed like an offense against everything that was sincere and worthy, an offense against music itself. Malcolm's shtick was to present himself as the students' friend; but he wasn't really their friend, not when he made them think they were better and more knowledgeable than they were. In Henry's view this was not friendship but pandering. Also his friendship seemed a little thin. He could be seen smiling and joking with them, but he also didn't hesitate to disparage them to his colleagues.

What became especially hard for Henry was when Malcolm started pulling the department leadership in his direction—indeed, to some extent even the administration. He was regarded as a rising star and his methods were adopted and touted. Henry was bewildered by Bertram and his willingness to go along with

Malcolm's schemes. He had nurtured Bertram and prepared him for leadership, thinking he would restore some sense of purpose and humanity to the department; but the more Bertram rose, the more he was drawn into Malcolm's orbit. The gravitational pull seemed irresistible, and Henry could not understand why. Couldn't he see how shallow Malcolm was? Couldn't he see through the whole credentialism thing—the complete disconnect between it and music education?

There had been problems in the department when Henry was a young man, too. The leadership was just as dissolute and directionless and the politics even more brutal. At the time, Henry had been able to push the tawdriness out of his mind because of Hope; because he was still anticipating a glorious day when truth and beauty would prevail. But he was not a young man anymore, and he no longer had this hope. The great enlightened leader he dreamed of, the philosopher prince, never seemed to materialize. At first he thought Bertram might be the one, but it pained him to look at Bertram now. Malcolm was determined to make the department seem more "professional"—purely a surface value, in Henry's mind—and Bertram was perfectly willing to go along.

This clash was at the core of his frustration with Malcolm's attitude toward Alicia. To Henry, she was the Quality. She was the end to which all musical education should be directed. She had the skills, but more importantly she had the depth to draw her students into the Promised Land. She loved the great composers for their own sake, loved the music and was not simply using it as a platform for success. In fact she was the very opposite of the courtier climber. She did not dress for success or care what people thought of her. She was all about the music and paid no attention to the rest. This made her a danger to mediocrities like Malcolm—but also to herself, as Bea pointed out. She was like Beethoven, unkempt and unbending in her integrity, but did she have Beethoven's talent to carry her through? No one did.

Henry was worried about her. He loved her deeply in a non-romantic way, even though he hardly knew her—loved what he perceived to be her integrity—but he wondered if she was made for this world or would ever find a niche where wolves like Malcolm could not get her. He wanted so much to protect her because of this love he had for her, but at the same time he wanted to push himself away from her and stick his head in the sand and pretend he had never known about her. He did not feel he could afford to love her the way he did—not just then. It was too dangerous. There were too many things going on in the department for him to divvy up his energy for her, especially when she did not give the impression of having any will or desire to help herself.

But Margie was drawing him in. He could not help himself. Not just into the politics, which was bad enough, but into the heartache. Henry would see Malcolm or Jeff or even Bertram in the hallway and he would just burn inside. He would smile and nod and give his usual greeting, but inside he was burning up. The very fact that they smiled back made him burn even more. He knew those smiles were fake. He knew they were his enemies and were plotting to get rid of him. They had been plotting for some time. Jeff had a friend who was purported to be a good violinist and a verified academic. He could see her in Henry's position. After all, Henry was old. He was creaky and had gray hair and was an embarrassment when they caught him napping in a department meeting. It was time for him to move on and give some deserving young person a chance to have a career and succeed.

Yes, Henry had made his promise to Margie and been rewarded with another get-together, but he was out of his comfort zone for the first time in a very long time. Just the simple act of walking around the hallways caused his blood pressure to spike and his face to turn pink. In fact a number of his friends commented on it— "Why is your face so pink?"—and he would go to the nearest bathroom and stand at the sink and look at himself in the mirror; and yes, his face was quite pink. They weren't joking. He could feel the high blood pressure inside him, which he knew was entirely stress-related, and he could see confirmation of it in his face. They were making him sick, Malcolm and his friends.

Then there was the little dust-up. He was unlocking the door to his office one cold morning when Malcolm happened to walk by. His erstwhile friend stopped and asked him if he would have his reports in on time and Henry just lost it. "What business is it of yours when I get my reports in?" he snapped. Malcolm backed away. "Just trying to be helpful, buddy. I know how you hate to do them, but they're due next week. Don't want to see you get in trouble."

Yes, he did hate to do them. He hated all the paperwork and folderol that was being foisted on the department in the name of professionalism. It had nothing to do with teaching, in his view, nothing to do with education, and it was not leading to any palpable improvement. Forcing professors to do more paperwork did not make them better professors. An obsession with metrics cannot change mediocrity or improve education. All it could do was to abet the careerists. More humanism was the approach Henry favored, not more meaningless numbers. But numbers were where the department was going.

Then Henry started to feel bad about his little outburst. Malcolm's tone was not unkind or sneering. Had he overreacted? Maybe Malcolm really was trying to help him, as he implied. Maybe he wasn't the evil monster Henry had built up in his mind. He had snapped at him and he never snapped. He couldn't remember the last time he had snapped at anyone. There was a reason why he never allowed himself to get involved in department politics, and this was it. Frankly, he wasn't very good at it. He was all about playing his violin and making beautiful music. He was all about trying to give his students a valuable education; education in the deepest sense, not the shallow stuff Malcolm and Jeff were pushing. He wasn't the glassy-eyed "scurvy politician, who seems to see things he dost not." His thing was his authenticity. But you can't be authentic if you want to be one of the players. You can't lose your temper and have petty outbursts at the puppeteer who's pulling the strings for the department leadership.

It was a long week for Henry, a long week of suffering and pink faces, and the only thing that kept him going was the delightful prospect of Thursday night and the chance to spend some time alone again with Margie. He was not disappointed. They went back to the same restaurant and seemed to take up right where they left off. He bought a pricey bottle of white wine, showing off a bit. He did not particularly care for white wine, but it was what Margie liked. He surprised himself by how talkative he became after a glass or two. In general he was content to let his music do the talking— unless he was lecturing, which was the kind of talking he enjoyed the most—or used to anyway—although even that had been getting a little stale lately.

But he found himself very much wanting to talk with this pretty girl sitting across from him and a glass of good wine in his hand, especially after the stress he had been feeling all week. He wanted to share his stress with the only person who he thought would really understand it. He opened his mouth and blab, blab, blab—it all just came out. Margie seemed to be enjoying it. His feelings of outrage were very much in tune with her own, particularly when it came to Malcolm. He found this gratifying. She was an ally, and they were precious. He talked more and revealed more about himself than he had in years.

As much as she enjoyed listening to him kvetch, Margie did want to talk about the dean thing.

"Does she know all of the details—why Malcolm wants to get rid of her?"

"You mean because he's jealous?"

"Yes."

"Well, I don't know how much she knows about that. I didn't mention any specific names. My strategy was about diversity and how important it is to the university—and so forth. I told her diversity comes in many forms, and Alicia was being treated unfairly, in my view, or at least not being given the credit she deserves, because she doesn't conform to some people's ideas about pedagogy."

"But you didn't tell her he was jealous of her. You didn't tell her about the incredible performance she did and why he and his buddies really want to get rid of her."

"You can't go there with the dean. She's thinking about the big picture. The main thing for us is to save Alicia, if we can. I'm not so much interested in exposing Malcolm's sociopathic behavior as I am in making sure she gets a contract for next year."

"But it doesn't really make sense if you don't tell her about that. She won't understand why this is important unless you come right out and tell her Malcolm has it in for Alicia because he's jealous of her, because she's better than he is and he knows it and everybody knows it. You have to say that or she won't respond or know what to do. You have to make it personal."

"That's not exactly my style," Henry said with a nervous laugh.

"I know it's not, but trust me, I know what I'm talking about. You have to think about this from a woman's point of view. She's going to be interested in the personal involvement. That's the main thing. Somebody getting hurt and it's just not fair. She won't get it if you go in there and just talk about high-minded stuff like diversity. She won't understand why it's such a big deal or why you really care. She's going to think you have something up your sleeve, cause you're a guy."

"I hadn't thought about it that way," he confessed. "To tell you the truth, she didn't seem overly receptive the first time. It could be I didn't make it concrete enough for her to understand what was really going on. I was trying to keep things at a high level."

"There, you see? You can't do that. Look, when women use the word 'diversity' they're usually talking about things that actually happened to them or their friends. It's not an abstraction for them. It's not just a concept. It's something they actually feel. "

"It's an abstraction for me because I'm a clueless male."

"No, it's an abstraction for you because you're too good. You've never had to deal with the kind of crap that's going on with Alicia, and of course you would never do that sort of thing yourself. So for you this is all very high-level. But that's not how women see it. For them, it's all about the outrage."

"Well, believe me, I'm feeling the outrage myself—as I guess you can tell. But basically what you're telling me is I have to go in there and make a direct accusation against Malcolm."

"Well, it's true, isn't it? The guy just has a real problem with women. He treats them like dirt. You told me yourself this has been going on for years and no one ever does anything about it. You won't get anywhere with the dean unless you make her understand this about him. I mean, she deserves to know what's going on in the department, right? Otherwise how can we expect her to make good decisions?"

"Okay, that's true. And it could be he's able to carry on with impunity year after year because the stench simply hasn't risen to the higher echelons."

Margie leaned forward and took his hand in hers. It was like an electric shock for him.

"Promise me you won't go all fuddy-duddy when you talk to her. Promise me you won't walk out of there without her understanding what you're trying to say."

"Okay, I promise," he said, laughing at this characterization of himself. He certainly did not want to go all fuddy-duddy, whatever that meant; not with those soft, warm hands on his.

She seemed satisfied. The conversation moved on to other things. The outrage had worn them out. At one point Henry was telling her about conversations he was having with the Moes about a new violin with a certain tone he was looking for when playing Mozart and Haydn, a more delicate singing tone.

"You know, I have an old violin, I inherited it from my grandfather. Supposedly it's pretty good, but of course I have no way of knowing."

"So what are you doing with it?"

"Nothing. It's just sitting in the closet in my apartment."

"That's not good. It should be played. It should be maintained. Violins are funny things. They don't like to just sit around and be neglected. They like to be loved." Henry blushed after he heard these words out in the open air. Fortunately it was dark in there.

"Do you think you could come look at it? You can tell me if it's worth anything. My apartment is just down the road. You could follow me over."

The conversation went on to other things but Henry's mind stayed right there. Even when he was holding forth eloquently on some arcane subject he was really thinking about the invitation he had just received. He couldn't think about anything else.

The check came and it was time to go and they stepped outside into the chilly night air and started walking to their cars. Henry's heart sank. Had she forgotten about the violin? He didn't want to remind her—seemed too forward—and she didn't mention it. But when they reached her car she pointed down the dark road. "So we just head in that direction for about a mile."

"Sounds good," Henry said nonchalantly. He was in a state of elation. He practically ran to his car.

Her sense of distance was a little off. It actually turned out to be almost two miles. But before he could quite believe it Henry had parked his car near hers and he was getting out and he was joining her and they were walking to the stairs to the front door where she took out her keys and let them in, and they were chatting as if all this were quite normal and there was nothing different about it and they were just going to go in and Henry was going to look at the violin and that was that.

Henry kept talking, mostly out of nervousness, as if they were there for talking, which as far as he knew they were; and before long they were standing in her apartment and she was turning on the lights. He looked around and tried to acclimate himself, tried to pick up some signs about the mystery girl from her environment, but her approach to decorating was, well, minimalist. There were bookshelves with music on them and there was an oboe (her instrument) lying in an open case and a baby grand and a TV; other than that it could have been pretty much anybody's apartment, it was so generic.

She went to the aforementioned closet and pulled out a battered, dusty violin case. Henry opened it and saw an attractive instrument. He picked it up and felt it and inspected it and started tuning, breaking the e string in the process. He played some and couldn't resist showing off a bit.

"Well? What do you think?"

What he thought was he wanted to be positive. "Very nice. It has a nice tone and is well-made. You should definitely take it to someone and see about having it set up."

"Oh, I don't know if I can afford that."

"Don't worry. I've got just the guy. He takes care of all my violins. And he's very reasonable."

She seemed pleased by this. She offered him a glass of wine, which he accepted, and they sat and talked happily for half an hour or so. All this time he was latched onto her in an unseen embrace. He was talking and he heard his voice coming out and he seemed to be making sense but in fact he was out of his senses because he wasn't really talking, he was looking at her while talking, he was taking her in his arms and holding her with all the passion he felt inside, holding her the way a violin never could be held, no matter how much he loved it.

But at the same time he was aware that she did not seem to be aware of his passion and did not evince any similar feelings herself, at least not openly. In fact she seemed almost—cool. He could not read her. He did not understand her. Was it really just about the violin? He had not touched her at dinner, he hadn't dared; but she had touched him. She grabbed his hand in a moment of exhortation. What did that wonderful touch mean? Was she interested in him? How so—and how much? She was always smiling at him. She was completely focused on him when they were together, like he was the only thing that mattered in the whole world. But beyond that he could not tell what she was thinking or feeling—and she was not giving anything away.

Perhaps it was because she didn't have anything to give. Perhaps she was not experiencing the same passionate feelings that held him in their sway. She was pleasant enough, appeared to enjoy his company, but nothing more. A thought passed through his mind about getting out of the rocking chair where he had planted himself and strolling around the room and casually sitting next to her on the couch. "The aura of election is upon you." But he never got around to this bold maneuver. It was too obvious, too cliché. He was not really a seducer. That was not how he saw himself or what he wanted to be. He was a lover, and he happened to be in love with her; but did she love him?

No, he did not get up. He sat there feeling quite awkward and self-conscious. In one sense he was enjoying himself—after all he was with her, this girl he had been thinking about for weeks—doting on—all alone with her in her apartment—but in another sense he was in agony. Was it just friendship she had in mind after all? Can a man and a woman be friends when one of them had the feelings he had for her? Did he even want to be her friend in that sense? One thing was sure—he had not come up there with just friendship on his mind. Actually he did not know what he had in mind. If it wasn't exactly friendship, neither was it lust. Not in its pure degraded form. But what then? Love, a promise, something fresh and new, redemption—what? He looked at her as she talked and did not dare to look into her eyes but just looked at her and sighed inwardly, deeply sighed from his heart.

What in the world was he doing—malingering in her apartment at this time of night when he should have been home acting his age and practicing for next Saturday's concert, which was a challenging one? What business did he have to feel the way he felt about Margie, who had all the freshness of spring? He was the mildew to her fair rose, the corruption of the very thing he doted on. It wasn't just because he had lost the youthful spring in his step; it wasn't just the aches and pains that come with age. No, it was the baggage. Men grow old in their bodies but also in their minds. Experience leads them inevitably to disappointment in the world—and also in themselves. This is what makes them unfit for any but the most charitable interactions with youth.

Did he have any right to take advantage of the illusions she had about him, especially when he knew they were just illusions? To her, he was a renowned artist who could be found at places like Town Hall with his famous group Forum playing some of the greatest music ever written and surrounded by adoring fans. But this was not how he saw himself. He was not always on the stage.

He was not really a god. Most of time he was just a guy like any other guy, with the same foibles, the same weaknesses, the same foolishness. "Age doth transfix the flourish set on youth."

Another half hour went by in this agony and then he knew it was time to go. He did not want to wear out his welcome. Margie seemed a little surprised when he abruptly stood up but made no attempt to stop him. She walked outside with him to the landing. There was an awkward pause as they stood looking at each other, or at least it was awkward for him. Then she surprised him by reaching up and giving him a winking little peck on the cheek. He turned and ambled not very adroitly down the short flight of stairs and across the street to his car. He pulled out carefully, still glancing in the direction of her apartment. She had gone inside. He shook his head and drove off.

With all of these distractions he did not see the white Accord parked in the shadows. He would not have known what to make of it if he did.   .

UNDER THE MICROSCOPE

IT HAD BEEN AN ASTONISHING EVENING, with many highs and some lows, but after all was said and done Henry was left with a very prickly proposition. He had promised to expose Malcolm to the dean. He lay awake all night under a bright full moon pondering just how to carry out this dubious commission. First of all, it went against his core values. He did not believe in denigrating one's coworkers to their superiors. It was the sort of thing Malcolm did all the time, and Henry despised it.

At the same time he could not quite bring himself to have faith in Margie's strategy. He understood what she was trying to say. He knew about "the personal is political," at least in the sense of its prominence in the dialogue—who didn't?—but this was the first time he had tried to come to grips with what it actually meant. Margie seemed to be saying that the political situation with Alicia hinged on his ability to make it somehow personal for the dean. If he could not or would not make it personal, then Camilla would see no compelling reason to act.

This made sense, now that someone had explained it to him. And Henry had nothing against the personal being political for women. His problem was that the personal was not political for him. He did not frame politics in personal terms, especially workplace politics. To him, the political was based on the ability to convince others of the validity of your ideas; but Margie seemed to be saying that this abstract approach would not work with the dean. In order for her to know how to act, she had to know how much Alicia was suffering and why she was suffering—which meant bringing up the contretemps with Malcolm.

Henry understood the theory, but implementing it was a different matter. It would require him to go against his own aversion to personalizing the workplace. It would require him to descend from his lofty perch and get down into the dirt with Malcolm, which he was very reluctant to do. Perhaps most of all it would require him to make a leap of faith, precisely because he was not a woman. He did not know if what Margie was telling him was true—had no way of knowing from his own frame of reference—but he had to *act* is if it were. He had to act against the dictates of his own reason.

Remember, Henry did not know for certain that Malcolm's opposition to renewing Alicia's contract was in fact personal. He was pretty sure it was; everyone he knew seemed to agree. They all assumed that Malcolm wanted to get rid of Alicia because he was jealous—because she had shown him up with her concert in the fall—but this was mere supposition. There was no way it could ever be proved, short of a confession from Malcolm himself. It was possible, after all, that Malcolm was perfectly sincere. Not likely, but possible. And unfortunately Henry was not shallow enough to be unaware of this possibility or to avoid having his righteous indignation mitigated by it to some degree.

Then again, what other explanation could there be for this madness? How could they even think of letting Alicia go with all of her talent and promise unless her presence there was an affront to someone's massive ego? Oh, they could posture all they wanted about her master's degree and perceived lack of "professionalism" in her teaching methods, but it just seemed obvious that what they really resented was her success. The better she did, the more talent she exhibited, the more they hated her and wanted her to go away. Henry understood this dynamic very well. It was the same one he had been dealing with his entire career.

The appointment with Camilla crept up on him and before he was ready for it he found himself sitting in her office in the same chair as before, with her looking more formidable than ever. Women look formidable to men even when they are not formidable, but Camilla had precisely the clear, crisp manner that Henry found daunting. She greeted him cordially but not, he felt, with the same open enthusiasm as the first time.

"Just wanted to follow-up on our last conversation—about our favorite adjunct," he said in his most ingratiating manner. "You mentioned you were going to look into things. I thought I would drop by and see how 'things' were going." This little attempt at a joke did not come out quite right and made him feel even more self-conscious.

Camilla smiled a tight unforthcoming smile. "You already helped by coming forward. I appreciate that. We need people to step forward, not bury things. We need transparency. And you can be sure I took everything you said very seriously. I know you command a lot of respect around here."

"Well, thank you, but it's not really about me. I didn't want you to do anything on my account. As I said the last time, it's really about the university and how we think about our mission to the students."

"No, I appreciate that. I agree with you—it's important to think seriously about these things. I did make some calls after we talked. But I must say, I got some rather interesting responses."

"Really? Can you share?" Henry said, as if he didn't know.

"I don't see why not. I talked to Bertram. I thought that was appropriate, since he's the department chair. To tell you the truth, he seemed a little puzzled by the whole thing. He didn't see any kind of discrimination going on when it came to Alicia. As far as he was concerned, they were just following the directives we had from the administration about cutting costs for next year."

"Right. That's what he told us, too."

"But you don't agree with him."

"Bertram's a good guy, but in this case I think he may be a little biased."

"Biased? In what way?"

Henry sighed. "Let's just say that if there's a problem there, a problem of the kind I described, he's not likely to see it. He is too close to the situation. I'm not saying Bertram is causing any problems himself, but sometimes your perception of reality can be affected by your—well, your allegiances."

"'Allegiances'? Not sure I'm following you."

Henry looked at her. He had a decision to make—whether to stop right there or forge ahead and fulfill his promise to Margie. He forged ahead. "As I said before, what we have here is basically a conflict of styles. You're going to hear some things from some quarters about Alicia's supposed 'competence,' but it's not about that, I assure you. There is nothing wrong with Alicia, nothing whatsoever. She has all the 'competencies' she needs to do her job well—very well. In fact she's as competent as anyone I've ever seen at this level. No, this business about competencies is being used to mask something else. Alicia does things a little differently from some others in the department, and they are perhaps not as open to this difference in style—yes, this diversity—as they might be."

"Who's not? Bertram?"

"Well, no, it's not Bertram. Alicia gave a very fine concert last fall. I believe I told you it was one of the most remarkable concerts I've ever heard here. And I'm not the only one who feels that way. Many of my colleagues agree with me. This young woman has a remarkable talent. But the thing is she has a very different style and different methods from what we generally see with the orchestra, and, to be honest, from modern performance concepts in general. And that's where the problem is, as I see it."

"Yes, I get it. The orchestra," she said, and Henry perceived a slight shift in her tone. "So is this about Malcolm, then? Are you saying Malcolm is the problem?"

"Look, I'm not interested in calling out any individuals. That's not why I'm here. Malcolm is a talented guy himself and has made many contributions to the university. I'm just here on a positive note, out of a desire to put in a good word for someone who I believe deserves our support, someone who definitely has a lot to offer, even if she's a little rough around the edges. After all, we were all a little rough around the edges when we started. Teaching is a high calling. It takes time to grow into the role—and I think she deserves to be given more time. She's a raw talent with unlimited potential. She needs to be nurtured and encouraged. Not only would it be a crushing blow not to renew her contract, but it's in the best interests of the university to hold onto this young woman as long as we can."

"Okay, understood. But you are talking about Malcolm, right? Essentially what you're telling me is Malcolm is opposing to her because she does things differently than he does, or maybe he's not too happy about her being there. That's what you're saying."

Henry smiled. "There's a little thing called human nature. We all have it. I think when someone enjoys great success there may be a tendency not always to feel too happy about that. To make a long story short, I think some of the criticism coming her way is not necessarily based on purely objective criteria but may have something to do with feeling threatened, or misunderstood."

"Well, this is being direct. Basically you're saying he's jealous. He feels upstaged by her and now he's out on some vendetta to put her in her place."

"I don't know if I would put it quite like that. All I'm saying is that it's easy to confuse our own standards of value with high standards, to make ourselves the standard of what is good and think everyone else should be just like us. It's natural to feel that way—I feel that way myself sometimes—but it isn't always equitable or right. Different people do things differently. That's just a fact of existence. And it is also the very soul of diversity, as I understand it; the idea that differences can contribute to the integrity of the whole. I think we should encourage the differences, if we can; embrace them, as long as they lead to quality results. It's the end result that matters, not so much how we got there."

She looked at him. "Diversity is part of the mission of this university, and I would be very disappointed to find out that there are some who are not on board with it, especially people in leadership positions. But I do see one little problem with what you're saying. Bertram is the one who brought all this up. Bertram is the one who came up with the plan for the adjuncts for next year. He doesn't conduct the orchestra; why would he be jealous of Alicia?"

"Well, again—Bertram is not necessarily a disinterested observer. At least not in this instance."

"Bertram is taking sides with Malcolm? Or Bertram is somehow in on it with Malcolm?"

"Bertram and Malcolm have both managed to convince themselves she needs to go. How they arrived at that consensus I don't know. I happen to disagree with the decision. I think it diminishes the university. I think it diminishes us all."

"I must say, I wish you had told me all this the first time around. It would have saved me from going on a wild goose chase. And I certainly have a much clearer picture now of why you wanted to talk to me, why you feel this sense of urgency. You're not the kind of guy who goes to the dean with every problem you see. I get that. But if you don't mind me asking you again—what is it exactly that you want me to do for Alicia? Put yourself in my position. I have literally dozens of situations like this to deal with. How can I help you without being unfair to all those other well-meaning professors who have someone they feel needs to be protected or needs special treatment?"

This stopped him. "I'm not talking about special treatment. I don't want that, and I don't think Alicia does, either. As for what you should do—to tell you the truth, I don't know. I fully understand your predicament, believe me. I didn't particularly want to come here. It's just that I seem to have a burden for this gifted young woman. Frankly, I find the whole thing kind of frustrating and bizarre—that there should even be a question about keeping someone of her caliber. But that's my problem, not yours."

"Of course it would be frustrating to see someone cut loose when you have strong feelings for that person. I totally get that. And I'm glad you came to me to talk about it. Don't get me wrong. But here's my dilemma. In reality, the only way to get any kind of formal inquiry started would be for you to press charges. I mean, I could make some more calls for you, if that's what you want. I could try some other people in the department and see what they have to say. But I can't say for sure what would come of it."

"You would be willing to do that? I don't want to impose."

"Of course! I'm not going to turn a deaf ear when someone like you comes in to talk to me. I take this very seriously."

"Well, hopefully they'll be frank with you. What's happening right now is people are reluctant to speak up. There is a lot of support for Alicia, but I seem to be the only one talking about it. Maybe if they hear from you directly that will change."

"I'm happy to do it. I'm happy Alicia has such a strong supporter."

Henry did not attempt to obtain a more firm commitment from her or a clear explanation of what she meant by "some other people." He preferred to assume it meant someone other than Malcolm or Bertram—which, frankly, was good enough for him. On the whole, he was pleased with this meeting. He thought it had gone as well as he could have expected, perhaps even better. He had done what he came to do. Malcom's name had come up. He may not have used the direct route that Margie probably would have preferred, but he had done enough. He hadn't gone "all fuddy-duddy," whatever that meant. Yes, from his point of view he had done more than enough.

He went directly to her office to report.

"Well, I did it," he said, sticking his head in the door with a beaming smile.

"You did what?"

"Told her everything. Just like you said."

"You did! I'm so proud of you."

"Yes, we had a very good talk. She's a good person. She doesn't want to see anyone mistreated. And you were right. She hadn't done very much up until now because she didn't know the specifics. Now she knows the specifics, so we'll see what happens."

"Did she have any idea about Malcolm—what he was trying to do?"

"No, she seemed quite surprised. But people at her level don't see Malcolm the way you and I do. They see a nice-looking young man who's bright and enthusiastic and seems to know his business."

"That needs to change. He's doing a lot of damage around here."

"Well, I planted the seed anyway. We'll see what comes out of it. She is still looking into it. Maybe it's time for a little of his nonsense to come out."

"But what did you say? I mean what exactly did you tell her?"

"Just what we talked about. I made it clear that the opposition to Alicia was not based on a fair assessment of her capabilities. In particular, I told her that some people may not have been happy about her success with the orchestra. She caught right on. I give her credit. She knew exactly what I was talking about."

"But you're sure she knew you were talking about Malcolm?"

"Of course! She was the one who brought up his name."

"Really?" Margie said, seeming surprised. "Did she say anything about him?"

"Well, no. That would not have been appropriate. But the personal connection you were talking about was definitely made. I could see it on her face."

Margie looked like she was going to say something but stopped herself. "Well, that's really good news. I can't wait to tell Alicia. I just don't know how I can thank you."

"Not a problem. Happy to help."

Henry closed the door quietly and headed toward his office. There was a little bounce in his sixty-two year old step. He even thought about whistling. But what does one whistle when one is a music professor? A passage from the Seventh? Vivaldi? Henry smiled at these silly thoughts. He felt rather silly, or giddy, having just delivered his good news to Margie. He looked up and saw Bea coming toward him down the hallway and smiled at her, too. She gave him a queer look, but he didn't think anything of it. He didn't mind. He felt like smiling.

SETBACK

HENRY FELT GOOD, overall, about his second meeting with Camilla, and especially good about the effect it had on Margie. He was glad he had stepped forward for her and her friend. He had done something for them they could not have done for themselves, made himself useful for the first time in years.

The weekend and a rather dull Monday went by without any further contact with Margie. Henry thought about her smile when he gave her the news. He longed to cash in, as it were, on that smile, at least to the extent of seeing her again, but did not know how. He certainly did not want her to think he was cashing in. But then it was Tuesday and the sun was shining and the weather turning and he was sitting in his office looking over the music and markings for an upcoming concert when who should walk in the door but Margie herself!

"Hey there," she said in all good humor.

"Hey yourself. You're looking—great," he blurted.

"Thank you! You look great too. How was your weekend?"

"Oh, it was all right I guess, in spite of the rain," he lied. Actually the weekend had been torture. He had spent the entire time thinking about her and hiding from Gabrielle, who was in a strange mood for some reason. "How was yours?"

"It was good. A little lonely. All my friends were away."

"What about me? I thought I was your friend."

"Of course you are! I mean my girlfriends that I usually hang out with. I don't know—with this long winter people seem kind of desperate to get out of town."

71

"How come you're not desperate to get out of town?"

"Oh, it's too fun here. Just can't wait to see what's going to happen next."

"Are you expecting something to happen?" he said, thinking this could mean a couple of things.

"With you on our side, anything can happen."

"I don't know about that. We'll see."

"So are you going to say something tomorrow? At the meeting?"

Henry looked at her blankly for a moment. She was adorable with that smile. "I could. Camilla said she was going to look into it, but there's no reason why I couldn't put in another good word for Alicia."

"Oh, would you? I'm just so nervous about it. I mean, when do they have to decide?"

"End of next month, I believe. But no, I'd be happy to say something. You know Alicia can count on my vote." He just couldn't bring himself to say anything that might take the scrunch out of that face.

"Well, just thought I'd stop in and say hi. Hadn't seen you for a couple of days."

"I know. It seems like forever, right?"

"You're so funny. Are we going to get together again one of these nights?"

"Sure, I'd love that."

"Me too!"

She skipped off leaving poor Henry a bit dazed.

What had he just done? Had he completely lost his mind? Was he really going to say something at tomorrow's meeting? He had already spoken up in one department meeting and gone to the dean twice. As far as he was concerned, it was enough. No, it was too much. But he couldn't help himself. He just could not bring himself to say no to Margie. He should have said no—every rational part of his being told him to say no—but when he opened his mouth it said yes. It was almost as if his mouth and his mind were not connected.

Henry was a little upset—at Margie. He had done so much already; did she really expect him to do more? Was it really that important to her? She was adorable, yes, but he was not Superman. He put his pants on one leg at a time. And at his age it was getting harder and harder. In fact on the very morning of the meeting he was putting his pants on one leg at a time when he lost his balance and almost fell down.

Gabrielle: "What's the matter? Are you all right?"

Henry: "Oh, it's that numbness in my left foot again. I'm fine."

Gabrielle: "Don't you think you should go see Dr. Corso about that?"

Henry: "That quack? I'll probably walk out of there with fifteen prescriptions."

The thing is this little balance problem annoyed him. He was tired of being the "old man," as some of the wags in the department called him. He was not ready to be put out to pasture. Not yet. Suddenly he found himself *wanting* to tangle with Malcolm and Jeff. He was sick and tired of the lack of respect. In the past it had been carefully veiled—the scornful attitude they exhibited toward his humanistic approach to music, toward him. But lately the attacks had become more pointed and personal. Like the thing with Alicia. It wasn't just about her; it was a proxy assault on him, on who he was and what he stood for. He was sure of it. And all of his friends agreed.

Supposedly her conducting technique was "not very good." This was the authoritative judgment Malcolm was sharing with all who would listen. It simply infuriated Henry every time he heard it. It was an indictment on those who did not bow down like slaves to *la technique*, by the minions of Mordor who were not soulful and did not understand what soulfulness means. "Conducting technique"? Oxymoron! Did they not understand that the only technique that matters is the one that draws love and tenderness out of the players? There is no technique for what the spirit orders. That which is spirit is spirit, and that which is flesh is flesh.

Henry felt rebellious. He who had never overtly tried to have an impact on the department found himself very much wanting to have one now. It wasn't enough to go to the dean and trade platitudes; he wanted to win this battle. He wanted to get Alicia her contract—but most of all he wanted to put Malcolm in his place. Would he speak up for Alicia? Of course he would! He was not the sort of person to go back on his word. Besides, he was encouraged by the dean's openness. She seemed to understand what he was trying to say. She agreed with him about diversity of methods. He did not think she would side with Malcolm and the good old boys if push came to shove. There was a change in the air. Their way of doing things was becoming obsolete.

The time for the meeting came and they were all gathered in the usual place. It seemed to him there was electricity in the air, a sense of anticipation. Margie came in and gave him a little wave of the hand. He was charmed, but it was not just about Margie now. It was about himself and self-respect. He was ready; he knew what he had to do. They were not going to surprise him like the last time. Unfortunately he never got the chance. There was a guest speaker from HR who droned on and on for what seemed like forever about the new sensitivity codes and gobbled up the entire ninety minutes. Afternoon classes were beginning. There just wasn't time for anything more. Bertram didn't even bother making the usual last call for questions or comments. No one wanted it. They were all worn out.

Henry was disappointed—or was he? To tell the truth, he wasn't quite sure. Part of him really wanted to have an opportunity to take the floor and filibuster against the unjust severing of Alicia Baptiste; part of him wanted to break out of his shell and show his fiery side. Then again, he didn't really want to do this at all, did he? Eisenhower's adage: Battles never go as planned. Lee thought he had the advantage at Gettysburg, Napoleon at Waterloo. It is too easy to talk yourself into thinking you have the upper hand. Foes like Malcolm are never to be taken lightly. He could try to stay positive, but he couldn't prevent the trolls from trying to hijack the discussion and taking it in their usual negative direction. Once battle is engaged, you must be ready to pursue it to the end and never waver. Was he ready?

He went back to his office and sat down and gazed out the window, where the sun was beginning to appear from behind icy clouds. Margie walked in and closed the door—she was not happy.

"What happened? I thought you were going to say something."

"You saw how it went. The topic never came up."

"That's because no one brought it up."

"There wasn't time," Henry said defensively. "That poor woman went on forever."

"There was time. After the presentation. Everybody was waiting for you to say something."

"What do you mean 'everybody'?"

"Everybody! They knew you were going to defend her. You could see they were all waiting for you to do it. I don't know why you didn't."

"It wasn't the right moment," Henry said weakly, torn between wanting to accept her implied flattery and wanting to defend himself. "I had it all worked out—what I was going to say—but it would have taken too long. People had to get to their classes."

"But you promised. I told everybody and now I look like a fool."

"You shouldn't have told *anybody*. That was not a good idea," Henry said, becoming alarmed.

"Oh, don't try to pull that one on me. Everybody has been waiting for you to speak up. You just sit there and you don't do anything. It's like you're afraid of them or something."

"I'm not afraid of them," he protested. "But you have to pick your moments. You have to be smart about these things."

"Yeah, well, good for you. You go ahead and be 'smart' about things. Meanwhile they're going to get rid of her and nobody's going to do anything about it."

She stormed out. Henry sat there stunned. He had never seen her angry before. It was shocking. Was this really how she saw him—as a coward? Afraid of Malcolm and Jeff and even Bertram—his own protégé? Was that how they all saw him? Did he really have a reputation in the department for just sitting there and saying nothing because he was afraid of what might happen? Such a thought had never entered his head. It was disturbing. He did not see himself as a coward. He saw himself as being philosophical. He was not in the habit of fighting battles in the department because they were not his battles.

What he fought for was his ensemble, and staying in playing shape, which took up several hours every day, and publicity, and getting concert dates, and actually playing the concerts. There was no one else in the department who had the moxie to do all this and to keep on doing it for forty years. There was no one else who had what it takes to be a first violinist in a chamber group and have to lead the way through the most challenging repertoire and get up on stage and put everything on the line not just in front of adoring fans but sniping critics; not just when you're feeling good and confident but when you're feeling not so good and do not know how things are going to turn out.

Courage? They had no idea how much courage it took to do what he did. For that matter, it also took courage to keep his mouth shut all these years, like Cordelia before her raging father: "Love, and be silent." He had been maligned, abused, mistreated, misinterpreted. He had sat there and listened to the most outrageous insinuations being floated about him and his motives and said nothing. No courage? Really? He had bled for them in his desire to help them become the kind of department they should be, the kind of department they easily could become if the obstructionists would get out of the way.

He marched down to Richie's office.

"Howdy."

"Doody."

"Do you think I'm a coward?"

"Define 'coward.'"

"Do you think I'm too afraid of the Nazis to say anything?"

"I think you've found your hiding place and that's a good thing—for you."

"So you do think I'm a coward. You think I'm afraid of them. Because that's what I'm being told. Everyone thinks I'm a coward for not saying anything about Alicia today."

"They were probably just amazed at what happened last time you opened your mouth and looking forward to a good show."

"It's hilarious that they think I'm the coward. I was the only one who spoke up."

"Yes, you did—and what were you thinking? You know what they're like."

"So now you're saying I *should* be a coward."

"I'm saying it doesn't make sense to tangle with people like that. You have a handicap because you have a conscience. You're too honest. There's no way you can win."

"But that's just not right. Why do the liars always have to come out on top?"

"Because they can! They want the power more than you do; that's why they lie. If you don't want it, you're not going to be willing to do the kinds of things you have to do to get it."

"So that's the choice, then? Lie and cheat or give up the fight?"

"Lying is the path to power, and people in power are the biggest liars of them all. Generally speaking. Or at least I haven't seen anything to make me feel otherwise. Then again, I'm a young man. What's your excuse?"

WALPURGIS NIGHT

HIS CONVERSATION WITH RICHIE did not necessarily make him feel any better. Don't go to a wit when you're looking for sympathy. But the person who really shook him up was Margie. He did not know what to make of the abrupt change in her. Up to that point she had been all sweetness and light, smiles and compliments; now she was like a prickly hedge. It wasn't just the tone—it was the fierceness. People get angry and people get nasty, but these were two separate things in Henry's mind.

Oh, he could understand why she was upset. Alicia was her friend and Alicia's position was in jeopardy. It was natural to feel some urgency—and after all, he had failed to speak up after promising he would. But the change was just jarring. It hinted at a possible dark side to Margie, which frankly was something he did not want to think about. Was this what she was really like, deep down? Or what was she like? He realized he did not know much about her. He had hardly known her at all until that fateful day when she walked into his office—they traveled in very different crowds. Was she another one of the troubled young women he had seen come and go through the department over the years? Had he managed to stick his unsuspecting head into a hornet's nest?

But then again he did know her. Didn't he? Of course he did. He'd spent quite a bit of time with her over the past couple of months, and very pleasant time it was. She would sit there in the candlelight smiling sweetly while he held forth on music and culture and the arts or whatever. It seemed like they were in

78

agreement on almost everything, especially Malcolm and his shortcomings. Maybe it wasn't so much Margie's fiery reaction that was troubling him as his own embarrassment. He did not want to disappoint her. He liked the heroic image he seemed to have in her eyes. Was that why her anger stung so much? Because he was afraid of losing it?

On the other hand…it wasn't his fault that the evil HR lady had droned on and on with her dreary slide presentation. There was no way to shut her up, and by the time she did shut up there was no way to bring up Alicia. The timing had to be auspicious for discussing such a sensitive topic. There had to be favorable headwinds as well as plenty of opportunity for people to overcome their reticence about speaking up. This had not been the case at the end of the meeting, not by a long shot. Everyone was worn out and irritated by the presentation. Henry could see it on their faces. And they had to get to their classes.

In short, Margie's reaction seemed all out of proportion to the offense—if that is what it was. It also showed a lack of gratitude, as far as he was concerned. He had probably done more for her than for anyone else on the faculty in his entire time at the school. On top of that, he doted on her! Did it count for nothing that he was so utterly bewitched and bewildered by her? Wasn't his affection worth something? Then again—how would she know? He had done nothing to make his feelings clear. And maybe it was a good thing she didn't know, based on what he had just witnessed. Maybe it was a good thing he had not exposed himself.

Maybe the shocking outburst was actually rather fortunate. It might bring him to his senses and make him give up this ridiculous infatuation. After all, she had not come to him as an angel of love. No, she came looking for a mentor and defender. He was a senior member of the department, and her friend was in a desperate situation. She needed his help, not his adoration. Being a mentor was something Henry happened to enjoy. It had taken many years and much suffering to reach mentor status. He liked the idea that someone like Margie would come to him when she needed help.

He was her mentor and he would stay her mentor—if she still wanted him. Now was the time to make this all-important metamorphosis in his mind. No lines had been crossed. Nothing had been done or said to betray his infatuation. He was still a father figure in her eyes; disinterested, caring, distinguished, experienced, wise. These were just the things he wanted to be; just the things he had labored so hard and long to become. Why risk an honorable identity in a foolish attempt to become something else, something impossible? Why?

And yet—he could not let go. The truth was he was smitten. He had barely even known her before that fateful day when she walked into his office; but then she smiled at him, she let him take her out to dinner and invited him up to her apartment—and he fell in love. He thought about her day and night. Sometimes he sat in his office in a daydream, writing her name in the condensation on his window and then rubbing it out again and shaking his head at his own idiocy. One day he was walking across campus and suddenly called out her name—right there in the middle of the street!

He wanted her to love him and at the same time he didn't want her to love him. He wanted her to give herself completely to him but another part of him wanted her to go away and never come anywhere near him again. He did not know what to think and he couldn't think. All he knew was he was always thinking of her. For every part of him that said "no" there was a fresher part that wanted to dote on her and longed to see her again. He tried to scold away these tender feelings but they would not be scolded. They mocked him every time he tried. He reasoned with himself, told himself it was foolishness, insisted that nothing good could come of it, but the thing he was dealing with was not reasonable. No, it would not be reasoned away. It was a tyrant, and the worst thing was that he was inclined to be in love with its tyranny.

He tried to shake up the psychological status quo by changing his habits. He stopped coming to the office so much, which he had started doing purely on account of her. He stopped parading around the hallways pretending he was on some sort of mission when the only mission he was really on was to catch a glimpse of the adorable Margie. But nothing changed. He could stay away all he liked—he was still thinking of her. In fact it seemed like he was thinking of her more and more. He who always had a cure for the love woes of others now found that he had none at all for himself.

A cold, rainy week went by and then another as winter lurched uncertainly into spring; then came some fine April days and the birds started to sing—but still there was no sign of Margie. Henry would sit in his office waiting for the little knock on the door that never came. He tried composing an email to her but would just sit there staring at the drafts. He could not formulate the language in the way he wanted, in a way that was safe and yet not too safe. He did not seem to be able to use the language of reconciliation without crossing over into affection and love—but then when he took out all the affection there was nothing left. It seemed like a letter from the insurance company, and just as pointless.

Another week went by and still there was no contact between them. Then he received the planner for the April meeting and felt a jolt of excitement. There it was, right at the top of the agenda: "Discuss adjunct faculty needs for next year." He printed it out and practically ran to her office.

"Hi, there!" he said cheerily, trying to act as if there were not several weeks standing between them; trying to make it seem like there had been no disconnect at all, no angry outburst, no misgivings on his side, no endless agonizing.

"Hi!" she said, lighting up with a beautiful smile. "It's so good to see you! Where have you been?"

"Oh, busy with concerts. A lot of rehearsing and all that boring stuff." This was not completely untrue. There had been a concert just the previous weekend at a chamber festival in New Jersey.

"I was getting worried. I thought you forgot about me."

"How could I forget about you?" he said a little more fervently than intended. He held up the printout of the meeting planner.

"Did you see this?"

"What is it?"

"Agenda for next week's faculty meeting. Check out number one under 'old business.'"

"Alicia?"

"Well, adjuncts anyway. I think it's pretty much implied. I'm sure they know it's going to come up."

"Oh, promise me you'll say something!"

"Of course! That's why I'm here. I need you to help me figure out what to say. I want to make sure I do you right."

This did not quite come out the way he intended, but she did not seem to notice. "I'd be honored to. I'm flattered you even asked. But I don't know what I could tell you that you don't already know."

"Oh, you'd be surprised." Now he was really getting tangled up. "It's so beautiful out—how about a little walk? Maybe we can get a cup of coffee or something."

They went to Starbucks and then headed for the town park at the edge of the campus. It was a glorious day after a long, cold winter; the kind of day when everything seems so right with the world and so sweet. The banks brought forth their fresh daffodils, a legion of field fairies bearing joyful yellow diadems. Among them rose the dark-haired queen, in Henry's mind, robed in purest white with periwinkle and snowdrops at her waist, bearing in her delicate hands an embroidered pillow on which there lay a shining golden ring. The flower legions nodded their approval as she glided with light feet to the hawthorn break and then down the hill into a wooded copse.

Here nature's own memorials stood low and still, their faces made of granite; on them flowed the fleecy sedum and the sturdy stonecrop with tendrils clinging delicately to every crevice. A flock of hens and chicks made their way into the festive hall in their various handsome burrs of blue and purple, turning their heads to watch as the queen approached and all was made ready. Lady slippers bore her to the crystal basin strewn with lilies and ivy flowing down into a glistening stream. She paused to dip her pale finger in the water as the birds sang the vernal chorus.

"Yield up your precious charge to the water," the surly grackle commanded, "for I have been plucking worms from the hard ground and must see the end of all that was begun."

"Would you disturb her reverie?" reproved the goldfinch, sitting haughtily upon a winter-worn thistle. "Pay no attention to the fickle bird, my queen. You must do as you see fit, for spring is the time of flowers, and in spring the flowers hold their sway."

"Yes, yes, follow your heart," chimed in the tiny wren. "Pay no attention to us. I have found a place to nest, a snug little nook high up in a chestnut tree, and have nothing more to ask."

The queen lifted her face up to the trees and smiled at the feathered colloquy but did not lay down her pillow or cast its precious cargo into the pool. She stood as if waiting for a signal as the ferns waived in the breeze and the azaleas displayed their coral glories. Then like one who has endured many winters and seen many springs she gently drew the pillow up into her bosom and enfolded the ring against her breast, and once again the turning of the seasons was complete.

Henry and Margie meandered along for the longest time, taking every trail they saw. He was on fire. He had made a lifelong study of botany and was able to identify all of the flowers and many of the attractive plants along the way, both in their common and their Latin names. He was enjoying himself, his excitement was real; there were few things he loved more than a walk in his beloved Nature. Margie smiled while he talked. She seemed to enjoy both his knowledge and the attention he was showing her.

Soon the topic returned to Alicia and the upcoming meeting. "Did they put it on the agenda because they were told to? Is that your take?"

"I can't make that connection explicitly. All I know is I had a good conversation with the dean—and now it's shown up on the agenda. It seemed like a good sign, like things might be turning our way."

"So do you think they're finally on to Malcolm then?"

"Oh, I don't know about that. I don't know if you can count on anything happening there. The best thing as far as we're concerned would be for Alicia to get her contract."

"But he's the one who's blocking it. He's the one who's causing all the problems."

"I know that; everybody knows that. But Malcolm is—let's just say resourceful. He has a talent for landing on his feet. I'm going to focus on the positive value Alicia can bring to the department."

"But it's not fair. What he's doing is not right."

"I know. Believe me, Malcolm has been a veritable aquifer of unfairness ever since he arrived here. They're never going to get rid of Malcolm. They love him. But this will kill him, if we manage to bring back Alicia."

"Oh, I hope so. He's such a pig. He's always saying inappropriate things—it's embarrassing. And this whole thing with Alicia is so obvious. Everybody knows he's jealous of her. That's why he wants to get rid of her. That's the only reason."

"I wouldn't give 'everybody' quite so much credit," Henry said with a laugh. "I know a lot of people who are impressed with Alicia, but a lot of people are impressed with Malcolm, too."

"How could they be? He's such a phony."

"I don't know. It's a mystery. I feel the same way, but he seems to have a lot of friends and admirers. He certainly wins a lot of awards. The local critic is in love with him."

"Yeah—literally," she smirked. "He has his own issues."

It was a very pleasant conversation, a healing conversation after all the agony Henry had endured, and in such an exquisite setting. He felt they had managed to get back to the place where they were before the outburst. Walking with her in the spring sunlight—he could not even put his feelings into words. The more she seemed to take him into her confidence, the more he thawed inside. He stole a glance at her and her beautiful black hair and his mouth went dry. It was one of the greatest days of his life, the day of reconciliation.

Later on they were sitting on a stone bench, watching the swans float dreamily on the pond and gladly soaking up the sun. Henry could feel her sitting next to him. They weren't actually touching, but he could feel her, that's how strongly his soul went out to her.

"Look at them. Aren't they beautiful?" he said.

"I love swans. They seem so delicate. And I love the fact that they mate for life. There's something so romantic about that."

Henry sat in the deafening wake of this comment for some time. He sat there with the word "mate" echoing around in his head and he heard the word "life" and he felt the force of spring bearing down on him and the closeness of her and of her hand, which was resting on the bench between them. And then he could not help himself, he put his hand on her hand.

"I am so in love with you," he blurted, staring straight ahead.

She smiled without looking at him. Then she took his hand in hers and kissed it.

UNTO THE BREACH

ENRY COULDN'T BELIEVE HE SAID IT. He could still hear the shocking words coming out of his lips, the words he did not intend to say but which were pulled out of him somehow by spring or swans or the scent of the year's first new-mown grass or some other irresistible force.

She did not reply. Indeed, neither one of them said very much after that. What was there to say? They walked back to school and went their separate ways with a friendly nod—a very friendly nod, he thought—but few words. He was waiting for her to speak, to respond; he longed to know what she was thinking. Did it seem like he was joking? He had heard young men say such things to pretty girls, just to see how they would react, although usually in bars after a couple of drafts. Was that what she thought he was doing? He found himself wishing it were—there was more dignity in it somehow.

Then there was the chance she was thinking of him as a romantic old fool. And she was right if she was. He was certainly old, much too old for a fresh young thing like her, nor could there be any doubt that this infatuation of his was making him foolish. He seemed to have lost all sense of his station in life, his stature in the music world, the eminence he enjoyed in intellectual circles as a music professor and classical artist. Was this the way professors talked? Love blather? Emotive outbursts? "Youth of course must have its fling," but the foolishness that is so attractive in young lovers seems a little stale in someone like himself, a man long past his physical peak. Even Orlando becomes tedious if he does not grow up.

Henry was ashamed of himself. He decided to stay away from Margie for a while. He did not go to school at all the next day. The day after that he had classes to teach, but he did not go anywhere near the faculty offices. At the same time he became determined to demonstrate his regard for her by speaking up for her friend. No one else was going to stick their neck out for an adjunct they didn't know or for a cause most of them didn't care about; no one else had the standing, even if they had the desire. Malcolm's behavior was becoming increasingly destructive. His disgusting campaign against Alicia provided a perfect opening for a rebuke, since Henry could use the diversity argument to his advantage.

The time for the meeting came. Henry was sitting there trying to look the same way he always looked as people filtered in and he made his friendly greetings. He was feeling confident and strong but also a little jittery. The confident part came from his faith in his rhetorical strategy; diversity was practically the sacred mission of the university now, and he was simply applying it in a new and—in his eyes—more interesting way. It also came from what had happened at the park two days earlier, the love that was so strong it was almost overpowering. The jitteriness, meanwhile, came from—what? Excitement? Anticipation? He did not know.

Margie appeared and she glanced at him and smiled and he thought he saw a little blush and he was charmed. Then Malcolm and Jeff came in doing their usual snark. He looked at them and felt rage—and more jitters. He looked over at Bertram, who was not giving anything away. If he was concerned about a battle looming, he wasn't showing.

The meeting was underway, and there were the usual presentations, and the usual discussions featuring the usual characters making the usual remarks about this or that new policy or directive or whatever, and Henry hardly heard any of it, since he was counting down the items on the agenda; except when Malcolm spoke up, and then he burned inside.

Finally the highly-anticipated topic came up.

"Now we have adjuncts on the agenda again," Bertram said in a somewhat weary tone, "because I know there has been a lot of discussion of adjuncts at our meetings, going all the way back to

January, and I just want to make sure we are all on the same page. *Are* we on the same page?"

Silence in the room. Henry looked at Malcolm and Jeff; one was fiddling with his Android and the other was staring at the ground with a strange smile. He started getting edgy. He could not allow the moment to pass when he knew it would result in Alicia being quietly shuffled into nothingness. If he was going to speak up at all it had to be now. Also Margie was watching him—he could sense it. He could not let her down. Not after what had happened. He felt a need to back up his tender outburst with actions.

"Well, just to clear the air, the issue for me is one of diversity. I think it's important to allow ourselves to look at things in new ways, ways that challenge our assumptions and paradigms. It's good for us as a department and good for our students."

"I don't think anyone disagrees with you," Jeff piped up. "Did you have something specific in mind?"

"I think you all know how highly I think of Alicia Baptiste, and it would be my hope that we could find some room in the budget to bring her back for another year. She adds a great deal to the university and is a remarkable talent. I realize there has apparently been some discussion of her methods, but there's no denying that they work—which after all is the important thing."

"Well, okay, everyone is entitled to his opinion, but what does diversity have to do with Alicia Baptiste?" Jeff replied with open scorn. "Are you saying we have to have her back because she's a woman? Most of the adjuncts are women. For that matter, more than half the faculty is women."

"That's just my point. There are different kinds of diversity. In this case we're looking at a diversity of styles. Sometimes we come across a style that is not our own and we find ourselves resisting it. Maybe it's just foreign to us, maybe we feel threatened—I don't know. But that doesn't mean the results are necessarily any less valuable than our own. They may even be getting better results from their strange style than we are. At least we have to be humble enough to consider the possibility."

"I really don't understand this. I don't know what you are talking about. Are you saying Alicia is better than the people we already have on the faculty? I mean, we have an orchestra conductor with a national reputation. We have someone who is dedicated to the students and trying to take the program to a new level and doing something exciting and unique, as has been widely acknowledged. His credentials are impeccable. Look at the awards he's won—somebody must think he's doing a good job."

"Of course he is," Henry replied diplomatically, although his heart was not in it. "I'm not making comparisons. As I've said many times, we have a good, talented department here, and we should keep it going and support each other. All I'm saying now is we should also be respectful of styles that are different from our own, styles that may challenge us."

"Again, nobody's disagreeing with you. But let's say we hired a violinist who had a different style than you. Let's say you felt this violinist was causing problems for the students because the techniques she was teaching were not the right techniques. So in your view, you just have to sit there and be silent and let her teach for the sake of 'diversity'? No matter how much it screwed up the students or hurt their chances for success? Speaking hypothetically, of course."

"Well, no, obviously. That would be rather counterproductive."

"So then the kind of diversity you are talking about is not necessarily always good. It's possible to use the term 'diversity' as a whitewash for bad technique or pedagogy."

"But that's not what we are talking about here. We are talking about someone who is eminently qualified and in fact has proven her qualifications."

"That's your opinion, you've stated it. I'm not sure it's everyone's opinion, and I really don't think we should be taking up any more of the faculty's time discussing it."

"I have to agree, Henry," Bertram said. "We all have our opinions about these things, but the fact is the decision has already been made. We have to cut back next year and several adjuncts will be affected by the cutbacks, including Alicia."

"I wouldn't do that—not until you've talked to the dean."

"I told you, the decision has already been made. And I talked to the dean. She's in full agreement."

Henry was thoroughly silenced. *De gustibus non disputandum*—but this was precisely what he was doing. He and Jeff were in equipoise on the question of Alicia. Things might have tipped in his favor if others had joined in, if a few brave souls had agreed with him about her sterling qualities; but of course this is just what did not happen. It was his old agony, his old burden coming back to haunt him again. It was his own playing and the fact that Opinion does not rest on depth or passion but on a dozen other things, most of them superficial. This was Henry's hell, and apparently he still wasn't quite ready to live in it. After all these years he still had not made peace with it. Not entirely.

He looked around the room. It remained silent. Some were looking at him; some were looking away in the awkwardness of the moment; some did not appear to be listening at all. The truth hit him. He had been discomfited, publicly thrown down and made to look small. The diversity argument was not as potent as he thought it would be, not out in the open where it could be deflected. No one spoke up to support him and his notion of diversity of styles. And the personal support he was anticipating for Alicia also seemed to be non-existent. He had taken up the challenge, risen to open combat with his enemies, and had been humiliated. Alicia could not be saved. He had known it all along. Why didn't he listen to himself?

Henry lost whatever confidence he came in with. He withdrew into his shell and managed to get through the rest of the meeting only by playing the slow movement of a Beethoven quartet over and over again in his mind. He did not hear what was said and didn't want to hear. Afterwards he went into his office and closed the door and stared out the window, trying to get his blood pressure back under control. He picked up some student papers and started to read the monstrosities half-heartedly. The words danced about on the page. Just when he thought he might be beginning to calm down again there was a timid knock on the door. He tried to ignore it. Then more knocking, more insistent this time.

"Come!" he said with as much enthusiasm as he could muster, which was not a great deal.

It was Margie. Something had changed. She seemed very business-like.

"I'm sorry—I didn't mean to bother you," she said. "How do you think it went?"

"Not well. You were there. No one spoke up."

"Yeah, I was surprised at that. I was sure somebody would say something."

"It seems we were both laboring under the same misconception. These people talk their heads off outside of the meeting but they won't say a word in it. I guess I can't blame them.

There's too much at stake to put a target on your back for the sake of an adjunct."

"But I keep telling you, this isn't about an adjunct. It's about Malcolm and the way he treats people."

"Listen, I know you think I have the power to do something about Malcolm. I don't. You notice he didn't even have to open his mouth. His friend Jeff did all the dirty work for him."

"I noticed you didn't try very hard. You went on and on about this stupid 'diversity' thing, but that's not what this is about. I keep telling you. This is about him abusing his power."

"I'm well aware of that. I know exactly what this is about. And I also know you can't make an accusation like that in a department meeting. Give me some credit for knowing how these things work. I've been here a long time."

"Okay, but what do we do now?"

"Now? There's nothing we can do. You heard Bertram. The decision's already been made."

"But we have to do something. It's outrageous."

"I think I've done quite enough," Henry replied with a chuckle. "Who knows, I may have been the one who got her fired."

She looked at him. "How?"

He shrugged. "I went to the dean. I went over Bertram's head. That's not kosher."

"Wait a minute. So you're saying they're getting rid of her because you went to the dean?"

"No. I don't know. Could be. I'm just saying I think I've probably done enough."

"But if you're the one who did it, then isn't it up to you to undo it?"

"I didn't say I did it. I was just laying out a scenario."

"Well let's say your scenario is true. Let's say you really did get her fired. You're okay with that?"

"No, of course not. But I don't know if that's what really happened."

"But it could be. You said so yourself."

Henry was trapped. "Yes—it could be. I doubt it, but anything is possible."

"Then you have to do something, make it right."

"What can I do?" he said defensively.

"Go to the administration. You keep telling me you're such great friends with the president. Tell him what's going on. Let's be honest—this is sexual harassment. They thought they could pick on her because she's a woman. They never would have tried this with a man."

"Oh, I don't know about that. If a man came in here and had the misfortune to upstage Malcolm, I'm pretty sure the result would be the same."

"No it wouldn't, because he wouldn't be able to get away with it. Malcolm would never mess with another member of the patriarchy. It's just the women he likes to screw over."

With that she turned and marched out. Twice now she had come to him to let him know that his performance in the great uprising against Malcolm was not up to par. Twice now she had shown an angry, even petulant side that was otherwise kept carefully under wraps. And why, oh why, had he tried to deflect her anger by blaming himself for "getting Alicia fired"? Come to think of it, he knew why. It was because he was imagining she had feelings for him. It was because he thought she would not allow him to blame himself; she would come to his defense and let him off the hook. He'd been too clever by half. He had hooked himself and made himself the focal point of her indignation.

Henry was stunned by this little conversation, unnerved in deep parts of his being. First of all there was the hurt lover in him. He had been falling hard for this adorable little thing over the last few months to the point of insensibility. Something had taken root in him and grown itself into him hard. There was the strange confession he made in the park. She smiled, but what did it mean? Was she smiling at his tender apostrophe or at her triumph—or possibly his foolishness? The terrible thing is he wanted it to be tender, even after the tongue lashing he had just received. He wanted very much to hold onto the delirious notion that there was something between them. But was there? Or was it all in his head?

After all, she had a right to be angry. She was worried about her friend and upset about the nonsense going on in the department. He was angry at Malcolm himself and probably would not have respected her if she didn't share his anger. Wasn't it the very thing that had drawn them together—their mutual disgust with Malcolm and his shenanigans? And she was right about his performance in the meeting, as much as he hated to admit it. Clearly the diversity strategy had not served them well. He had initiated a confrontation but was not able to follow through. He had brought up the elephant in the room but danced around it until it disappeared.

Still, he could not whitewash the tone she had used or her cold demeanor, no matter how much he adored her and wanted to make excuses for her. It made him feel small and ridiculous. He was beginning to get the impression that there were two Margies. One was all deference and softness and full of proclamations of admiration and even awe at his accomplishments while the other could be full of impatience and even contempt. Yes, contempt. That's the way her words and her tone came across. It was like being lectured by your second grade teacher. And this was dismaying. To be talked to in such a tone by someone he loved so much, someone for whom he had such tender feelings! He did not know who to be angrier with—Margie for her abuse or himself for his foolishness.

Who exactly was Margie Hart? He realized he did not know very much about her. They had talked a great deal, but always about impersonal things, never about themselves. Was there some truth in the warning he'd received from Bea? Had he rolled himself up into her web?

THE COUNSEL OF FRIENDS

ENRY SCARED HIMSELF. There was a reason why he was reluctant to be drawn into department politics. He had lost his job one time for speaking his mind. He had simply spoken the truth then, too, spoken what was on everyone's mind about some outrageous boondoggle that was going on; he had lost his temper and ripped into the wrong person, a prominent member of the department who was well-connected. It did not happen right away. It took a couple of years. But his enemy had an opportunity for revenge as a member of the tenure committee. Henry didn't have a doctorate. They sent him packing.

He still didn't have a doctorate, and the wound of that strange and terrible interlude in his life had never quite healed. True, things had changed. Forum had become one of the most well-known chamber groups in the world. He had prestige as an international artist that he did not enjoy as a young man. He had been at the school for thirty years, was an institution there. He was on friendly terms with the administration and had tenure.

Yes, much was different—but the old paranoia had never really gone away. Henry did not realize it until now, until he violated his ironclad rule. A certain terror came over him as he sat there going over what had happened in the meeting. He could still hear the ominous silence in the room, the complete lack of any sign of support from the others. Why silence? Because they were afraid. Because he had trod upon sacred ground. Because they had homes and cars and debts and needed their jobs just like he needed his.

Because they knew what Malcolm was like and did not want to become targets.

Henry was already a target. Actually it started when his hair went gray a few years back. He figured it was because of the stress he was under, especially with Forum and all the things he had to do to keep the group happy and in the limelight, but also the politics at school. Malcolm's hair was never going to turn gray because he never felt the kind of stress Henry experienced. He didn't feel stress; he caused it. Henry still felt youthful, for the most part, still felt vigorous and did not look like a man of sixty-two. But it didn't matter. In the eyes of some he was the "old man." He'd had his time in the sun; now he was expected to show some common decency and get out of the way.

There may have been a time when the elders were venerated, but that time was long gone. Did all of Henry's years of experience and accumulated wisdom count for a mite on those rare occasions when he opened his mouth and tried to speak? Not at all. No one was listening—perhaps they couldn't afford to. It was not wisdom that was honored in the world in which he found himself; it was ambition and show. It was the tall men, like Malcolm, the big talkers. It was the ones who, without having any particular gravitas in the sense of depth, were able to feign this precious quality through vague intimidation.

Henry had exposed himself to his enemies. He knew it all too well. They'd been looking for a pretext to push him out, and now he had given them one. He said some things in the meeting he did not really mean to say, things he never would have dreamed of saying if it had not been for Margie. He softened them, spoke in vague generalities, but they were not the kind of things you say if you treasure equanimity and are trying to keep a low profile. They happened to be true, but that didn't make any difference. In a political world it is not truth that has value but careful positioning within the prevailing winds of power. Those words would be used against him. He was sure of it.

He felt ill. He couldn't sit. He ran down to Richie's office. Seems like he had been doing a lot of that lately.

"What did you think?" he said to his good friend.

Richie put aside his usual whimsy. "I thought it was kind of rough, if you really want to know. There were a lot of wide eyes around the room."

"I deserved it. I broke my own rule: Don't waste your time on these people."

"You got involved in a good cause. Nobody can fault you for that. You just didn't realize the cause was already lost."

"Did you think I was out of line?"

"Not at all. I think everything you said was obviously true. You were out of tune, perhaps, with the times, but that's a different matter. I think the real problem is you can't really say what you want to say without drawing Malcolm into it. You tried mightily, but it just can't be done, because in fact what happened was he let his ego get the best of him."

"I didn't want to. Believe me, I was showing all the restraint I could."

"I realize that. But the cold, hard reality is he wants her out of here because she makes him look bad. Those are the facts, and it's hard to talk around the situation and still help her. Especially when he's out slamming her every chance he gets."

"But why didn't anyone else speak up? It was three against one. Just one other advocate or perhaps two could have turned things in Alicia's favor."

Richie chuckled. "I was tempted, especially when Jeff started in on you. He really is a loathsome little toad. For God's sake, lose the moustache. But then you brought up the dean thing and that kind of took the wind out of my sails."

"You mean because they said it was a fait accompli?"

"No, not that. The way you said it made me realize you were staking a lot on her. And I had a pretty strong suspicion this faith was misplaced."

Henry blinked. "What do you mean?"

"Well—her and Malcolm, of course."

"What?"

"You don't know? No, of course you don't. You're always surrounded by your gaggle of admirers at these faculty klatches, so you don't get to observe the two of them together."

"Don't tell me they're shacking up."

"Who knows? Anything's possible. The flirting, however, is pretty outrageous."

Henry was stunned. This was like running into a wall. Richie was right—he was banking heavily on Camilla. If she had a thing for Malcolm, then he had just delivered himself into the hands of his enemy. Malcolm would rip him to shreds.

"Just when you thought it couldn't get any more bizarre," he managed to sputter.

"Around here there's always some new layer of bizarre that can be added on. You don't know the half of it. You're always off gallivanting around the world and hobnobbing with the rich and famous, and I never bother to tell you."

"So that's it, then. I'm toast."

"How do you figure?"

"I basically accused him of being incompetent and vindictive. They'll crucify me for that."

"No, don't be silly. They can't touch you."

"I wouldn't be so sure. The thought police. They're very big on this campus right now. And if he has Camilla on his side—there are a lot of things he can do. Why didn't I see it? So stupid. I did notice something in her body language when Malcolm came up. I should have known."

"You actually brought up Malcolm with Camilla?"

"Well, not directly. I described the situation, and she made the logical deduction. At the time I thought it made her clever. Silly me. They'll get rid of me now. That's what they're trying to do."

Richie scoffed. "They can't get rid of you. They keep talking about how they want us all to have international reputations, and you are the only one who actually does. No, they won't get rid of you. They'll just punish you severely."

"Oh really! What did you have in mind?"

"Well, you know how you love music appreciation classes. I can see a couple of those in your future."

"No—don't tell me. I'll shoot myself."

"What else? I know! Didn't they tell you they were thinking about having you conduct the orchestra in the fall, since Malcolm is involved in the musical? Now watch them change their minds."

"Stop! You're killing me. It's practically the only thing I live for now."

"And then there's this residency thing you've been talking about for, oh, twenty years or so. Lately you've had some encouraging signs from the administration, right? Well, that can change. I'm sure they're going to be taking a second look at that."

"They wouldn't dare. They don't know who they're messing with."

"They know exactly who they're messing with," Richie said with a laugh. "A big pussycat. They've been lying in the weeds all these years, envying you and keeping a distance because they were afraid of you. Now you're wounded. It time for the little people to come out with their little spears."

Richie had reverted to his usual jolly self, but to Henry it was poison. Everything he said seemed all too plausible. They were going to make him pay for his honesty, and whom did he have to blame but himself? On the other hand, Richie's punishments were rather comforting, in a way. What really scared him at this stage in his life was the thought of being pushed out against his will. He was afraid of losing his income and having his pension devalued. He was afraid of losing face.

Compared with that, a couple of extra classes and the other things didn't seem quite so bad. Unpleasant, but not crushing. Richie didn't seem to think he was in any real danger. Henry took refuge in his certainty.

THE DREAM

THE END OF THE SEMESTER was coming and thank God because Henry almost couldn't drag himself to school anymore, in fact almost couldn't drag himself out of bed in the morning. He came in and he was in terror of seeing people, even people he had been on good terms with for years, because of what he had done; because of the trouble he had stirred up with his ridiculous attempt at instigating a coup, like Prometheus; because he did not want to see the knowing looks in their eyes.

He especially did not want to see Malcolm or Jeff. The animosity between them, which he had taken such pains to conceal over the years, was now out in the open. It was a contest between him and Malcolm and Jeff, especially Malcolm, only Henry would not fight. Malcolm would fight. His mouth was going all the time, stirring up trouble in sundry and insidious ways. Henry would not fight back because he was not a fighter. He hated confrontation. It was like blood-letting in his brain.

They talked about him all the time—he knew they did—people came to him and told him some of the ridiculous things they were saying—pointed things, recycled stuff from years ago, warped or untrue—but he did not respond in kind. He shook his head and kept his mouth shut. He should have kept it shut before, when it really mattered. He should have stayed in his Zen zone and not tried to act like one of them. All he could do now was maintain a dignified silence. It was too late, which made it not so dignified. No, from his side it seemed more like silent shame.

He liked to think of himself as a principled pacifist, a peacemaker in a violent world, but the real reason he had to keep his mouth shut was that their mouths were stronger than his. And he knew it. They were more determined and more devious. He found it difficult to lie and twist the facts, which to them seemed perfectly natural. He found himself having to go back into his cave, not because he was wrong but because he was weak. He simply could not compete with them on their own ground. Put him on a stage with a violin and he could compete; but in a war of words he was no match for Malcolm.

Henry had his supporters, of course; they spoke up for him when they could, when they felt they were in a position to do so without incurring Malcolm's wrath. So he was not alone. It was not as if the entire faculty was against him; not even close. He may have even had a majority. But it seemed that way to him. He was a transgressor in his own mind, and he transferred these feelings into the minds of others. He was his own harshest judge and he made everyone else his judge, whether they were judging him or not.

Even in the best of times there were not a great many friendly faces on campus, at least among the faculty. Too many old wounds for that. But now Henry took this generalized gloom and made it personal. He forgot about his colleagues being mad at life and thought they were mad at him. They were not. Most of them weren't, anyway. But he had no way of knowing this. They did not come to talk to him and tell him how they felt. Some were too afraid of Malcolm. Frankly, some were too afraid of him. Others simply didn't feel they knew him well enough to enter into such a personal conversation and weren't sure what to say even if they were inclined to try.

In the epic war that was waged there was waxing and there was waning. Malcolm struck on some gold when he complained about Henry's attitude toward those who were not performers like himself—the attitude he had apparently been hiding all these years but exposed in the meeting. Since this comprised most of the department, he won some sympathy from others who were also concerned about their status. He exaggerated it and made it sound much worse than it really was, made Henry sound intemperate and arrogant, and the clamor against Henry grew; and then he overplayed his hand, because he couldn't help himself, because he really was a small person when you come right down to it—and then the tide turned in Henry's favor for a while, like the Trojans and the Greeks.

So it went in the tumultuous weeks following the meeting. The department was in an uproar because Malcolm would not let go and kept fanning the flames in every quarter. Henry heard about it and he also sensed it, and he was mortified. He had never been in this position before. He had always been the supportive one, the gracious one, the one with the kind word. It was the persona he had carefully cultivated over the years because it was a persona he valued. And now it was smashed, ruined. He had made himself the bad guy, the outcast, an enemy of the people. He felt it acutely and was depressed.

He was determined to keep his mouth shut from now on. What was the point of crossing swords with them? He knew he could never win. It was clear from what happened at the meeting that he could not win when it came to Malcolm and Jeff and their prevarications. First of all, he was not glib like them. He could be eloquent when inspired by truth and beauty, or when holding a violin in his hands, but not in a petty cause. Not to justify himself. Not to tear down others the way they tore him down. And more, he lacked the will to do it. Henry was not like them. He wanted beautiful music. He wanted beautiful friendships. He wanted the sun to shine in the rain.

Then there was Margie and her Jekyll-and-Hyde behavior— what was he to make of that? She had stormed out of his office not once but twice now. Was he being manipulated? Something told him he was. Something told him she was trying to get him to help Alicia and that was the only reason for her interest in him. But then something else stepped in and told him not to be so hard on her, so cynical. Maybe she was just passionate like himself. Maybe that was why she stomped out.

Passion was a good thing, especially in a just cause. He could not blame her for being upset with the ruling caste. What had happened to Alicia was truly disgusting. The boys didn't like her because she made one of their own look bad and the boys had gotten their way again. They always got their way. No, there was nothing wrong with Margie being angry about the situation. He was angry too. He was sick about it and tired of them and their evil ways. Her passion was also his passion.

But what about this seeming rage of hers? It scared him. He was a passionate person—no one could be more passionate on stage—but he never went into a rage. It just wasn't done. In Henry's mind to be in a rage was to give oneself over to dark forces. It was to let go of the very thing that makes us human, the distance we are able put between ourselves and our destructive animal natures. He sensed darkness in her rage—but then again was it really darkness? Or was his lack of rage just a deficit or defense mechanism of his own? Was he wrong about rage?

The thing was he so wanted to be wrong. He'd had such strong feelings about this girl—this young woman—he wanted to be wrong about her rage. He wanted to love her rage—because he was in love. Or was he? For a while there he had been head over heels in love. He had allowed himself to lean in her direction—and then he allowed himself to fall. He had never fallen in love before because it threatened his music, his first love; not even with Gabrielle. Now he had gone into a new world and for a while it was a happy world. It was a joyous world flooded with light and beautiful colors. It was laughing inside and it was the smell of flowers. It was the dead come to life.

Or was it? What did he really know about this girl, and why did he think he loved her, beyond the fact of her obvious endowments? Was he just another old man making a fool of himself? He wouldn't be the first. Old men had been making fools of themselves forever. Could there really be love between January and May? He scoffed when he saw other men his age indulging themselves in this way, the rich ones, as if they did not know why they had those young things on their arms. Why wasn't he laughing now?

Then there was the dream about her. It was the last day of April and it was a dark and stormy afternoon, lightening flashing and thunder crashing and rain pounding the dark streets below his office window in wind-blown sheets. He was standing by the bookshelf, near the door, in a state of abstraction, looking for the Pastoral symphony and its stormy section, looking for the well-worn score he had not seen in many years, not since he did the third and fourth movements with the orchestra. He had been a mere sophomore in high school the first time he played it, in that special youth orchestra they put together for Lincoln Center. He was the concert master. Ah, those were days!

Anyway, he was standing there in abstraction, listening to the thunder and the rain, and then he felt a small hand on his left arm and looked up startled and it was Margie. And suddenly she was very close and just as suddenly a great ravine seemed to open up between them. His first impulse was to open his arms and reach out and hold her with all the tenderness of his soul, but his second impulse was to leave his arms just where they were and smile and say hello as if all those feelings he'd had before—and maybe still did have—had never been.

Which is exactly what he did. Only this was no dream. This was a very real storm blowing in out of the Catskills and this was Margie herself standing at his side with a happy expression on her face, the one he had seen many times before. She was real and it was real, although it took a few moments for him to rouse himself from the distant lands of reverie.

"Hi!" she said with that bewitching smile. "I saw you as I was going by and thought I would stop in and say hello. It seems like forever since I've seen you."

Henry looked at her and did not know what to think. Was it déjà-vu? His mind was a jumble and his mouth was dry and his lips were dry. He wanted to kiss her, but his lips were dry, old-man dry.

"Well, you know, I've been so busy. End of the semester and all that. Concerts."

"Yes, I know, lots of concerts. I don't know how you do it all. So how have you been?"

"Good, good," he lied, forcing a placid smile through the pain and strangeness. "You?"

"Oh, I'm fine. I've been worried about you, though."

"Worried?" he scoffed. "Why?"

"How you're feeling. That was pretty bad."

"Oh—you mean the meeting. I'm fine. I'm always fine. 'Whatever doesn't kill me makes me stronger.' As long as I don't wind up in an asylum."

"But the way they treated you...it was shocking."

"Don't think about it," he said with a wave of the hand. "Believe me. I've been there plenty of times before. They were just doing what they do. My mistake was in thinking I could change what they do."

"I guess I made the same mistake," she replied smiling. "Well—off to class. Great to see you!"

"Yes—great. Let's get together some time."

"I'd like that."

This was not a dream, this was real. But it felt like a dream—it came out of a reverie and was as strange as any dream, her voice coming to him as if from far away—but the light touch of her small, dainty hand on his arm was not a dream, it was real. It was like a dream because he could not make any sense of it. He did not understand what had just happened or what it meant.

She had shown up at his side and put her hand on his arm at a time when everyone else in the department seemed to have deserted him, even his friends. Why did she do that? What did it mean? He knew what he wanted it to mean. He wanted to be her lover. Part of him wanted this and wanted it in spring, which is the season for lovers.

This is what the old man thought as he contemplated her unexpected appearance, and there was a sweetness in his soul that was not usually there, a youthfulness and sense of joy. He was not an old man then, not with those feelings or those thoughts, not when that bright-eyed young lady had her hand on his arm and let it linger there in a scattering of stardust. He was not an old man then and he found himself very much tempted to be young again.

But he *was* old. It was a fact. He knew about the delusion of youthfulness. He knew middle-aged people never saw themselves as middle-aged. They do not see themselves as others see them, as they actually are, but are "forever young" in their own minds. Henry knew it well on an intellectual level. And on that level he stood apart and he looked at himself talking to this fetching young woman and he had to laugh. Old man! Wake up!

The problem was he could not wake up, not entirely. He could not let go even when he was convinced in his own mind that it was an illusion. Margie was a very desirable young woman. He wanted her to be in love with him and he wanted to be in love with her. Part of him did anyway, some strange part over which he did not seem to have much control. His feelings for her were the one bright spot in his life just then. The workplace had become a disaster of his own making. The classes he had been teaching for thirty years were almost intolerable. Even the work with Forum was getting a little stale. He had been doing the same thing with the same people for all of his adult life. Now when he looked at them they just looked old.

But Margie, this exquisite little thing with the shining eyes! That was different. That was new. He was like a completely different person when he was with her. There was fun in him. There was a sense of mystery and intrigue. There was the vanity of thinking he could still be attractive to such a comely young lass. Most of all there was this feeling of being in love, of immersion. It was just like in the Puccini operas he had always laughed at. Only he wasn't laughing now. He was a Puccini melody.

On the other hand, he could not make her out. There was something troubling in her behavior. Just what was this ferocity she had shown on two occasions? Was it righteous indignation on Alicia's behalf? Because it could be—he wanted to believe this is what it was. Or was it something else, something darker and strange? He could not hide these misgivings from himself. He wanted Margie to be special because he wanted to be in love. He wanted the colors to come back and the sense of drudgery to go away. He wanted to feel young again and have hope.

For a long time now he had not had hope. It may seem strange to say for someone in his position, a renowned classical musician and revered professor—but we mean hope for happiness. One thing young men have that old men lack is this beautiful sustaining hope. With age comes the realization that happiness is a mirage. The world is what it is, what it has always been, and will never change. What keeps it going in spite of itself may be something of a mystery, but its deficits become self-evident. It cannot come into the light. There are always people like Malcolm and they always find their way into positions of power. There are always our own foolish limitations constantly making themselves known.

With Margie those feelings of hope revived. Her sheer attractiveness and youth, working perhaps on his male hormones, or on other more mysterious forces inside, caused him to feel light and happy. But now he was all mixed up again, because he had seen both sides of Margie and did not know which one to believe. Who was this person who had the power to inspire such tender feelings? Was she the fairy whose hand had just rested so lightly on his arm in the middle of the storm—or was she the storm herself in its fierce anger? She was not like a piece of music. She could not be interpreted. He was a master of notes written on a page but not of the human heart.

And yet there was the addictive joy, the hope, the feeling of elation he'd just had with her standing there beside him and her hand on his arm. All of these disparate feelings were merged in the obsessive attachment he had formed. He had been clinging to Margie like a life raft—sometimes it seemed like he thought about her all day long—but was she really his savior? Was she the adorable little thing of his imagination or something quite different?

DISCLOSURE

I T DIDN'T TAKE LONG to find out.

On the last day of classes Henry was sitting in his office absentmindedly grading papers and receiving visitors with a weary end-of-the semester smile when he realized someone had come in. It was one of those things where you know you're supposed to know who this person is but you just can't place them—or in this case, her.

He looked up. "Yes?" he said.

"You don't know who I am, do you?" she said bluntly. She was smiling but it wasn't really a smile and her tone was not overly friendly. "I'm Alicia Baptiste."

"Alicia! Of course! I'm a big fan of yours," Henry said, bumbling to his feet.

"I understand you were the one who got me fired."

Now that was an opening. Henry's first reaction was she must be joking, so he laughed, but on closer inspection she did not seem to be the joking type.

"On the contrary," he replied soothingly. "I was the one who tried to get you rehired. I was very impressed with that concert you gave last fall. I think you're a great asset to this university and I think if they had any sense at all they would do whatever they could to keep you."

"According to Margie, you said you got me fired. You were trying to settle some old score or something and got everybody riled up."

"Margie told you that, did she?" he said steadfastly maintaining his smile. "I think there may have been a misunderstanding there. They made up their minds about you long before I entered the picture, unfortunately. Actually Margie was the one who came to me and encouraged me to stand up for you. Did she tell you that?"

"She wasn't accusing you. She was just saying what happened. That you made things worse by going to the dean or something."

"Well, I really don't think it had any impact on the outcome. In any case, I am very sorry about what happened. It was a travesty of justice and a disgrace, as far as I'm concerned. And I don't mind saying so. You did more with those kids than anyone in the thirty years I've been here."

This was heartfelt, but Alicia wasn't listening. A light seemed to have gone on in her head. "So Margie came to *you*. Is that what you're saying?"

"Yes. Why?"

"Let me guess. She tried to get you to go after Malcolm."

"I wouldn't put it quite that way. She was upset about what they were doing to you. I guess she figured the old man would be out of the loop, and she was right."

"I think I'm starting to understand what happened here. How much do you know about Margie? Are you friends?"

"Not…really. Or at least not until this came up. Why?"

"You've never heard anything? Any gossip?" Here she did something funky with her hands.

"I can't tell for sure unless I know what you have in mind."

"About her and Malcolm," she said forthrightly. "Did you know about that?"

Henry went white. "What about her and Malcolm?"

"She has it in for him. She's hell-bent on getting him back, and this must have been her way of doing it while pretending to be noble or something."

"A lot of people aren't too crazy about Malcolm," he replied carefully. "There's quite a long list of folks who would like to see him get his comeuppance—and you can add me to it, if you like."

"Not like her. It's an obsession with her. A sick obsession, if you ask me."

"What is the source of this supposed obsession?"

"He seduced her—at least that what she says."

Henry blinked. "Malcolm seduced Margie? When did this happen?"

"Oh, I don't know—last fall or something. And then he dumped her. He made her believe he was madly in love with her but apparently all he wanted was—well, you know what he wanted. It's the same thing he always wants. As soon as he had enough of that he dumped her and went running back to his wife and kids."

"How do you know all this?"

"She told me. That's how I know. We used to be close."

"Used to be?"

"Well, yes, until I realized she was using me. I never wanted to be her *cause célèbre*. I never asked for that. If she hadn't made such a big deal about it, going around telling everyone how much better I was than Malcolm, I might have had my contract renewed. I might have had a shot of getting on the faculty."

"So your theory is she went around bragging about you to make Malcolm look bad. It wasn't really about helping you; it was about her and Malcolm."

"Duh! And then the rumors started about certain adjuncts not being invited back—I guess that's when she decided to take it up a notch and enlist you in the effort. Of course I didn't know anything about it. It was all done without my permission."

"Well, she shouldn't have done that. She should have talked to you before she came to me."

"Like you talked to me before going to the dean?" Alicia said.

Henry stared at her blankly for a moment. "No, you're right—I didn't. In hindsight, I probably should have. It might have saved all of us a lot of grief."

"Yes, it would have. Look at me now. I don't have anywhere to go and no prospects for a job. You all had your fun—where does that leave me? I have $125,000 in school debt and rent to pay."

All of a sudden she started to cry. Henry thought it would stop, and then when it didn't he tried to soothe her, patting her hand in a paternal way and eventually even feeling compelled to take the poor girl in his arms stroke her hair when it seemed like she was headed for downright hysterics. Apparently she had been holding it all in under that steely exterior.

She calmed down a little. Henry counseled her as best he could, told her about a couple of his contacts at other schools and promised to call them, encouraged her and let her know how special he thought she was. He was patient and kind, but to tell the truth he couldn't wait for her to get out of his office. His brain circuits were exploding. He needed to be alone and think about what she had just told him and the implications. The implications.

Finally she left, acting like he was her best friend in the world, and he was alone again and closed his door and locked it and turned off the lights and sat there in shock. Malcolm! Was it possible? Had he been her lover? Margie, the fresh-faced pixie? The adorable little innocent one with the doe eyes and great burden for her put-upon friend? This was how he had seen her, a fearless young crusader for justice, almost virginal in his mind. This was why he had fallen for her—or one of the reasons.

But this idealism was completely overthrown by the image of her in Malcolm's arms. Malcolm was young, handsome, athletic, charming, a rising force. She was in love with him. That was the reason for the rage. That was the reason for the coy behavior. Henry did not know anything about Margie. He knew nothing about her family, where she had gone to high school, who her best friends were, what she did when she was not with him. The one thing that had been completely firm in his mind was their alignment in principled opposition to Malcolm, and now this conviction had been shattered.

Had he been played? Had she heard about his disenchantment with the handsome Machiavelli? Was that why she came to him—to play on the animus between him and Malcolm? He had allowed himself to articulate his bitterness openly. He had been fulsome in expressing his contempt for Malcolm and all the chaos he was creating in the department. Was this the reason she had come—while he convinced himself it was something else?

All this time he been had acting like the sage in his relationship with this young and untutored colleague. She would sit there in rapt attention as he would go on and on with fascinating stories from the music world and his heartfelt opinions on the difference between music-making and being a metronome and many, many other topics of great interest, too many to recount. He thought she was smiling because she was happy to soak up the pearls of wisdom that fell from his lips. Now he wondered if that smile meant something else. Was she was laughing at him?

And then he was seized by particularly dreadful thought. Were they *all* laughing at him? The others in the department? Was that why they remained silent when he spoke up at the meeting? He remembered the peculiar look on Bertram's face many months ago when he saw Margie coming out of his office. A cold terror crept over him. He was deeply compromised in his relationship to Margie. She had taken his principled objections to Malcolm and turned them into something unprincipled. If others knew, Henry could be in deep trouble.

He went to the place he always went when he needed to know what was going on—Richie's office.

"So you'll never guess who just came to see me."

"Alicia?" Richie said, with a bored look.

"How did you know that?"

"I'm clairvoyant. Did she come to say goodbye?"

"No, she came to say much more than that. She had some interesting news about our friend Malcolm. But maybe you know what I'm talking about."

"There's all kinds of interesting news about Malcolm. What did she say?"

"Well, we've all known for some time that he was a bit of a Lothario. We've heard him make comments to coworkers that would land either one of us in the dean's office."

"Don't go there. The dean's office, I mean. You really shouldn't go there, you know."

"Believe me, I'm not. But it seems Camilla isn't the only one he's been interested in," Henry said, leaning over with a confidential and utterly fake smile.

"Really? Who did you have in mind?"

"Whom do *you* have in mind?"

"Wait a minute, I don't have anyone in mind. You're the one with the hot rumor."

"You haven't heard anything about Malcolm and another faculty member, something that may have ended rather badly?"

"I've heard lots of rumors of that nature. Can you be more specific?"

Henry was doing everything he could to avoid naming names, but his friend, it seemed, was not going to let him off the hook. "Well, according to Alicia, there was something between him and Margie Hart."

Richie burst out laughing. "Oh—that."

"So it's true?"

"How do I know? It's a rumor. But they say ninety percent of every rumor is true."

"I'd like to know how they arrive at exactly ninety percent. And besides, how can only ninety percent of this particular rumor be true? Either they did or they didn't."

"Well, let's say the rumor is they like each other, they spent a lot of time together, they went out on dates together, they slept together. Even on the face of it, there are four parts to the rumor, so you could say half true or mostly true, or just a little bit true, and that's even before we start parsing things like what does 'a lot of time' really mean."

"Thank you for that brilliant analysis. So are they saying those things about them?"

"No, that was just a hypothetical rumor. As far as I know all they said about them was they slept together."

This was delivered with such a perfect deadpan that even Henry had to laugh, although it was a dagger in his heart. "What a pig. I wonder if his wife knows," he replied—and then blushed down to his bones as the bright light of self-consciousness descended.

"That's what we've been asking all along. Just how much does she know? You would think she would have to know, he's been so—active."

Henry started to reply and then stopped. Strangely, in all the time he had spent with the captivating Margie he had not been thinking of his wife. But now he was like King David and Nathan. He applied his outrage at Malcolm to himself.

"So is this—common knowledge?" Henry said at last, dreading the answer.

"Umm—pretty much! In fact I'm surprised you didn't know about it. I thought everyone did."

"No, I didn't. And I must say, I'm rather shocked."

"Don't be. As they say, the lady must have been willing."

Of all the things that Richie could possibly have said, this one hurt the most.

COMING OUT OF THE GATE

ENRY HAD A HOT MESS on his hands. He had allowed himself to fall in love, and he had allowed himself to be used. He'd put his position at the university in jeopardy for a lie—a lie he told to himself, by the way, since Margie never told him she loved him, never gave any definite indication of being interested in him in that way. Even when she kissed his hand in the park it was just a young woman having pity on her fatherly colleague. He had imagined everything else, and he had allowed his imagination to make him bold and get him mixed up in things he had no business getting mixed up in.

It was bad enough when he thought he was doing it for love. Even when he thought of himself as the chivalrous knight who was coming to the aid of the fair maiden—even then he was amazed at how foolish he had been to abandon his successful thirty-year run of avoiding politics. But Margie and Malcolm? Really? It made everything rancid. She was the complete opposite of what he had imagined. She was not some pre-Raphaelite maiden walking around in a garden thinking deep thoughts while the birds sang in the trees and the sunlight kissed the flowers. She was a major game-player, someone who used her feminine charms to manipulate men, and he had fallen right in.

He thought about his many interactions with her and was mortified over and over again. There was the night in the restaurant when he patted her hand. What tenderness and emotion he had invested in that gesture! More than the most exquisite passage on the violin! He could only imagine what she was thinking. He thought of the walk in the park and his outburst in the sunlight on the stone bench—oh God, did he really have to think of that? Wasn't there some way to wipe the memory of that awful day out of his mind? It was too humiliating.

Meanwhile his conversation with Richie brought another level of humiliation into view. It occurred to him that he and Malcolm were just the same—or at least not as different as he liked to think. The sheer tawdriness of what went on in the department, the soap-opera quality that had disgusted him over the years, was also now his own tawdriness. Malcolm's seconds! The thought made him ill. He had been accustomed to railing against his young antagonist's indiscretions. "How could he do this to his poor wife!" was a refrain often heard from his cultivated lips in cultivated tones, as if all he cared about were her feelings, as if he were an exquisitely delicate soul.

Now that the shoe was on the other foot, he wished he'd kept his mouth shut. It was not pleasant being exposed as a hypocrite. It occurred to him that old men have all the vices of youth and none of the promise. They think and feel the same uncivilized things young men feel but can no longer look forward to some blessed day when they will live up to their own expectations. Instead they find themselves in the awkward position of having to face the truth. The human creature is not a beautiful creature. Not where it counts—not inside. All of its beauty is on the outside; all show.

He had always been faithful to Gabrielle. They married at twenty-five, pretty much fresh out of school, because their mentors thought they should marry and encouraged them. They would sit down with these older teachers and have serious, elevating conversations about the benefits of such a marriage and how it would be different from other marriages. Nothing was off the table when they talked about their future together, even sex. Part of the reason they were going to marry was the acknowledgment that human beings have certain needs. There was to be no bourgeois shame in any of this. They felt very wise and adult to be talking about these things, openly and in a calm and rational way.

It would be wrong to say that this arrangement made Henry perfectly happily. He struggled a great deal, especially in the early years. Gabrielle did not withhold herself from him but neither was there anything resembling passion in her love-making. She was not sexless but she did not seem to need sex or, for that matter, to like it very much. She seemed to be interested mostly for his sake. She was like a vestal virgin for music, and this made it hard for him to make love to her, first because he almost felt like he was violating her, not having assurance of her full consent, and because it was hard to give himself to her when she would not respond in kind.

And then there was the part about having a family. They were both so busy and working so hard that he did not spend a great deal of time thinking about it at the beginning, while his career was taking off, but this definitely changed as the years went by. They would visit his brother or sister and their happy families and he always came away feeling depressed. Then the next thing he knew they were turning forty and Gabrielle was still on birth control and they were still concertizing and teaching and still too busy to think about a family. He resigned himself to childlessness, but not without suffering.

Barreling into middle age, Henry rededicated himself to music. This was what made sense of his life. He became more monkish in his ways as the years flew by. Then menopause came along for Gabrielle and she became even less interested in conjugal pleasures. It was not unusual for two or three months to go by without making love—or six. It seemed actually painful for her. Henry reconciled himself to the change. The embers of lust seemed to be cooling, and wasn't it a good thing after all? It left him more time and energy for his music. He told himself he wanted them to cool. Sure, he was frustrated sometimes; but he had his violin. He would pick it up when that other mood came upon him and practice late into the night. He would practice with a vengeance on his violin until exhausted.

The problem with all this, Henry now realized, was he was proud of the seeming spirituality of his marriage to Gabrielle. He was not like Malcolm. He wasn't walking around making untoward remarks to female coworkers or chasing every skirt that walked by. He despised anything coarse and loved women the way they should be loved. Moreover, he was scornful of Malcolm's lack of discipline. It prevented him from realizing his potential, from working as hard as Henry worked to perfect his craft. Henry had allowed himself to take undue pleasure in this difference over the years. Malcolm was weak in the flesh and incapable of rising to the spirituality of music. After all, how could someone with his swinish sensibilities understand the sublimities of Brahms and Beethoven?

But that was before Margie. That was before Henry had lost his way and shown himself to be just as swinish and as foolish as Malcolm—even with the same girl! Good Lord, even the same girl. He turned a deeper shade of red every time he thought of it. No, he was not different from Malcolm. He was exactly the same. If by the grace of God he had managed to stay faithful all these years to Gabrielle, what credit was that to him? He was faithful with his body—but what about his heart and mind? No, the truth is he was far from being pure. He had managed not to succumb, but that did not mean he was immune. The difference between him and Malcolm was merely one of degree.

And then there was the outburst, the fateful moment when he lost control of his id in the department meeting and said things he had no intention of saying, implied things he did not want to imply. It was true that he was an international performing artist. It was true this made him different from everyone else on the faculty. It was also true that much of the mean behavior directed his way over the years had come from jealousy; not from anything he had done—he had always gone out of his way to treat his co-workers with respect and kindness—to the best of his ability—but because they could not help themselves. They could not keep from letting their jealousy spill out in mean and little ways.

Still, their pettiness did not justify his lashing out. He had invested his identity in the idea of suffering for the sake of "love, love, love." He did not return meanness for meanness because he wanted to be kind. He believed in the Golden Rule; it was his beacon. The more he was mistreated, the more he focused on making himself a fountain of graciousness and tolerance. After all, he could afford it. He really was the one with the international reputation. He could afford to be magnanimous because he had the very thing they all wanted and would never be able to obtain. It was his good fortune to have it—not just on account of hard work but of all the other things that figure into success—and he had been careful over the years never to forget this.

So why had he forgotten it now? It was too easy to blame Margie; what was the real reason? Sure, it was because of her special pleading that he had stepped up for Alicia. But the things he said in the meeting had nothing to do with Margie per se—and little to do with Alicia. He did think highly of Alicia. He did think she was getting a raw deal and suspected some involvement on Malcolm's part. But the real reason for lashing out—for the things he said and especially the way he said them—was the simmering feud between him and Malcolm. It was the resentment he had built up over the years. Margie and Alicia were just the pretext. The rest was his doing.

He thought back to the words he had used, the things he had implied, and wanted to die. He had an unspoken arrangement with his fellow department members. He would allow them not to be professional musicians like himself or to have attained his level of notoriety—and they would allow him to be famous and enjoy some of the perks of fame, like taking time off from teaching when there were concerts in foreign lands and workshops to be done. This unspoken arrangement was mutually beneficial, but now he had broken it. His implied attack on Malcolm indicated that he was calling in his debts after all these years. He was going to try to force the issue and discredit Malcolm on the basis of artistry and authority. He broke the unspoken accommodation.

Again, it was pride that made him break it. And this was unfortunate on two levels. First, he did not want to wound his fellow laborers. He was not the arrogant diva—he hated that sort of thing with all his soul. He loved his coworkers in spite of their flaws, in spite of the many ways in which they had hurt him over the years; loved them at least in the abstract, and as much as he was able in the particular. Besides, many of them had never done anything to hurt him. They were the innocent victims of his arrogance.

Second, he could not afford to break the arrangement. He had mortgage payments and car payments and was helping to support his ensemble. This was perhaps the main reason why he had stayed out of department politics all these years. No matter how much he was suffering, no matter how much they slighted him and schemed to keep him under their thumb, no matter how wrong-headed he thought they were about the purpose of education or how disrespectful of him and his accomplishments—through all this he had maintained his smile and dignity and most of all kept his mouth shut.

But now in a moment of madness he had gone into their temple and tried to pull the whole structure down on their heads. Only he had not succeeded. The temple was the world and could not be destroyed. All he had managed to do was to destroy himself.

Destroy himself? Really? Why did he feel this tremor in the center of his being? Wasn't he tenured? Well, yes; but tenure is no guarantee of employment. He had seen tenure set aside when it suited the purposes of the administration. After all, they did not have to fire him outright. They could find some way to force him to retire. He was over sixty. He was making too much money for the work they were asking him to do. There was no guarantee of surviving a storm, if one should come; not at his age. And he was pretty sure a storm was coming. He had called their competence and integrity into question under the guise of diversity. Oh yes, there would be a storm.

Pride goeth before a fall, and Henry was looking at a hard one. He decided to take immediate action. He would annihilate himself. No—not that. Not the bare bodkin. This annihilation would take place in the mind. Henry had gotten himself into trouble by raising his head up too high; now he was determined to bow it down as low as possible. After all, he valued humility. He believed in it as the only rational response to the ephemeral nature of man, to his smallness in the universe, to his ignorance. He could not tolerate the unbounded conceit of the world, which for the most part was based on nothing, the brash and idiotic boasting of poseurs and politicians of all kinds, like Malcolm. The greatest artists he had known were, for the most part, very humble. This was also true of his greatest teachers. It was true of his own father. Greatness, in his mind, was associated with humility.

But Henry wanted double humility—because he wanted double repentance. His arrogance and the mess and hurt he had made demanded it. He did not want to be the person he had become in recent months. He was deeply ashamed of that person. And his way to repent was to use his sins as a wrecking ball against his own self. He consciously set out to dwell upon his sins and his vanity as a way of destroying sin and vanity in himself. He dredged up all the bad memories he had been storing over the years and gorged on them. Usually he tried to push them away, hold off the pain they caused, but now he embraced them as a way of knocking himself down to size, as a way of leveling the mountains of the human ego so that some freshness and new hope could creep in.

The struggle, the strain, of being a front-line artist was wearing him out. The fine stout resistance of youth was gone, the pride of the performer with upright posture and clear penetrating eyes. Even the music had begun to lose some of its charm. This was something so terrible and unexpected that he could hardly admit it to himself. At a young age he had put Beethoven and Brahms and Mozart on such a high pedestal that he thought their charms would last forever—but nothing in this world lasts forever. There hadn't been any new "classical" music in over a hundred years, or not much that anybody wanted to listen to, and very little of the chamber variety, since there were no longer dukes and duchesses with a need for music for intimate occasions.

Basically he and the ensemble were reduced to trotting out the same old war horses over and over again just to get people to come to their concerts and support them. It wasn't quite as bad as the poor pop star who has to sing his big hit until he is too old to sing anymore. After all, the music was universal. But it was a bit of a chore to have to practice pieces he first learned as a teenager in order to get them performance-ready. He did not want to become like those musicians he despised—the mercenaries who showed up with dead eyes and played the music perfectly but with no passion and no apparent love. But was that what he was in the process of becoming? Was the music becoming cold to him now?

Henry wanted a return of the sweetness and freshness of music. He wanted a revival of the excitement of youth—and not just for music, but for life. And it seemed to him now that the way to obtain it was to blow up all the baggage he had accumulated over the years, all the weight of being who he was perceived to be and all the false responsibility that came with it. These things were nothing but burdens. They got in the way of the music and true happiness. At one time he thought that being on top of the world would make him happy, but this was far from the case. All it did was make him mindful of the emptiness of existence. But he had been truly happy once—when he was a young man, pursuing his dream. At that time the music was like a drug to him. He could take it every day and be exhilarated and never have to pay the price of a hangover later on.

Could he have this happiness again? If he annihilated this false appearance of himself that had been created and accumulated over the years? If he put away the confident smile and put his head down and let his sadness be seen by the world? He set about his new endeavor immediately. He let the wrecking machine of painful memory reduce him to nothing. He became deeper; the colors of the world deepened around him. Now when he met someone in the hallway or on the street he would greet them with a sad smile and a kind word. One of his old professors had taught him about the concept of the mensch. This is what he now aspired to be, with all his heart; and the particular idea he had in mind was a mensch who has a sad face because he knows he is not worthy; because cares for others; because he is willing to put others first and to suffer if need be for the sake of this ideal; because a laughing face is an arrogant face, and arrogance is oppressive to the spirit.

To his delight, this new plan seemed to be working. For a couple of days after his conversations with Alicia and Richie he was in a constant state of anxiety and disorientation like someone who anticipates a great fall. But annihilating himself had the beneficial effect of leveling his world and restoring his reason. Gradually he started to feel better as the days went by and he went on greeting people in his pleasantly subdued new way and being greeted in new ways. It was quiet. It was the end of the semester and the numbers were dwindling. There were no ominous emails from Bertram or the dean. There was no sign of Margie. None of his allies or acolytes came running into his office to warn him about some great plot Malcolm and friends were cooking up for him. He began to wonder if he had imagined it all. It wasn't really as bad as it seemed.

A week went by and then another week before Henry finally began to feel grounded again and get over the shock of learning about Margie and Malcolm to some degree. Exams were over and grading was over and everything seemed to have returned to normal. But Henry did not want to return to normal. No, he liked his new robes of solemnity. He liked the new person he was making. He could see the results right away. It was changing his relationships in the department. It was giving him a new enthusiasm for the art of performing. He thought he could discover a whole new approach to bringing the music to life. The key was to annihilate the façade and bring the great masterworks directly into the soul of the audience. The key was to set aside all the distractions and everything that was not nourishing and whole.

Henry began to feel his recent near disasters had been good for him. "The fear of the Lord is the beginning of wisdom"—and sometimes the fear of the Lord can be as simple as the threat of retribution for some wrong that has been done. He had been getting a little too smug, a little too complacent in recent years, too full of himself and his supposed grievances. To an alarming extent he had allowed the walls of pride to go up between him and his colleagues, and now those walls were coming down, and he was glad. From now on he was not going to take anything for granted. If perchance he was confronted by some sweet-voiced young woman with black hair he would know better than to imagine himself a paramour. He knew he was an old man. He'd had a first-hand encounter with his mortality.

Then disaster struck. He came home one Friday night in May, a beautiful, balmy spring night, and found Gabrielle in a foul mood. This was surprising. Gabrielle was not one for extreme moods of any kind. She almost always kept herself on an even keel, but there were storm clouds in her countenance. Henry was sensitive to this sort of thing. He knew something was very wrong.

She was banging around the kitchen when he came in, doing something of indeterminate significance. "Is everything all right? You seem annoyed," he said, feeling self-conscious as he said it.

"I don't know if everything is all right. You tell me," was the ominous reply.

"Tell you what? I'm sorry—I must have missed something."

"You missed something, all right. What you were doing at that woman's apartment—at night? You tell me that, and I'll tell you if everything is all right."

For a moment he just stood there looking at her, the blood draining out of his face. Whatever self-assurance he had been able to restore in the last couple of weeks was completely gone.

"What 'woman'? What are you talking about?"

"That little tramp from the orchestra department. I always knew she was a tramp. I just didn't realize you went for tramps."

"I don't know who you mean."

"Sure you do. The oboe girl. Margie, or whatever her name is. You know exactly who I mean."

"I don't understand. Where is this all coming from?"

"I got a nice little email today. It said you were having an affair with her. You were seen coming out of her apartment in the middle of the night."

"What! That's outrageous. I don't know why anybody would say that."

"There was a picture. Apparently somebody has been following you around."

Henry's mind went blank. "A picture? Of me?"

"Yes, standing in her doorway and looking very taken with each other. It was nice of you to stand right in the light like that. Very obliging."

"Who sent this email?"

"I don't know who sent it. It came from a university server."

"What did it say?"

"I don't know what it said! What difference does it make?"

"No, I want to know. What specifically?"

"Something about 'it's my unfortunate duty to let you know that your husband is having an affair with another faculty member.'"

"In those words? That's a complete lie."

"Well, no. There was more. I don't remember."

"Can you at least show me?"

"No, I can't. I deleted it. I didn't want that filth in my in-box."

"I wish you hadn't done that. I wish you had at least given me a chance to defend myself."

"For God's sake, Henry, there was a picture! What is it about this that you don't understand?"

"What I don't understand is why someone was so interested in what the heck I'm doing."

"What does it matter? The real question is why you were doing it. I thought we had an agreement. I thought we were partners and we were going to grow old together and have our 'golden years' together, to use your own words. Did you forget about that? Or maybe you just figured it's time to dump me and go find yourself a trophy wife. At your age. What a joke."

Based on his recent determination to humble himself and level his pride, Henry decided to confess. "No, I'm not going to dump you. That was never what it was about. And I don't know what happened to me. She came to me, I didn't go to her."

"So it's true, then."

"All right, I screwed up. I admit it. Big time. It was like I lost my mind. She wasn't even interested in me. She was just using me to get back at Malcolm."

"Malcolm! Get back at him for what?"

"I don't know—I guess they had a fling or something."

"And that's your excuse? She was using you, so you had an affair with her?"

"It wasn't an affair…"

"Did you love her?"

"I don't know how I felt about her. I told you, I was all mixed up. I wasn't seeing things clearly."

"Did you love her?"

"I guess I had some feelings for her. I'm sorry—I don't know what happened."

"Well, I have a pretty good idea. You saw some cute little thing who came to you simpering over the 'great violinist' and all that nonsense, and you fell for her. You fell in love with her."

"I'm sorry. I can't even tell you how sorry I am. Can you forgive me?"

"That's it? I'm supposed to just forgive you now and move on? I don't think so. It's one thing for something like this to happen, but for it to be so obvious that other people know about it! For me to actually get an email with a picture of you and this little slut in her apartment! It's too much. I'm sorry, it's just too much."

"What do you mean 'you're sorry'? What are you thinking?"

"I don't know what I'm thinking! I'm going to my sister's. I need to figure out what I'm doing with my life. You can stay here and try to come up with a better answer."

"Don't go. Really. I don't want you to go. I admit it, I've been a jackass. I've been a fool. But that doesn't mean I don't love you or care about you. That doesn't mean I want to lose you. If you go I don't know what I'm going to do."

"You should have thought of that before. And as for 'love,' I don't even know what you're talking about. When did you ever tell me you loved me? Never. I can't remember you saying it once."

"Oh, come on. You know I love you."

"Sure, right. That's why you had an affair."

With that she stormed off toward the bedroom, where apparently she had done some packing, because she emerged just a few moments later with a suitcase and bags in her hands.

"You're kidding," Henry said. "You're not really doing this."

"Watch me."

"Is there anything I can say to get you to stay?"

"Save your breath. I wouldn't believe anything you said."

THE CONFRONTATION

ENRY'S WEEKEND BEGAN with his wife of 35 years walking out on him.

He had never felt so alone. Over the years, through everything, Gabrielle had truly become his friend. With their crazed schedules they did not see as much of each other as other couples, but when they did they always talked about what was going on in their lives and the world and always had a good talk. They agreed on most things. They very rarely argued. Sometimes over finances or the dishes, but not often. They both worked hard on the things that had to be done to keep the household in good order, removing the friction that often builds up between couples over time. They were true partners.

Actually, now that he thought about it, Gabrielle was probably his best friend. You know that old cliché—well, there it was. They might not have been terribly romantic but they were quite close in their own way. She was a good person and he valued her goodness. He enjoyed spending time with her; he didn't have to force himself. He liked coming home to her. He liked the way she treated other people, the good she did for them. He was proud of her for that. Actually he was proud of her generally. He liked the way she carried herself in company, her genuineness. He liked the way she cared for her parents and for his father when he was dying. She was a very giving person.

It had been decades since he had been alone, and Gabrielle did not have to be gone very long before he realized he did not like it.

At all. He enjoyed sitting down with her in the evening to read or watch TV or scour YouTube for performances they wanted to see or new music they wanted to hear. He liked going shopping with her on the weekends and or for an impromptu drive to the Catskills or Lake George or wherever. If he was going out for a walk around the block on a warm spring day he wanted her to come along and she was happy to oblige. She never turned him down. They would walk and they would talk—or sometimes they would just walk. Either way they were comfortable together.

He trusted her judgment. If Forum was practicing at their house, which happened often, he always wanted to know what she thought, and he almost always took any suggestions she made to heart and incorporated them into what he was doing. She was his counselor on all matters relating both to the university and to the group and its various enterprises. Men joke about the value of "yes, dear," but the sometimes reason they say it is they love and trust their wives. Yes—Henry realized it now. He loved Gabrielle in a way that was maybe deeper than the more florid depictions of love seen in books and movies.

He couldn't imagine life without her. He was not cut out to be alone. He had not done well when they were apart for extended periods of time, during concert tours or whatever. But now he was alone, very much alone on a dreary Saturday morning, feeling somewhat nauseated, heaving heavy sighs, not fighting the hot tears when they spilled into his eyes. He tried to think of how he could fix what he had broken but nothing came to mind. What could he do? Get down on his knees and beg forgiveness and profess unending love? That was the problem right there. She was right—he'd never told her he loved her. He never could see himself saying it. He wasn't sure she wanted him to say it. But in that case it seemed ridiculous and self-serving to start saying it now, just to exculpate himself.

He wanted to show her he loved her, but how? Send flowers? A box of fancy chocolates? He did not think she could be impressed with such conventional gestures. She was trying not to eat chocolate, and they rarely had flowers in the house. True, this was partly because he never brought her any—but was it too late to try? Could he be like Fred Astaire in those movies they both loved so much and send her a huge box of flowers? Would this have any effect on her, other than to make her scoff at his extravagance and obviousness? What else could he do? Give her jewelry? She hardly wore any. He did not know if he could soften her fury by giving her things. She might say he should have given it to the animal shelter or the children's fund. He could see her saying something like that.

He did love her in his own way, but he had never given her any reason to think so. His anniversary cards were always artsy and somewhat impersonal, always "fondly," never "love." He had never gone to Hallmark like all the conventional husbands and bought her a card with a treacly poem. He would not be caught dead in such places. No, his cards were more likely to come from the Met or Barnes & Noble, with sentiments that could have been scratched off the dry end of a piece of chalk. But if he could not appeal to love, then how could he expect tenderness? What reason did he have to think her heart could be touched? He called her cell, but there was no answer. He called his sister-in-law, but there was no answer there, either. Clearly she did not want to talk to him.

Actually, Henry was clueless about his wife. In reality it was love that stood between him and Gabrielle now. The very thing he felt he could not say to her was the thing she needed to hear and longed to hear. Gabrielle had always wanted him to love her—the way she had loved him, almost obsessively, with pure devotion. She may have put on the appearance of practicality in their marriage but she did not have a cold heart. Far from it. She didn't marry Henry because she agreed with their desiccated professors and wanted to have a practical professional relationship with him. What a ridiculous idea! She married him because she adored him and hoped that he would come to feel the same way about her.

But this never seemed to happen. They were fine together—he treated her well—he was considerate and not at all demanding—but he never showed any sign of returning her deep and enduring affection. He acted as though he really did see their marriage as a partnership to help them meet their professional goals. If he saw it as anything more, he never let on. The years went by and nothing changed. There was always this distance between them, she felt, created by him; not a wall, exactly, but more like a barrier. A formal quality. The more things went on like this, the more fearful she became of losing him. She would see him with attractive young students or attractive colleagues and almost die inside, because she did not feel she had a real hold on him, because she did not know where she stood, because she was afraid he would fall in love and never give her the happiness she longed for.

She was very careful around him. She was afraid if she ever let him know how she really felt it would drive him away. She had made a compact with him and gone into it with open eyes and was afraid of letting him down. She was afraid of making him feel she had deceived him or was using him in some way. She didn't want to use him; she was in love with him. They had made a high-browed arrangement with the blessing of high-browed professors whom she knew he idolized. Could she tell him she loved him and still be considered high-browed? If she showed him this weakness, would he turn away from her? Would he think her shallow? Would trying to drive him into her arms actually drive him away?

And the sex thing—her perspective was so different from his. She could not give herself to him as long as she felt it was just an arrangement. There was something creepy about it. Sex just for the sake of sex was hard precisely because she loved him so much. To tell the truth she was a little ashamed of it. Sex without love—what was that? As the years went by she almost began to dread it. She felt like she was not even there, in his mind, when they were making love, like it could have been anybody as far as Henry was concerned. There were none of the usual tender caresses or meaningful looks, and this broke her heart. But she would never have dared to breathe a word of this to Henry. It would be breaking their agreement. It would be tumbling from the image she was trying so hard to maintain as a liberated young woman who has a career on her mind and does not trouble herself with sentiment. It was why she turned her back to him in bed; not because she didn't love him, but because she loved him too much. He never saw the tears. She made sure he didn't see them.

Although they were the same age, he seemed so much older to her. He had an air about him, everyone was conscious of it. The first day of school he had walked in and was promptly installed as the concert master of the orchestra. That just didn't happen. Everyone said it didn't happen, but no one could do anything about it, no matter how much they might burn with jealousy. He was clearly the best player and a natural leader. He seemed completely comfortable in the most conspicuous chair. Gabrielle would sit there looking at him in wonder.

Throughout their marriage she had suppressed herself and pushed herself down to avoid offending him in the hope that eventually he would come to her and love her. Yes, if there were breakfast dishes in the sink, and they were his dishes, and there was dry egg yolk bonded to the plate, she put aside her pride and swallowed her anger and did them; and if there were underclothes on the floor, because let's face it Henry could be a bit of a slob at times, she would pick them up for him and put them in the hamper in the hope that someday he would come to appreciate all she had done and go beyond the friendly relationship they shared to something deeper and more beautiful.

What Henry did by allowing himself to get tangled up with Margie was to strike directly at her deepest fear. This girl, this talentless little charmer had bewitched him and taken the love she longed to have for herself. Yes, she knew who Margie was. She'd met her at faculty parties and couldn't stand her. Pretty little vixen, that was her first and enduring impression, very full of herself and conscious of her charms. And now Henry had apparently fallen in love with her! This was what drove Gabrielle almost to distraction, into a rage she had never felt before in her life—the thought that little Margie had the love she coveted for herself. She was sick to her stomach when she finished reading the vile email, sick to the soul. After all she had sacrificed! To be displaced by a meretricious little schemer—it was simply too much.

Of course Henry knew nothing of all this. All he knew was that Gabrielle was gone and he was sick about it, bouncing around the house alone and not knowing what to do to with himself. And then there was the overwhelming feeling of shame. He was naked, like Adam and Eve in the garden. All of his pretenses had been exposed. He had ruined himself in Gabrielle's eyes, he could hear it in her tone of voice. Everything she said about his foolishness was completely true. He knew it better than anybody. To have been unfaithful to her was bad enough—but with Margie! Malcolm's girlfriend! She was right. He was no better than other men.

To have fallen so far in Gabrielle's eyes! Her disgust and body language were still fresh in his mind. The one person whose good opinion he valued more than any other was Gabrielle. He realized this now. The whole world could hate him, the whole world could desert him, but he could still hold on as long as he felt he was something in her eyes. Critics had praised him lavishly and critics had panned him; colleagues had worshipped him and colleagues had dismissed him as an overrated hack; but through it all his rock was Gabrielle. She was the one who brought stability to his struggle. She was the one he could depend upon for comfort.

Oh how he wished he could go to her right then and throw himself at her feet! How he wished he could beg her for forgiveness and tell her everything and see if she could still love him! His foolishness, his weaknesses, his instabilities, his fears and vulnerabilities—all of it! All this time he had been trying to build himself up in her eyes, casting himself as the hero in a story he was making up for her. Why? Because he valued her good opinion. Every conversation, every action was the unfolding of a story, and all of it was based on the nobility to which he aspired, the high-mindedness, the devotion to music and the finer things in life that he wanted her to see in him. She was too good for anything less.

All this time he had been afraid of taking a tumble in her eyes— and look how he had fallen! Humpty had fallen and could never be made respectable again. From now on and for all eternity his image would always be a broken and a shabby one to her. There would always be something out of place, an unshaven patch of stubble, an untied shoelace, pants that were a little faded, creases that were no longer sharp. He had been exposed and there was nothing he could do to change it. The tender stem of identity was corrupted and would never be whole again.

Could she still want him? Could she accept him as himself, as he really was, a fallen man, in many ways a shallow man? Did she even want him to come groveling now full of confessions and belated honesty? All through life the masks we wear are gentle masks. They keep us on the light side in our minds. Others never see us as we really are—they see our masks. Henry had destroyed his pleasant mask, and unfortunately it was the mask that made him feel worthy of Gabrielle. Was he still worthy now? Even if she would have him back, could he have himself? Could he live with himself after what he had done, all the pain he had caused?

Mixed in with white-hot shame was a deepening paranoia. The email completely unnerved Henry—not just its effect on Gabrielle but the fact it was sent at all. Who could have sent it? Who hated him enough to do such a thing? To spy on him? Take pictures of him with that girl? And there was something else. So far there had been just one email, but there could be more. The email came from a university server. It could be sent to the entire department simply by tipping in the group address. Someone had incredible power over him, potentially held his entire future in his or her hands. What else did they know? What other pictures did they have?

And most of all—who? Malcolm? It had to be. Henry's mind immediately went to something a little strange that happened on Friday. He was in his office when Malcolm stopped at the door. He seemed to want to tell him something, but a distraught student pushed by him to cry about not finishing her final and he drifted off. Henry noticed the funny look on his face. Was he trying to warn him? Or maybe gloating? They almost never talked anymore. There didn't even try to pretend to be friends. There was too much antagonism. It seemed unlikely to be a coincidence, coming on the same day as the email.

Lord knows, Malcolm had a motive. Henry had embarrassed him in front of the entire department, hinted that an adjunct was a better conductor. Okay, maybe more than just hinted. Apparently this was the message that had been taken away, although not the one he intended. Besides, his antagonism toward Malcolm was well-known among his friends. It was their favorite topic of conversation. You have to have something to talk about when you get together, and there was nothing more fascinating than Malcolm and his outrages and arrogance. They were all in perfect agreement on the riveting subject of "Hitler," as they often called him.

But it was one thing for Henry to disparage him in private and quite another to have openly taken him down in a department meeting. Henry himself was shocked by it, by what he had implied. He did not start out to imply it. He had no intention of disparaging Malcolm when he spoke up in support of Alicia. Somehow it just happened. He felt badly at the time and even entertained some thought of apologizing. But what would that accomplish? Malcolm wasn't gracious enough to know how to accept an apology. Plus there was no way to apologize without admitting his guilt. Also he did not know for sure that Malcolm felt he had been disparaged, which would make an apology rather awkward.

What Henry had done was to break the truce. There was a war going on in the department and almost everybody knew it, between the Credentialists and those who believed in more organic teaching methods, but the key to waging this war was to remain patient and strive for advantage and not total victory. The way to "win" the war was to wage the war without trying to win it and thus to avoid losing your job. This required staying within certain bounds. Administrators and faculty were always coming and going. The dynamic in the department was in constant flux. Sometimes the Credentialists were ascendant, and those on Henry's side were cowed; but just when all hope seemed lost there would be a subtle change—it was not always clear why—and then Henry and his sympathizers would have their time in the sun.

It was an accommodation; not a truce but more like a perpetual stalemate tacitly accepted by both parties—as long as neither one became too bold and tried to annihilate the other. Malcolm wasn't stupid. He and his faction were well-aware that Henry brought tremendous value to the department, no matter how annoying they found him or how much they resented the "cult of personality" that had grown up around him, as Jeff referred to his enduring popularity with students and many of the staff. They were willing to let him more or less go his own way and not conform to the rules they dreamed up as long as he did not try to force his idiosyncratic views on them; as long as he showed respect for them and the value they were bringing to the department.

Unfortunately Henry had broken the rules and opted for all-out war. He had issued a direct challenge to the bubble Malcolm and his friends had created for themselves, the mutually self-reinforcing rhetorical glow in which they were said to be doing "groundbreaking" work and being "visionaries in the field" and "setting an example of excellence" for the department and the whole university. In his more charitable moments, when he was not outraged by all this empty bluster, Henry saw it as a sign of insecurity. Someone who is actually doing remarkable things does not need to boast about it. Malcolm and friends had to boast because they were not doing remarkable things. They were music professors in a middling college, not musicians. They could not have gone with Henry to Carnegie Hall and played Beethoven for a sophisticated New York audience.

To Henry it was all an illusion, a sleight of hand. He doubted that ten truly gifted teachers could be found on the entire campus, should it be threatened with sulfur and fire. They wrote reams and reams of incomprehensible dreary gobbledygook that they published in obscure journals, created just for that purpose, and then they demanded that you read their awful dispiriting prose so you could claim to be erudite, too. They went to graduations wearing their moldy old gowns and hoods and paraded in ahead of the student hordes, but Henry couldn't help noticing that some of the most prominent marchers were also the biggest poseurs. He knew them personally and had worked with them on those dreadful committees. He knew how empty it all was.

Having such subversive views was not a problem in itself. It was not a fatal weakness to be out of step with the world as long as one could find a way to conceal one's disillusionment and fit in. Indeed, millions and tens of millions of Americans were doing this very thing every day, in foolish and dispiriting workplaces all across the land. But no one can openly hate the world and also live in it. In the past Henry had always been able to conceal his contempt for what went on in the department. He'd made a point of getting along with the leadership no matter how much it cost him. But now he had indulged his subversive fantasies. He had allowed his opposition to be seen. He may have done it for a noble cause—for Alicia, who was deserving of support—but you cannot set about to reform the world if the world does not want to be reformed. You cannot oppose the world without being opposed.

Henry had been tolerant for thirty long years. He had smiled blandly and gone along with all the idiocy and nonsense and kept his mouth shut because he knew in his heart that resistance was futile. But now he had gone and opened his big mouth and spoiled everything. Worst of all, he had betrayed his own self. He was all about the love. This was the fundamental difference, in his mind, between him and the Credentialists. It was love that drew him to music and love that he wanted to express through his music; not ego, not power. But his attack on Malcolm was not based on love, or at least not on any great or magnanimous love. No, it was based on his foolish infatuation with Margie.

Henry knew he had an ulterior motive in attacking Malcolm. Outwardly he was supporting Alicia, but inwardly he was thinking of Margie. There was also too much self-love in the attack. Whom was he really supporting when he went after Malcolm? Yes, it was Alicia—but wasn't it also himself? Wasn't he really thinking about his own worth and predicament? In some sense, wasn't Alicia's cause, worthy as it may be, also a proxy for his own private war and the long agony of abuse and neglect he had endured over the years? He did not need to attack anyone in order to praise Alicia. No, the attack itself had come from somewhere else, from a part of himself he did not recognize until later on, after it had produced its inevitable consequences.

Malcolm had the motive to send the email. He also had the meanness. Henry could not think of anyone else in the department who would do such a thing. It was true that Jeff had hardened himself in semi-open opposition to Henry years ago, but he couldn't see him doing *this*. For one thing, he was too lazy to follow people around on a frigid winter night. Plus, it wasn't Jeff that Henry had attacked at the meeting. Bertram? No, close the book right there. Henry did not put Bertram in the same category as Malcolm and Jeff. He was their friend, but he was not like them. Also whoever had done it had used a university server. They had to be highly motivated to run the risk of exposure. This seemed to rule out both Jeff and Bertram.

No, it had to be to Malcolm. Wasn't he supposed to have been Margie's lover? Maybe he was still in love with her. Maybe that was why he was following them around. Henry felt himself getting worked up into a rage as the weekend dragged on and he had nothing to do in his lonely house but think too much. All of the other feelings—the shame, the guilt, the regret, the paranoia—started to find their way into the anger that was building towards his nemesis. He was determined to confront him. He went to work Monday morning bristling for a fight. What would he do if he saw him? He wasn't sure. All he knew was he had to know the truth. He had to know who had sent the email. Not to know was killing him—wondering who his antagonist was and what else they had in store for him.

Henry practiced a new piece he was working on and graded exams and fidgeted and found ways to spend much of the day at school. There was no sign of Malcolm, however. He kept going to the window and looking out at the parking lot and his usual spot, but the handsome one did not appear. At last he was the only professor left in the building on a beautiful spring day, so he decided to go home.

As soon as he walked in the house he knew something had changed. He sensed it before he understood. Gabrielle removed her Presence. She had come while he was at school and taken everything she considered a personal belonging. Henry felt the change like a physical blow. He actually had to sit down on the sofa to recover and regain his bearings. It was not just about moving out. It had nothing to do with wanting what was hers, because she was not materialistic. No, it was an act of spite. She was sending him a message, telling him she was through with him. She was making her displeasure known.

He called her cell. She did not answer. He left a message, and then he called again and left another message. He needed to talk to her. Wouldn't she please talk to him? It didn't do any good just to cut him off. There were things he wanted to say, things he needed to say. It was complicated—it wasn't what it seemed. All right, he had acted like an ass and he was sorry. He couldn't even tell her how sorry he was. Wouldn't she at least talk to him?

He left these heartfelt messages and then he made himself some supper he didn't really want and went out for a walk and came back in and sat in the twilight in agony, waiting for the phone to ring. It didn't. It was silent and the house was silent and he was miserable. He wanted Gabrielle to come home. He wanted her to walk through that door like she always had, with a little smile on her face, and come in and sit down and talk to him as they had done for thirty-five years. He kept looking at the door, hoping for a miracle, but it stayed shut.

The night wore on and it got dark and it was dark inside because he did not bother to turn on the lights and he sat there in the same place in his misery looking at the door and still there was no sign of Gabrielle. He beat himself up over and over again, sitting there in the gathering gloom, half-wishing he were dead. He had been feckless. He acted like a jerk. She had seen a photo of them standing outside Margie's apartment, and yes it was real. It really did happen, although it wasn't what it seemed. Or was it? At the time he had hoped it was. There was no point in trying to deny it. He had been crazy about Margie. He had forgotten Gabrielle.

He was caught, there was nothing more to be said. But was that the end of it—of them? Was there nothing he could do to make it up to her? He was willing to do anything—but how did he know what to do when she wouldn't even talk to him? She was being unreasonable. It surprised him. It wasn't like her. She had every right to be angry, but couldn't she at least hear what he had to say? Wasn't there anything in their thirty-five years together to sway her or make her at least willing to listen?

It was a restless night, a sleepless night for Henry. He went to bed early, not having anything else to occupy him, and lay there thinking, churning, turning, getting twisted up in the sheets. He was angry with himself. He fully deserved what had happened. He had gone and blown up everything for nothing—destroyed his marriage for the sake of an illusion. His restless mind turned to the email that had ruined his marriage. That email really scared him, the invasion of privacy, people in his business. The more he thought about it, tossing on his bed, the more he felt it had to be Malcolm. The son of a bitch had outdone himself this time. Henry wanted to kill him. He imagined himself doing all kinds of violent things to him. He wanted to do them right then.

Yes, right then! At about two in the morning he bolted out of bed and threw on some clothes and actually drove over to Malcolm's house seething with rage. He parked the car across the street and turned off the engine and just sat there. The house was completely dark on a dark moonless night. There wasn't even a night light to scare away burglars. Were they home? There were no cars in the driveway. There might be in the garage, but it didn't matter. Henry knew he wasn't going to do anything. He had made his big heroic gesture. He had driven over to Malcolm's house in the middle of the night. Now he suddenly felt very tired. He started the car and drove home, slowly, not really wanting to get there, not wanting to be alone with his thoughts.

He got back into bed, now wide awake again after his heroic foray. It was a long night and morning was a long time coming. He dragged himself out of bed because he wanted to go to school. He wanted to confront Malcolm, and Malcolm was usually there on Tuesdays. He didn't bother with breakfast. He didn't stop for his usual cup of coffee. It was a strange drive in—a cloudy May day—and he was so tired he was groggy and everything seemed a little unreal, as if viewed through a filter, and he could feel his senses focused for some reason in the point of his nose.

He pulled into the parking lot and immediately spotted Malcolm's car and parked as far away as he could, although the whole point of coming in was to see him. Henry trudged wearily up the stairs and down the garishly lighted hallway. The door to Malcolm's office was open. He walked right in.

"Hi, there," he said menacingly.

"Henry! How are you?" the Evil One said, with a disarmingly friendly smile.

"I've been better. But I suppose you know all about that."

"No, I don't know. Something happen?"

"Aren't you the one who sent that nice little email?"

"What email?"

"To my wife."

"Gabrielle? No, I didn't send her any email."

"It had to be you. It was someone at the university. Who else would have done it?"

"I don't know, but it sure wasn't me. I don't even know her email address. What was it about?"

"Some nonsense about me and Margie."

"Margie Hart? *She* probably sent it. She's a bit of a psycho."

Henry felt his tower of righteous indignation crumbling. "So you're telling me you did not send an email to my wife?"

"No, of course not. I don't have any reason to send her an email."

"Well, whoever did it should be really proud of themselves. She moved out."

"Oh—*that* kind of email," Malcom said in surprise.

"I don't know whether to believe you or not. But I can promise you one thing. I will get to the bottom of this. Whoever did this, they're messing with the wrong person."

"I can't blame you. I'd feel exactly the same way, if I were in your position."

That was the end of that. Henry had worked himself up into a lather for nothing. Malcolm had not given him an opportunity to show how manly he was. He stayed perfectly calm in the face of Henry's storm. It was this calm that told him Malcolm was telling the truth. He did not know anything about the email. Henry was disappointed. He really wanted to believe it was Malcolm, and not just because he had gone ahead and made the open accusation. He wanted it to be Malcolm because if it wasn't Malcolm—who was it? Who had it out for him? Who had secret knowledge of his business? What else did they know?

He had gone and made a huge unforced error, perhaps the worst error he had ever made in his career. He had given his enemy power over him. Because of his stupidity, Malcolm now knew about an explosive email that had caused Gabrielle to move out, and he knew this email had something to do with Margie. It was hard to miss the obvious conclusion. He could count on Malcolm not missing it from the look on his face. He could also count on this information being passed around the department. Malcolm would never keep something like this to himself, not if it made Henry look bad. It would spread like a brush fire.

But there was something else that was disturbing—although he really didn't want to think about it—the comment about Margie being a "psycho." Henry's first inclination was to consider the source, but the comment seemed perfectly spontaneous. Worse, it struck a chord. He thought about her behavior and the fierce anger she had occasionally shown. There was definitely something off-color about the whole thing, something he could not quite put his finger on. He wondered—was Margie the one who sent the email? Then again, what motive could she possibly have? Was she was trying to break up his marriage so she could have him to herself? He was not vain enough to think this was the case. Was it purely out of spite for having failed to perform up to her standards? This also seemed unlikely. She was taking a big risk sending such an email, incriminating herself with Gabrielle.

This thought sealed it. Margie would never have sent an email accusing herself. It just didn't make sense. Still, Malcolm's characterization made him uneasy. He had laid himself completely open and bare to her. Was she really a "psycho," and if so, what else could she do to make his life miserable?

BROKEN HEARTS

A COUPLE OF WEEKS WENT BY and graduation was over and Henry was finally free for the summer. Normally he would have been rejoicing in his freedom except the summer did not look to be a happy one. He was alone and each new day reminded him of how much he did not like being alone. It was strange going home to an empty house, waking up alone in bed, completely alone. It was strange not having someone to talk to. He realized how much he had come to depend on Gabrielle and how important their relationship was to his happiness and peace of mind, unconventional as it might be.

Another daunting thought dawned on him as the rose month of June approached: there was a mortgage payment coming up and car payments and electricity and gas bills and everything else. The household income had been cut almost in half with Gabrielle's sudden departure while the expenses remained very much the same. There was enough in the bank for him to pay June and probably July, but here too there were difficulties. Not all the money was his. It was their joint checking account.

He remembered all those articles he had seen over the years about the impoverishing effects of divorce, only now he was living it. The house was supposed to be their investment, their nest egg, but he knew he would not be able to afford it on his own. More than just a relationship had been damaged through his foolishness. The future they had so carefully planned together also grew dim.

He had to see Gabrielle. He was longing to see her. He had called her and left at least ten messages on her cell phone in the three weeks since her departure and there had been complete silence on her end. Even the way she took her things was disconcerting—coming when she knew he would be at school and simply cleaning them out. She had not taken more than she should, had not touched anything that could be considered his or even theirs. The big things were not touched—the large flat-screen TV and the stereo and silver and Macbook and other things of high value. Mostly only her personal things. Still, it was unsettling. She was obviously very angry.

It was becoming clear to him that she would not answer her phone and had no intention of returning his many calls, and yet he had to talk to her. He had to see her and see if he couldn't straighten this whole thing out. It was not as bad as it seemed. After all, nothing had actually happened between him and Margie. All she wanted was payback for Malcolm. He hadn't seen or heard from her since the last strange interlude in his office. He assumed he had outlived his usefulness.

But how to explain all this to Gabrielle? How to explain the email and the damning photo of him outside Margie's apartment? What Henry wanted more than anything was for Gabrielle to come home, but how to accomplish this? He could deny everything. After all, in one sense he was perfectly innocent. The photo implied something that simply wasn't true. He had gone to her apartment to look at the violin—and that was all he did.

What should he do? Should he insist there was nothing there? What about taking her to the restaurant? What about the time he touched her? What about the park and his ridiculous outburst? What about the photo? What in the world was a married man doing at the apartment of an attractive coworker at night? He could protest his innocence all he wanted, but he respected Gabrielle too much to think he could convince her not believe what she had seen with her own eyes.

Since she would not answer his calls, he would have to go see her in person. He would drive over to Dagny's condo and knock on the door and make her talk to him, whether she wanted to or not. After all, it was for her own good. She was angry with him, he knew it, but he wanted to give her a chance to get beyond her anger. There was no point in cutting herself off from a man who really did care for her and with whom she had spent three decades building a stable and financially secure arrangement. There was no point in throwing all that away just because of a foolish mistake.

All right, a terrible mistake, but what about love? Isn't love bigger than mistakes? He knew she was a good person, a generous person, kind-hearted. Couldn't she allow herself to be guided by love and set aside her wounded pride if he came to her on his knees and confessed that he was a foolish old man and begged her for forgiveness? She was better than he was. He knew it. He gladly acknowledged it. She was a better person, truly good. Couldn't she find it in her heart to forgive?

But what *about* love? Was that what they had together? He had not been very loving in his treatment of her, essentially humiliating her. Nor had they spent very much time talking about love during their thirty-five years of marriage. It never came up. It was not part of the arrangement. They were in love with music—wasn't that enough? Now he realized it wasn't. Not when he really needed love. He did not know if Gabrielle loved him enough to give him another chance—or if she loved him at all.

He loved her, however. He was sincere about this. The whole blow-up with Malcolm and Margie and Alicia and Camilla had made him realize just how much he loved her and needed her, how much he relied on her goodness, her loyalty to him. She was his ally, not a small thing in the lonely profession they had chosen for themselves. She was the one person he could trust, who would never betray him or play games with him and his fragile ego. But could she trust *him*? Hadn't he shown her that she couldn't? Did he himself feel trustworthy? No, just then he felt rather dangerous.

Still, he was going to try. After all, he had to do *something*. He was miserable sitting there in the house they used to share. Everything he looked at and everything he touched reminded him of her. The longer she was gone, the more painful these reminders became. He just couldn't imagine the future without her. He couldn't imagine starting over, not at his age. He didn't want to start over. He and Gabrielle were a thing. His identity was invested in their relationship. He wanted everything to return to normal. He didn't realize how much he appreciated normal until it was gone.

The idea percolated in his mind for a week or so until he finally decided he just couldn't wait any longer. She was still not answering his messages or emails; he had to see her in person. It was the last Friday in May, a warm, glorious spring morning, birds singing in the trees. He was sitting on the deck, fidgeting and drinking his coffee in gulps and thinking about Gabrielle when suddenly he reached the decision point. It was early, not yet nine, but he had a forty-five minute drive to get there. He wanted to strike while the iron was hot and his plan and resolve were fresh in his mind.

As he drove over the familiar roads he thought of all the times they had driven over those same roads together, for holidays, birthday parties, etc.; all the good times they'd had at Dagny's condo over the years. He had a great relationship with Dagny. She was funny and smart and fun to be around. Maybe a little too smart—maybe that's why she had never been married, although there had been a couple of close calls. She was a good friend to Gabrielle, for which Henry was grateful. And at least until recently she had been a good friend to Henry.

He began to feel a little nervous as he drove into the condo complex, like before a performance, but he was determined. He had to talk to Gabrielle, and this was the only way to do it, since she refused to return his calls. He parked in front of Dagny's garage bay—next to Gabrielle's car—and felt extremely self-conscious as he walked around to the front door. Had they seen him? What were they thinking? How would they react?

He rang the bell. There was no answer and he felt his heart sink. Had they heard him? How could they not?—he could hear the bell from outside. Were they ignoring him, then? He waited a minute and rang again, pushing the button with a little more fervor this time, as if it made a difference. He heard the chime, nice and clear, but still no one came to the door.

Now suddenly he lost his nerve. What was he doing there, uninvited? He thought about retreating. He turned to go—but no; his resolve returned as he thought about going back to an empty house. If Gabrielle was there, he wanted to talk to her. But what if she wasn't there? Well, he would just sit on the front step until she came home. It didn't matter how long it took. He had all day. And it was a beautiful day. He could see himself spending it on her stoop, like a doting Romeo. He was determined to see her, and this was his chance to show her just how determined he was.

This time he knocked. Strangely, there was a knocker in addition to the doorbell, and he gave the metal knob a couple of good vigorous clangs. Then he did it again. Still nothing happened. He sat down on the stone steps to wait. A couple of moments later the door opened behind him. It was Gabrielle.

"Henry, what are you doing here?"

"I came to see you," he said, jumping up rather sprightly for a middle-aged codger. "You won't return my calls, so I decided to come in person."

"Why?" she said with a pained look on her face. "I don't understand."

"I need to see you. I need to talk to you. It's been a month. Can we just have a conversation?"

"There's nothing to talk about. You made your choice, now let me make mine."

"There's only one choice I've made. I want to talk to you. I want to get past this. We're good together. We make a good team. I don't want to break it up now."

"Yeah, well, you should have thought of that before. It's a little late for it now."

"Look, can't we go someplace and talk? Just give me a half an hour. I need to talk to you."

"I don't have half an hour. I have a concert tomorrow night and I have to practice."

"Come on, half an hour won't kill you. I came all the way over here. Please?"

She stood considering him for a moment. "All right, come in. Dagny's out picking up some bagels."

Henry's spirits rose. This was working out better than he expected. They had a place to be alone and talk, which was just what he needed to push out the words he wanted to say. They went into the living room and sat down. It was all very awkward, this coldness between them, as if they were on a first date, as if she were a stranger and not someone he lived with for most of his life, but Henry was glad just to be in the house and alone with her for the first time in a long time.

"So," she said with a flat affect and not looking at him. "What did you want to talk about?"

"I want to get back together. I realize I made a terrible mistake and hurt you badly, but I just want to get back together. I can't live without you."

"'Mistake'? Is that what you call it?"

"All right—sin, blunder, crime. What do you want me to call it? I've been a complete ass. Nobody could feel worse about it than I do. But does that mean we have to destroy what we have? Do you really want to throw away thirty-five years of marriage over this?"

"I didn't throw it away, Henry. You did. You seem to want to blame this on me, but I didn't do anything. I took care of you for all those years. I did everything you wanted. And this is how you repay me. This is how you reward me for being a good wife."

"Okay, so is this a feminist thing, then? I'm not doing enough in the marriage? Because I can change."

"No, it's not a 'feminist thing,'" she said with a bitter laugh. "You were fooling around with someone else. You broke your vows, and that means the vows are broken."

"I wasn't fooling around. Nothing happened. I had dinner with her a couple of times to talk about Alicia. That picture you saw—I went to her apartment to look at an old violin she had that she thought was worth something. It wasn't. That was it."

"Did you love her, Henry?"

"No! Well—I don't know. I guess I may have had some feelings for her. But it wasn't love. Not really. She caught me off guard, that's all. It was like some kind of madness came over me. But I'm over it now. Believe me, I'm over it. She was just using me to get at Malcolm."

"But you told her you loved her."

"What?"

"That's what the email said—oh, did I forget that part? The exact words were something like, 'I know for a fact that he told her he loved her.' Do you deny it?"

Henry was reeling. What was this about? His spontaneous outburst in the park? How in the world could anyone have known about that?—except Margie? Did Margie send the email after all? It was certainly starting to look like it. But then who took the picture? That couldn't have been Margie. Or was whoever took the picture actually spying on them in the park? Was that even possible, in the middle of the day? And had his idiotic outburst actually been overheard? This thought was perfectly dreadful.

Henry was flummoxed. He sat there staring at his angry-looking wife as all the blood came rushing up into his head. He did not realize what was going on, what this line of questioning was really about. Gabrielle wanted him to say he loved her and not Margie. That was all she wanted him to say. It was all she had ever wanted to hear him say. She so much wanted Henry to love her the way she loved him. She would have forgiven him and gone back with him in an instant, right then and there, if only he said he loved her. But he did not say it.

Words could not express how much she regretted the arrangement she agreed to when they were married. Over the years she had come to see the wise old mentors who put them together as meddling busybodies who pretended to be interested in their welfare but were only interested in themselves, in perpetuating their legacy through Henry and Gabrielle, childless people or people with screwed-up children who wanted to adopt them as their spiritual heirs in the art of music. Well-intentioned or not, their meddling had produced a life of desperation. She was stuck in a bizarre marriage where the love was all on her side. Marriage is supposed to be love, but she was afraid to express her love because she thought it would drive him away. After all, he had never expressed any love for her.

Did he love her? She did not think he did. Oh, maybe in a way, but not in the way she wanted. Over the years she had almost come to see herself as his faithful amanuensis rather than his wife, or like the nurse who "marries" herself to the married doctor and his practice and goes through her whole life loving him and devoted to his career and never being able to say how she feels, because after all she's just his employee. That's how it was for Gabrielle. She was only Henry's domestic partner. She was good company for him, his household slave; that was all. He loved the little bitch Margie. He wouldn't come right out and say so, but it was the unspoken substance of his evasive words. If he loved that little conniving nothing, why couldn't he love her? Her heart was breaking all over again as she sat there waiting for the words that never came. Why couldn't he love her? Why? What was wrong with her? Hadn't she done everything for him?

The tragic thing was that Henry really did love Gabrielle. A forced separation had revealed this to him. They had a different kind of relationship and a different kind of love. Some people go into marriage crazy in love and lose it over time as the little insults of life pile up. Henry and Gabrielle had gone into marriage clearheaded and anything but crazy—as far as he knew—but his affection for her had steadily grown over the years. The irony was he could have said exactly what she wanted to hear. He could have said "I love you" to her right then and there and meant it with all his heart, if he had known such words were desired, or even welcome.

"Okay, I did tell her that," he said now, thinking a frank approach would impress her. "I said it, but I regret saying it. I admit it, I'm a fool. I'm not even going to try to hide it. I don't understand myself or the things that go on in my head. But that's why I'm here. I'm just trying to be honest with you and see if we can't get past this somehow. I don't want to throw away thirty-five years of marriage over nothing and my own stupidity. It just doesn't make sense."

"But it wasn't nothing. You were in love with her."

"I don't know what I was. I was crazy, I know that. Something happened to me, something I couldn't control. But you have to believe me when I tell you it didn't mean anything. I don't have any feelings for her. In fact I find her a little scary. Why would I lie to you? I'm being completely honest. I know what a jerk I've been. I'm just asking if you can forgive me."

"I can forgive you, Henry, but I don't think I can give you what you want."

"Think about it rationally. Think about your own self-interest, if nothing else. There's a mortgage payment coming up. We've been paying this mortgage ever since we bought the house, planning for our future, working to make sure we would be ready for retirement. It just doesn't make sense to throw it all away over nothing."

"Is that what this is about?" she said, looking at him wide-eyed. "Money?"

"No, of course not. I'm trying to talk reason with you and get you to see why it doesn't make sense for us to split up, even from a financial point of view, that's all. If we do this now, we're going to live to regret it."

At this point she laughed. "I think it's time for you to go."

"I don't know, maybe I'm not making myself clear. I can make a couple of mortgage payments on my own, but after that we're stuck. We're going to have to sell the house in a down market and wind up losing what we've worked so hard to build up."

"Sell it, I don't care. I don't want have anything to do with it anymore. Sell it all—the china, everything. I don't want to ever set foot in that house again."

"I don't understand. Why can't you be a little more reasonable?"

"No, you're right. You don't understand. You come here to talk about money and tell me I should forgive you so we can have a comfortable retirement. I don't want a comfortable retirement with you. I just want you to go away and leave me alone."

"You don't mean that. You can't really mean that. Not after thirty-five years."

"I mean it *because* of thirty-five years. Go. Just go, before Dagny gets back."

"Are you sure? I mean, is that what you really want?"

"I want you to go and take care of your money," she replied without looking at him as she stood up and walked toward the door. "You've got a house and a lot of stuff to sell. You're going to be busy."

Henry followed her meekly. At the door he tried to reach out and embrace her or even just touch her, but she pushed him away.

"Just go," she said. "This isn't helping you or me."

"I can't help feeling this isn't really you. Will you think about what I said and call me?"

"I'll think about it, but I won't call you. It's over Henry. And I'm glad. It's a relief. Honestly, after all these years it's just a relief."

With that she shut the door in his face. He didn't want to go. He knocked, he waited, but she did not return. He drove home in a daze. He drove to his empty house and he sat there in his driveway looking at it and shaking his head. Women are not rational creatures. He thought Gabrielle was different, but she wasn't. She would not listen to reason.

Later that afternoon he called a real estate agent and made an appointment to talk about putting the house on the market. His life was changing in ways he never could have imagined.

RED-HOT COALS

IT WAS MEMORIAL DAY WEEKEND and it was so sunny and unseasonably warm that Malcolm decided to throw an impromptu barbecue. He invited several coworkers. At one point he found himself alone with Jeff by the Weber, waiting for the hardwood charcoal to silver over and poking at the chicken and chops in the savory red sauce. They each held a bottle of beer. It was not their first.

"So, heard any exciting rumors lately?" Malcolm said, fishing.

"Not really. What did you have in mind?" Jeff replied, radar immediately on.

"Thought maybe you'd heard something about our old friend Henry."

"'Old' is the operative word. What did Henry do now?"

"Not exactly sure. I do know Gabrielle moved out."

"What! No."

"Yes. Last month."

"Wow. Unbelievable."

"That's not the half of it. Apparently it has something to do with Margie."

"Margie Hart? Whoa! Where did you hear that one?"

"From the horse's mouth, ass—whatever. He came bombing into my office and accused me of sending some crazy email or something. Of course I had no idea what he was talking about."

"So did he specifically say it was because of Margie?"

"He said Margie was in the email. But come on."

"Isn't he like a hundred years old or something? But it's funny. Bertram did say something about seeing them together in Henry's office a while back."

"When was that?"

"I don't know—a couple of months ago. But he was kind of struck by it."

"So it's been going on for a while. No wonder she moved out."

"I wonder if it had anything to do with him making such a damned fool of himself at the meeting."

"What do you mean?"

"Well, think about it. He never talks in those meetings. Now all of a sudden he's a freaking mockingbird. The whole thing was supposed to be about Alicia and standing up gallantly for her 'rights' or whatever crap he was spinning. Can you spin crap?"

"Your point?"

"Maybe he wasn't being so gallant. Or to put it more simply, maybe he was doing it for Margie."

"Maybe he was doing it in return for certain *favors* from Margie," Malcolm said, lighting up. "That's what you're saying."

Jeff laughed a beery laugh. "That's got to be it. Why else would he suddenly become so talkative? Too funny. How the mighty have fallen! But this is good for us. We finally have some ammunition."

"How so?"

"Come on! This guy's gotta go. If anything, this just confirms it. He's way overstayed his welcome at this point. I almost feel sorry for him. But the fact is he can't keep up anymore. He's lost it. Bertram told me there was some big brouhaha about one of his star students. Says he doesn't teach him anything."

"We've known that for years. He's been mailing it in ever since I got here."

"So don't you get it? That's what makes this whole Margie thing kind of interesting. If it's true then he's in hot water. He basically traded sexual favors for some big power play. Not good. Definitely actionable, from my point of view."

"So you're saying you think this information should be shared."

"Why not? He basically humiliated you in front of the whole department. I don't know if he's getting senile or what, but you don't stand up in front of everybody and just accuse one of your colleagues of being incompetent. Everyone is pissed off with him for that. Every single person I've talked to. He's been walking around here like the king all these years and everybody's sick of it. So maybe it's time for a little payback. I'm pretty sure you'd have a lot of support. He's not quite the superstar he used to be."

"Okay, but I don't really see what we can do."

"Well, if I were you, let's just say I'd start by finding a way to spend a little time with our cutie-pie dean."

"Camilla? Really?"

"Don't tell me you haven't noticed. She practically climbs all over you every time you're in the same room. And apparently Henry really pissed her off with this whole Alicia thing—that's from Bertram. She already feels like she's being used. So yeah— why not? Put on that handsome smile of yours and go for it. You've got nothing to lose but your chains."

"That would be too funny. Anyway, it's an idea. I know one thing. If this rumor ever gets around—look out. It's definitely a black eye for the old guard. One of their own, misbehaving."

"Particularly him, Mr. 'I'm-above-it-all.' It would be great to see him get taken down a peg or two. Come to think of it, there are quite a few people who'd like to see that. But I do feel kind of bad about Gabrielle. They were practically an institution around here— listen to me, I'm talking like they're dead or something. But think about it. All the concerts she came to, all the parties at their house. She put up with all that, and now this. It's sad."

"Well, maybe we can get her some payback. Lord knows she deserves it."

They laughed. Both young men got what they wanted out of this conversation. Malcolm had been dying to start a rumor, and was successful, because Jeff was easily the biggest blabbermouth on campus. And Jeff got what he wanted because Malcolm was intrigued. He immediately began to think about how to make sure this information reached the ears of Bertram and Camilla. Bertram was easy; Camilla was going to require some thought.

It didn't take long for the news about "King Henry" and the scandal to find its way around the department. Most people just heard some of the story. All they knew was that Gabrielle had moved out and some shadowy woman was involved. Others actually heard it was Margie, or guessed it from seeing her and Henry together. It was definitely the number one topic of conversation as spring turned into summer and parties took place around pools and there was fraternizing in various restaurants and bars around town. Everyone was shocked, although some claimed not to be surprised. They knew all along Henry had to have his Achilles' heel, in spite of what appeared to be a perfect career and a perfect marriage. Everybody does.

Henry knew nothing about the rumors, of course. No one was going to tell him; they were all enjoying them too much. But he did notice that all of Richie's predictions seemed to be coming true. First he received his course assignments for the fall. Two appreciation classes with the unwashed masses. Not just one but two! He hated those classes with a passion, hated having to try to inspire a love of classical music in smug, spoiled kids who just didn't give a damn and who clearly thought of him as an old fossil and had never seen him on stage and were invulnerable to his usual charms. With all the other assignments, his workload doubled. It didn't surprise him. He didn't bother calling Bertram to complain. Somewhere deep down inside he knew he would be punished.

Then came the second shock. He called in to talk about orchestra arrangements and was notified he didn't have to worry. It was "taken care of." True, there had been some discussion of him filling in; but after careful consideration, factoring in his workload and busy concert schedule, it was decided to make things easier for him and have Malcolm do it after all. He could handle both the orchestra and the play. This is what Henry was actually told! He almost threw up. Doing the orchestra was one of the few things he really loved at the university. He had already picked the music. He had already talked to some of the students about it and asked some of his professional friends to help out. Now he was going to have to give them the bad news. It was humiliating.

This one really hurt. Not just the fact that he wasn't conducting the orchestra, but the way he was told, brought in after the decision had already been made. He tried to pretend it didn't hurt but it did. Four long years had gone by since the last time they'd let him conduct. He loved standing up there on the podium with the students. It brought joy to his life. He loved to hold the baton in his hand and really try to do something special for them. He felt it was important, but it was not to be. All the planning and teaching and conducting he had done in his head—he had to give it up. He had to pull a cloud over it to hide his disappointment from himself.

Richie's prediction about the residency for Forum also seemed to be coming true. This one was especially dear to Henry's heart.

He had been working on it for years; decades, really. He had never given himself the luxury of hoping too much or being overly optimistic until the new school president arrived a couple of years ago. He came in knowing about Henry. He was a classical music enthusiast—that in itself was a first—and actually owned a couple of Henry's CDs. They'd had some very good talks, and for the first time Henry allowed himself to think his dream might come true.

He was about to be rudely awakened, however. He went to a department cookout at Bertram's house. He didn't want to go, but it was a command performance—team building and all that. Anyway, Henry was talking to Bertram about a concert he had coming up in Newport and Bertram was being very complimentary, which encouraged him to ask if he'd heard anything on the residency front. Bertram smiled one of his thin smiles and said he hadn't heard anything *lately*, but his last conversation on this subject with Camilla had not been promising because of the budget constraints that had hit the department.

Oh, well. Henry forgot the first and most important rule in the delicate art of negotiation: Never make it easy for people to give you bad news. His spirits sank as he stood there in the sun by Bertram's pool watching him shuck cherrystones while he jived his way through telling him what he didn't want to hear. Suddenly Henry felt very old. He stood there in his slacks and silk summer shirt with his unsipped glass of red wine in his hand and he looked around at his colleagues in their swimming suits and it struck him that he was Grandpa.

And tired. Really tired. It had been a long and tumultuous summer. The house did sell, amazingly, at the end of June, just before he had to make another mortgage payment—they had priced it to sell—but then came the ardors of moving and selling everything he owned jointly with Gabrielle and figuring how to divvy up the proceeds, all very complicated. She would not budge an inch; no, not on money matters—she was curiously flexible in that regard, almost to the point of negligence—but on her resistance to him and his desire to be generous. She would not allow it. She insisted on being generous herself, but somehow it didn't feel like generosity. It felt like a poke in the eye.

She was hard, cold; she would barely talk to him. Selling his home and dealing with her hardness took all the energy out of him, all the joy. And then he had to find a place to live! He was in a hurry and settled on pretty much the first small condo he saw that he felt he could afford. The night he moved in he knew he had made a big mistake. It was cramped, it was ugly—four purely functional rooms with no thought of aesthetics or comfort. It was too close to the city for his sensitive nerves. And when he tried to pick up his violin at ten o'clock to soothe himself his neighbor promptly called the super to complain.

There was more fallout from the rift with Gabrielle, unexpected. Her brother Karl was the cellist in Forum, and, after Henry, the most popular member among their cult following. He was good-looking and had all the moves on stage, and he also had a beautiful tone and expressiveness. Not surprisingly, Karl was unhappy about what happened to his sister. Gabrielle did not hold back when he asked her why she had moved out. They were quite annoyed with Henry, as a family, and they could be quite the family when they were annoyed. From their point of view, Henry had thrown away thirty-five years of their sister's life and ruined her financially for the sake of a frivolous little trollop. They did not know how Henry really felt, how much he loved Gabrielle, in his own way, and wanted to be reconciled to her. He could not tell them. It seemed unlikely they would want to hear.

But now it was causing problems in Forum. The group had always been a tricky thing to handle. Henry did not want to get locked into a traditional string trio or quartet and wind up playing the same repertoire his whole life. He had a vision for something new, something like a cooperative, where there were a group of core players but they could flex and change shape and configuration, depending on what they wanted to play. The great thing about this concept was that Henry was able to program musical evenings, as opposed to, say, string quartet concerts. He was able to be much more audience-centered and change things up so he could send his fans home happy.

The disadvantage was the challenge of keeping all the *players* happy. He was almost always playing—after all, he was the first violinist—but other players had to be willing to be flexible and sit out parts of the concerts, where appropriate. It was a delicate balancing act that he had somehow been able to carry off for four decades, in part because of the popularity of the group, but his main ally in keeping things together had always been his wise-cracking brother-in-law. They had an unspoken pact, as founding members, and family, to work together to influence, calm, smooth over, soothe, inspire—whatever it took to keep the group together and keep everyone happy and motivated to do great music.

Well, now Karl was no longer Henry's ally, and it made a big difference. Karl had not been himself since Henry and Gabrielle split up. He was curmudgeonly. The brilliant wit he always displayed took a darker turn, became taciturn. He was no longer the elfin young blond man with the boundless effervescence; he had aged like all of them and become a good deal more stodgy and gray. But now there was also an edge to his stodginess. He was not happy and did not bother to conceal his feelings. The group noticed and began to lose their cohesion, their contentment.

To tell the truth, it was amazing Henry had been able to keep them together for so long. Over the years things began to build up and little disputes blossomed into long-standing grievances and wounds developed that just seemed impossible to heal, even with the soothing balm of music. Henry had managed to patch things up and keep them going, in spite of many challenges, in spite of losing some of their original members over time and not quite being able to replace them satisfactorily. There had been many rough patches, and many dry spells where holding on was just for the sake of holding on, and through it all Karl had been his rock—but not anymore. The rock had become a loose cannon, not just rolling around but ready and willing to blow things up at a moment's notice.

Henry found it impossible to lead the group. He had always been the leader. It was an unspoken agreement. He had always been the one with the innovative musical ideas; and they, for the most part, had been willing to follow. After all, he was the entrepreneur and the impresario, the one who had brought them to their present level of success. But something changed. There was a rebellion, a breakout. It had been simmering for decades, which put an especially petulant spin to it. They began openly talking back and challenging him in rehearsal. It wasn't just a few things; it was everything. It was all the markings and the details and the very concept of performance and professionalism. Of course they knew about Gabrielle, and that didn't help. Everybody was on her side. All of them. Everyone blamed Henry for what had happened. After all, it was his fault.

This new development was terribly stressful for Henry. Forum was everything to him. It was his baby, his only child. Being part of a successful group is important to performance musicians. It becomes their identity, their thing, but also much more. It is where they go to integrate themselves into being. Players need a place to play or they stop being players. Henry was a player with a capital 'P,' and the prospect of having Forum fall apart on him was devastating. He was not going into an orchestra, not at his age. He was not crazy about orchestras, the politics, the palpable boredom and unhappiness of the players, the sham conductors. He was not going to attempt to become a soloist. That ship had sailed long ago. Besides, he didn't know the solo literature. The chamber literature he knew. He didn't have to kill himself to play it because he had been playing it all his life.

Also chamber music was what he loved. The conversation, the intimacy, the dance, the ability to say something as an individual while still being part of a highly sympathetic and skilled group, all walking a sonic tightrope together—these were things that appealed to him as a musician and as an artist. He lived for being on stage with Forum, touring with Forum, making plans for Forum, nurturing Forum, being innovative with Forum, trying to change the way people looked at classical music through Forum. He couldn't imagine his life without it. He couldn't imagine what he would do or be.

Well, now he was being forced to imagine it, because it felt like the group was falling apart before his very eyes. There were late calls with excuses from rehearsals. There was caviling about dates, even dates that had been set in stone long ago. There were quarrels about performance values. It seemed they were sick and tired of doing things his way. They had always done them his way. Maybe that's why the audiences were dwindling. Maybe it was time to modernize and do things a little differently.

The rehearsals basically degenerated into chaos. They weren't listening to Henry anymore, but they also weren't listening to each other. They were so used to following that they weren't terribly skilled at leading, at the art of compromise and finding middle ground. They argued on hot summer nights and old grudges came thump, thump, thumping back into the room like cave trolls and Henry completely lost control and began to feel like an outsider in his own group, the group he himself had created.

And there was something else weighing on him too, draining him and dragging him down—this email "someone" had sent to Gabrielle. Henry was trying to suppress the strange feelings caused by this email and its invasive message, but it was always there, in the back of his mind, lurking, threatening. How in God's name did this unknown mysterious person know what he had said to Margie in the park? How was it even possible? How?

At first Henry had assumed it was Malcolm. He was the only one who made sense, the only one with a motive and the nastiness required. But did he really make sense? It seemed like there were two possibilities. Either the sender was close enough to Margie to have heard it from her own mouth, or someone had been doing Bourne-style eavesdropping. The latter seemed highly unlikely. In a public park, in the middle of the day? But if it was someone close to Margie, a confidante, then that seemed to rule out Malcolm. According to Alicia, Margie despised Malcolm and was out to get him. Or was she? Was the story even more tangled and sick than Henry imagined?

Then early in August he endured another heavy blow, one more than he thought he could handle. Richie had invited himself over to see Henry's new condo. He was curious and summer-bored, and Henry was lonely and needed some company, so his good friend dropped over on a Friday night with a six pack of boutique brew, on which they proceeded to work while they laughed and joshed and Richie teased him about the condo and being a bachelor and they had a good time.

That is, until they stumbled onto the topic of Gabrielle. They were talking about Henry's new commute, and he was saying he didn't mind the distance but he did wish he had the Corolla for gas mileage, in case the prices spiked again. Gabrielle had taken it and left him the Jeep. "She thought she was doing me a favor. She figured I wound want the fun car with the four-wheel drive, but I kind of like the Corolla and being able to thumb my nose at the gas station as I drive by."

This innocuous little comment sent Richie down the fatal path. "How is Gabrielle? Have you heard from her?"

"Not really. I've tried to get in touch with her, but she doesn't want to talk to me."

"So you're what—separated?"

"I think she wants a divorce. She hasn't said as much yet, but I think she's working herself up to it."

"It's just so incredible. I mean, how could something like this happen?"

Henry instantly felt a wall come between them. Richie said these words with all apparent ingenuousness, but he knew him too well. His face and dilated eyes betrayed him. His friend knew something he wasn't saying and this was his way of drawing Henry out.

"These things happen," Henry replied cautiously, very cautiously. "People change. They grow apart. We're not the first couple that ever went through a divorce."

"True, but you and Gabrielle had such a great relationship. You were the envy of the department. I mean, it was all so sudden."

"Well, there's a lot to the story you don't know. Things were not always what they seemed."

"Really? In what way?"

Henry let out a sigh. "We had sort of a unique arrangement. In fact—I can't believe I'm telling you this—and don't you dare tell anyone else—we literally had a sort of an arranged marriage. We were put together by people at Julliard who thought they were doing us a favor. So it was a little different for us. We never really had the kind of closeness or intimacy that normal couples have."

"You think that's why she left? After all these years?"

"You've got another theory?"

"Well, I don't know. I was just wondering."

Henry fixed him with his gaze. "OK, obviously you're angling for something. What is it?"

"Well, it's just that I heard this rumor the other day. It was so unbelievable that I was literally walking around in shock. But it came from a credible source, so I didn't know what to think."

"What kind of 'rumor'?"

"Oh, you know, just the usual nonsense."

"No, tell me."

"Well, it's so ridiculous, you won't even believe—"

"Tell me!"

"Okay. Now don't blame me. This didn't come from me. But it seems there's a rumor—something about you and—well, someone on the faculty."

Henry froze. "Go on."

"Well—you know—that you're—involved—or something like that. With this someone. I told you you weren't going to like it."

"Does this 'someone' have a name?"

"That's what's so ridiculous about it. Supposedly it's Margie Hart. Some joke, huh?"

"Yeah, some joke."

"Please tell me there isn't any truth to it. I mean, you and Margie? I can't even imagine that. She's not in your league."

Henry blinked. "Well, I hate to disappoint you. But there's enough truth in it to kill a marriage."

"No, not really. Seriously?"

"I never claimed to be perfect. It's not what they think it is, but it doesn't matter. People like to hear bad news about people, and I guess it's my turn."

"Are you still—"

"What?" Henry laughed a bitter little laugh. "I was never really 'involved' with her. Why would she want an old man like me? But I managed to make a fool of myself anyway."

"So that's why Gabrielle left?"

Henry sighed. "That's why she left. As far as I can tell, she's never coming back. I want her to come back. I begged her to come back. She won't even listen to me. And I guess I can't blame her."

This conversation made Henry ill. Richie was his good friend, probably his best friend in the world. It hurt terribly to let him down. He could see it in his eyes—the disappointment. Henry hated to disappoint him. The conversation made him feel dirty, like when you haven't showered and your clothes are a little disheveled, like when something itches, like when you have a faintly unpleasant odor in your nose and the suspicion that it may be your own. Not until that moment did Henry realize how much he did not want Richie to know about Margie.

And if Richie knew, who was known to be Henry's close friend, then everyone knew. The cat was out of the bag and shitting all over the place. Henry felt like he did not have one single shred of pride or dignity left. They would all be whispering about him, cutting him up into pieces, gloating over his fall from grace. Oh yes, he would be made to pay for the notoriety he had enjoyed over the years. If the same thing happened to one of the less visible members of the department—say Johnson, the alcoholic—no one would have found it interesting. It was the very fact of Henry's prominence that made the rumor irresistible. He knew it and began to dread going back to school.

He would wear a big red "A" on his jacket. At least it would deprive them of the pleasure of knowing an astounding secret, take some of the smirking schadenfreude out of their faces. But no, he would never do that. He was too much of a coward, too worried about what people thought of him. This was the fear that made the idea of starting a whole new semester seem terrible.

RUMORS AND RUMORS OF RUMORS

IN ANY CASE, HIS FOOLISHNESS had been outed. Every time he looked at one of his colleagues he thought he knew exactly what they were thinking. The old man can't keep his pants on. He couldn't blame them. He was thinking the same thing himself, constantly beating himself up about it. What in the world had happened to him? He still couldn't say. All he knew was he had gone from having a reputation as a distinguished musician, professor, public intellectual, yes moralist, to being just another fool in nice clothing. He was not immune to the infection of love, the golden dart, whatever it was. It had struck him and unclothed him. It had revealed his clay feet.

Henry was still a little rattled when he thought of Margie. The intellectual side of him found it easy to condemn her. She had used him. She wanted revenge on Malcolm, and Henry had been recruited to help her get it. She never had any feelings for him. She was a coldhearted little vixen. But did this judgment really represent his intellectual side? Or was it the prideful side? Were these harsh judgments valid or were they the product of embarrassment and of being exposed as her would-be lover? It was Richie's reaction that had hurt him the most. A liaison with Margie was embarrassing because he was perceived to be too lofty for her. He wanted to be too lofty for Margie. There was a side of him that liked this perception.

Was that why love had turned so rapidly to spite? Not because of anything Margie had done, but because he was in love with her and embarrassed about being in love? He considered the evidence. First of all, she had never actually done anything to give the impression that she was in love with him. She did not lead him on. She did not respond in kind to his hand pats or romantic outbursts. She simply came to him to seek guidance for a friend who was in danger of losing her job. He had fallen in love with her, but that was not her fault. Second, what actual evidence did he have of being used by her? Alicia made the accusation, but she was a very distraught and angry young woman. She was obviously speculating, and there was no reason to think she was seeing things clearly in her disordered state. In fact there was every reason to think otherwise—because Alicia was looking for someone to blame.

What other evidence did he have of Margie's perfidy? None, really. There was Malcolm calling her a "psycho," but normally Henry would not believe anything Malcolm said about anyone. Besides, he had his own reasons for trying to discredit her. Maybe the most damning piece of evidence was the revelation of her liaison with Malcolm. But this wasn't evidence of any wrongdoing in relation to *him*, was it? It was embarrassing, because of his love for her, but nothing more. The truth is he didn't like being drawn to the same girl as Malcolm. He didn't like being dragged down to Malcolm's level.

On the other hand, there was the whole business of the email. There was information in it that only Margie could have known—what he said to her in the park. So either the email had to have come from Margie herself, or she had been talking to someone. If the first, then why? What motive could she possibly have for wanting to wreck his marriage? Was she really in love with him after all? Did she want him for herself? He could not bring himself to believe it. She had shown no sign of being in love, and therefore she had no discernible motive.

But had she told someone else then? If so, this raised a whole host of issues. First of all, why would she share this information? Was it in all innocence, was she making fun of him, or was there some terrible plot in play that he could not even imagine? And if she had shared it, and the person she shared it with had sent the email, then who was this diabolical person? What possible reason could they have for sending send such an email? Perhaps most of all, what other damage did they have in mind? Were there other pictures? Were more emails coming? Why?

There was unfinished business between him and Margie. He had rushed to judgment in his shame at being exposed, but it was not fair—either to her or to him. He needed to know what really happened. He could not leave things the way they were. To tell the truth, he did not want to feel badly about Margie. He'd made so many mistakes; was he making another? He wanted to give her a chance to explain herself. He wanted to know what she knew. If he had to play the part of the fool, at least he had a right to know the real reason for his foolishness. And there was only one person who could tell him.

The last week in August he went to his office to do some prep work before school began. With these same thoughts in his head he took the slightly longer route that went past Margie's office and was a little startled to find her sitting there. He hurried past her door, hoping he hadn't been seen, but stopped. There was no one else in the building—just the two of them, as far as he could see—there would never be a better time to confront her with the questions that were burning in his mind.

He turned back and tapped lightly on the metal doorframe with his knuckle. She looked up and smiled the same old smile she had always given him, like he was the one person in the world she wanted to see.

"It's so nice to see you!" she said, sounding perfectly unaffected by any consciousness of guilt or having wronged him in any way.

"Nice to be seen," he replied lamely. "Mind if I talk to you for a minute?"

"Of course! Anytime!" She jumped up to take a pile of papers and books out of a chair.

"That's all right, don't bother. I'll just be a moment. So—how have you been?"

"Good, good," she replied, walking up close to him. "You?"

"I don't know, not so good, I guess. You probably heard about my wife."

"No, I didn't. Is she all right?"

"Oh, she's fine. Nothing like that. No, we're just—not together anymore."

She smiled sympathetically. He did not know what to do with that smile.

"I'm sorry to hear that. Are you all right?"

"I guess it depends on what you mean by 'all right.' Not really used to being alone. Not really very good at it."

"Well, I know how difficult it can be, believe me. I'm sorry."

"Aren't you at all curious?"

"About what?"

"About why she left."

"I didn't think it was any of my business."

"Well, actually it is," he said with an awkward laugh. "She got a nice little email from somebody here at the school. About us."

"What do you mean, 'us'?"

"You and I. It seems we're having an affair."

"What? We didn't have any affair."

"No, we didn't. [He couldn't help turning a little red.] You wouldn't happen to have any idea who could have sent such an email? Or why?"

"No, none. Clueless. I can't even imagine someone sending an email like that."

"Well, see, that's what confuses me. Whoever wrote this email had some inside information. Things we actually said to each other—in private."

"Like what, for instance?"

Henry blushed again. "Well, you remember the time we went for a walk in the park? What I said to you? You probably don't remember."

"You said a lot of things."

"No—this was one thing in particular. I'm pretty sure you would remember it. When we were sitting on the bench."

She looked at him and her eyes seemed soft and kind. Then she smiled—"Of course I remember. I'll never forget it. It was one of the most beautiful moments of my life."

Henry stood there looking at her for a moment, blinking. "Well, you don't have to go that far."

"No, I mean it. You were so sweet. I felt honored."

"Well, I think you're just being kind. But whoever wrote this email seemed to know about it. I mean they actually knew what I said. And I know I didn't tell anybody."

"I didn't tell anybody, either. I can't imagine who could have known."

"Are you sure? You must have told someone."

162

"Oh—oh my God!" she said wide-eyed, putting her hand to her mouth. "I did tell someone—sort of. I remember now. I was so happy. I was on cloud nine. I went to a friend's house that night and after a couple of glasses of wine I just blurted it out."

"You told this friend about me?"

"No! Of course not. I would never do that. She just wanted to know why I was so happy, and I told her I went walking with someone in the park. Which was true. Okay, I did tell her what was said, but that's all. I didn't say anything about who said it. I'm not that stupid."

"Well, somehow she must have found out, because she sent a very nasty email to my wife. Can you at least tell me who it was?"

"I guess so. It was—" She stopped herself. "No, I don't really feel comfortable doing that."

"But she sent this email. I have to find out."

"I can't. It's not right. Besides, how do you know she sent it? I really can't imagine her sending an email like that."

"Well, it's either her—or you."

"Not necessarily. It could be somebody else."

Henry got a little hot. "Okay, but here's the thing. Alicia told me about you and Malcolm."

"What about me and Malcolm?"

"She said you were out for revenge. Supposedly that was why you came to me. Not to help Alicia—to get Malcolm."

"She actually said that? I don't believe it. She was all for me talking to you."

"She said she didn't know."

"That's ridiculous. Of course she knew. You think I would do something like that on my own?"

"I don't know; I'm just telling you what she said."

"Well, I guess I can understand why she might have said it. I mean what happened between Malcolm and me was pretty bad. But believe me, that was not the case."

Henry let his curiosity get the best of him. "By the way, what did happen that was so bad?"

She paused for a moment and looked at him. "He got me pregnant."

"What!"

"I know. It was all so strange. He'd never paid any attention to me in all the years I've been here. In fact I didn't even think he liked me—hardly acknowledged my existence. Then we wound up going to a conference together last fall. He was all over me. He claimed to be madly in love with me, couldn't live without me. Supposedly he was leaving his wife."

"But he didn't mean a word of it."

"No, of course not. As soon as he found out, he dumped me." Her eyes filled up with tears.

Henry wanted so much to take her in his arms and console her. Instead he backed away and went to his office and closed the door. He did not bother turning on the lights. Something was wrong. He felt ill. It was like nausea but it wasn't really nausea, it was something else. There was a pressing feeling in his upper arms and his face was tingly pink. He put his hand on his heart; it was pounding, pounding, out of control. There was nothing he could do to stop it. He took deep breaths. Didn't help. He tried biofeedback, but there was no effect. He was too scared.

He lay down on the leather couch and tried to calm himself. Calm, calm; still, still. The episode seemed to go on forever—and then finally he started to feel a little better. He could breathe normally again. Little by little he started to recover but he did not move. He just lay there feeling stunned. There were so many thoughts and feelings crowding into his brain that he could not sort them out, but the one predominant feeling was his hatred for Malcolm, his overwhelming, all-consuming hatred. He thought of Margie's sweet face while she was telling her tragic story and was filled with hatred all over again. The guy was a pig. Absolutely cold. He had no regard for others, no humanity. He was ruining the department and now he was ruining the people in the department.

Who knows how long he lay there in the pale indirect light obsessing over Malcolm. It might have been an hour, maybe more. Finally the terrible topic exhausted its fascination and he began to think about other things. The first was the business of Margie telling someone about what he had said to her. At least now he knew it was a she. But who could it possibly be? Who were her female friends in the department, and why would one of them want to use this information against him? He lay there for another hour going over the entire female faculty one by one. He knew most of them. He couldn't imagine any of them sending the email.

Did this news make things better or worse for him? It took away some of his paranoia. To know exactly what had happened, that it was nothing more than a carelessly placed word, was better than having an unlimited variety of scary scenarios running through one's head. He now knew it wasn't one of his rivals—Malcolm, Jeff or Bertram. They were the wrong sex. But on the other hand there was some unknown female in the department who appeared to have it out for him. This was unsettling. And what about the picture? How had she come into possession of something like that? It was all very strange. Henry did not know what to think.

THE PUTSCH

SCHOOL BEGAN and Henry was in a very bad place. It seemed like everything was going wrong. First of all, there was Gabrielle, not just her continued absence from his life but her complete unwillingness to talk to him or have anything to do with him or even acknowledge his existence. He continued to call, he continued to email, but she never replied. He was alone in his little condo, and each new day made him more aware of how much he hated being alone, really hated it. Some days just seemed like an eternity. Still, the hardest thing was how he had fallen in her eyes. He did not want her to think badly of him. It made him feel like nothing. But what else could she think?

At the same time, his work situation had become very strange. Just getting himself to walk into school on a sunny morning had become a major challenge. He felt his shame acutely and found it hard to look at the faces of old friends and acquaintances without reading things into them that might or might not be there. And of course there was Malcolm. He had been angry with Malcolm for months over Alicia, angry with him for years over his nonsense, but this was different. It was a different kind of anger. Every time he thought of Margie and every time he thought of her tears he became enraged all over again. He did not want to run into Malcolm in the hallway. He did not know what he would do.

Then there was the little matter of his workload. They said the budget cuts made it necessary for everyone to work a little harder. Henry also suspected he was being punished for what had happened at the department meeting. In any case he was not used to it. He found it exhausting, on top of all his private students and the practicing and the organizational work he had to do for Forum. He realized he really was getting old. He just did not have the energy to do what he had done ten years ago or even five. He found himself having to take shortcuts, make compromises, even in his concert preparation. He was not a compromising kind of guy, but there didn't seem to be any option.

Speaking of Forum, things continued to deteriorate on that front as well. Karl became more disruptive than ever, and the rest of the group seemed happy to follow his lead. It was a full-scale uprising, and Henry and his supposedly tyrannical leadership were the target. There was arguing in rehearsals. They seemed to *want* to argue and would break out over the littlest thing, making progress impossible. Some rehearsals were so tense and unpleasant that they made Henry physically ill. They became critical of his playing—and he couldn't blame them. He knew he wasn't practicing as much as he used to. Still, it was traumatizing to have so much discord. There were times when he wanted to quit on the spot, make a grand gesture by just walking away—but how? This was the group he had created. This was his baby. How could he walk away?

He wanted to walk away because he wanted to show them. He wanted them to realize how valuable he was, how important to the group, how much they needed him. But this was a futile gesture. He knew they would just go out and find someone else. In fact Karl already had a good friend lined up, a talented violinist he'd been fantasizing about bringing into the group for years. Henry wouldn't immortalize himself by walking away. He would simply hasten his inevitable fade to white. He knew he would be forgotten, just as Forum would be forgotten in time, as new chamber groups and new enthusiasms and younger stars came along. He just wasn't sure he was ready for it to start happening *now*.

Another thing that was weighing him down was the blasted arthritis or tendonitis or whatever it was in his left hand, which was acting up again after having been dormant for almost a year. He did not know exactly what it was because he refused to go to the doctor. He had only been to the doctor a handful of times in his life and was vaguely distrustful of the profession. He was afraid they would start tinkering with him and make things worse and then his playing days would be over. He'd been dealing with the pain for ten years, hiding it from everyone including himself, but now sometimes it was so sharp that it affected his playing in concerts. Was he getting too old to play? The thought terrified him.

Then there was the First Class gift he received in the mail one fine September day—divorce papers from Gabrielle. This made him sick all over again, so sick he had to lie down and finally went to bed, even though it was the middle of the day. But he did not sleep. He could not sleep. He just lay there on the bed with his shoes on and the manila envelope in his hands. How could he sleep when he felt like his life was coming apart? He wanted her so much, wanted her back; but this little love-package told him it was impossible now. She did not want him, and he could not make her want him. He stopped emailing, he stopped leaving messages. There didn't seem to be any point.

He was surprised by her behavior. He understood that his betrayal was terribly hurtful; he knew he had insulted her in the worst possible way by indulging himself—or at least his time and fantasies—with someone else. Obviously he could understand why she was angry. But what surprised him was the unrelenting heat of her anger. It wasn't like her, the Gabrielle he knew. One of the things he admired about her was her tolerance; which was his own ideal, what he aspired to be. She did not judge people. She didn't seem to hold the grudges that musicians often hold. She was very forgiving. Why couldn't she forgive him? Why did she seem so completely unrelenting?

His first thought was to refuse to sign the papers. It would be his protest. He would force her to get together with him and tell him why she was being so hard and unrelenting. He deserved no less after thirty-five years of marriage. But his anger and resolve faded with the day. He did not want to hurt her any more than he already had. If it would make her happy for him to sign the papers, then he would sign them. He even drove to the post office instead of jamming them back in the mailbox. As the envelope disappeared into the black void, a melancholy thought came to him—"There goes my marriage."

With all of these things going on, his first few weeks back at school had a nightmarish quality. But there was one more insult for which he was not prepared, news of which was brought to him by Richie, who came into his office and closed the door behind him. Henry was immediately on guard. Richie never did this. He looked uncharacteristically grim.

"So—how are you?" he began probingly.

"I'm good—I think. Why? Shouldn't I be?" Henry said with a nervous laugh.

"I don't know, I was worried about you so I'd just thought I'd stop by and see how you're doing."

"Oh—you mean the divorce. Yes, it was a bit of a shock. But I'm coping. I know there's nothing I can do about it, so I just have to cope."

"Oh, right—the divorce. Forgot about that."

"You had something else in mind?"

Richie looked at him. "So you haven't heard anything?"

"About what?" Henry said, bracing himself. Bad news was coming, he could feel it.

"You don't know about Malcolm and his latest inspiration?"

"No, nobody's said anything to me about it. There isn't much more they can do to me. I'm already teaching the equivalent of five courses."

"Well, I wouldn't be so sure about that. I'm sorry to be the bearer of bad news, but I think you need to know what's going on. The word is he's starting a little campaign to sort of encourage you to retire."

Henry waved his hand. "It's not the first time. He's been talking about that for years."

"This might be a *little* different. This isn't pub talk. Apparently he's got some information on you and he's willing to use it."

"Information? What kind of information?"

"Something about you and Margie."

"Now what? Will it never end?" Henry said exasperated.

"I know—he's always shooting off his big mouth. And I wouldn't be so worried if it wasn't for the dean. You know how she feels about him. Plus this is right up her alley."

Now Henry fixed him with his eyes. "Okay, what exactly are we talking about here? What is 'right up her alley'?"

"He's claiming the reason you went after him in the faculty meeting was because Margie asked you to."

"Well, actually, basically that's kind of true. She came to me and asked me to stick up for her friend. I thought I told you all that."

"Unfortunately that's not the way he's spinning it. He claims you did it because you were looking for something in return."

"Don't tell me you mean what I think you mean."

"That's exactly what I mean."

"Oh God, this is unbelievable! Is there nothing this man won't stoop to? She came to me and asked me to try to do something for Alicia, and out of the kindness of my heart I agreed."

"That's not what they're saying. Apparently there was a lot of loose talk around the department about you and Margie even before this came up. And he's playing on that."

"Of course there's a lot of talk! He's the one who started it!"

"So there's no truth to any of it."

"Are you crazy? You know me better than that. For one thing, I'm way too old for her. For another thing, why can't a man do something for a woman without having sex come into it? Why can't it just be me wanting to help out a worthy colleague? I mean, it wasn't Margie I spoke up for. It was Alicia. And by the way, they were treating her like crap. Yeah, Malcolm and his smooth-talking buddies. I notice she's gone. They managed to get rid of her. Why isn't anyone outraged about that?"

"I agree with you. They did treat her like crap. And I'm not saying you did anything wrong. I'm just telling you what Malcolm's apparently saying. I thought you would appreciate the heads-up, instead of being blindsided by one of his patented random attacks."

"And what about Bertram? Did he favor him with this little fantasy too?"

"I'm just going to assume the answer to that one is 'yes.' You know how tight they are. I can't imagine him not saying something to Bertram that he would say to the dean."

"Wait a minute—so you're saying he did talk to the dean?"

"Yeah—that's what I said."

"No, you didn't say that. You just intimated that he *might* talk to the dean. Now you're telling me this actually happened?"

"Well, that's the word on the street. All I can tell you is what I heard. Whether or not it really did happen is another matter. But I told you before—there's something between those two. I'm not sure exactly what, but something."

Richie didn't have much more to say. It was enough. He walked out the door and Henry closed it behind him and then he felt like he was going to die. He just felt like he would die. His heart started pounding again and did not let up. He put his hand over it and he could feel it pounding, like it was trying to leap out of his breast. The pounding would go away for a little while, and then he would think of Malcolm, he would see Malcolm's smirking face, and it would start all over again. This went on literally for days after his dreadful conversation with Richie. He would be standing in class, teaching, and his heart would start pounding. He would be standing in front of his bathroom mirror, brushing his teeth, and his heart would start pounding. He would be trying to play Beethoven or Schubert in a Forum rehearsal and his heart would suddenly start pounding.

A dark cloud settled on existence. They were finally out to get him. This time it was real. They had wanted to get rid of him for years. He was an obstacle, a dinosaur cluttering up the evolutionary landscape. They needed him to retire so they could modernize the department and get rid of all that nineteenth century cultural hegemony crap about the primacy of Western classical music and Western performance standards and other things kids weren't interested in anymore. They needed to put him out to pasture so someone younger and more energetic could come along and "revitalize" the string program, as they put it—in other words, dumb it down. Oh, he'd been hearing these sorts of things for years. Yeah, he knew all about it. They weren't fooling anybody. This was the kind of back room talk they indulged in when they thought no one was listening.

But now it seemed they were getting serious. This wasn't just the sort of thing the boys talked about idly when they were at the bar. This was an actual plan, apparently, with an actual charge being made. And the worst of it was he had no one to blame but himself. They were despicable; they were liars and posturers—especially Malcolm, the Lothario who had gotten Margie pregnant and then deserted her. But Henry had given them their golden opportunity. They were right; he had allowed himself to be sucked into the Alicia thing through Margie. His motives were not pure. On top of that he had acted like a naïf. He stood up in two faculty meetings and openly criticized them. He had gone to the dean and criticized them. This was something you just did not do. He knew you didn't do it. Why did he do it?

Well of course—it was because of Margie. It was because he had allowed himself to indulge in certain fantasies about her. What they were saying—according to Richie—was categorically false. He did not stand up for Alicia in return for sexual favors from Margie. There was no quid pro quo suggested and none even considered. But his behavior could easily be misconstrued by someone who wanted to do him harm. That someone was Malcolm. He would not hesitate to twist the truth.

Pounding, pounding. Henry could not bear what was happening to him. If he had Gabrielle—if he could go home and talk to her about it—maybe then. But not alone. It was maddening because he had tried to do something good for Alicia. And it was humiliating for someone who was a prominent player on the world music stage. The thought of these miserable talentless little rodents chasing him out of the department and blackening his reputation was upsetting and unbearable. Thirty good years he had given to the program. Thirty years he had toiled for the good of the students and university and bent over backwards to be nice to them and even support them in their various hare-brained schemes—and this was how they repaid him for his tolerance and kindness, his magnanimity!

Henry went into an unreal world. All he could think about was what Richie told him; what they were plotting against him; what fresh hell awaited him. He could hardly sleep at night. He didn't feel like eating, he didn't feel like working, he didn't do a whole lot of practicing—just didn't have the heart or the stamina. He taught his classes but it was almost like he wasn't teaching them. He was on autopilot. He heard himself saying the kinds of rote and clichéd things he never allowed himself to say, the things he hated when he heard other teachers say them. His driving became erratic. He scraped the side of the Jeep backing out of his garage and knocked a piece of molding off the door frame. He cut himself when he shaved. One day his hand was so unsteady he cut his ear. It bled for hours. He didn't wash his clothes. He didn't have the energy.

About a week went by like this and then he just couldn't take it any longer. He had to know the truth. It seemed worse not knowing. He went to see Bertram.

"We need to talk," he said to the laconic one, not in a threatening way but earnestly.

"Okay, let's talk. We haven't talked in a long time."

"No, that's true. We haven't. And I regret that. I know I told you when you became chairman that I would help you. I have been helping you, in my own way, but I haven't been a very good advisor." Henry was trying to keep the edge out of his voice but was conscious of not entirely succeeding.

"You don't have time. I don't know how you do what you do, never mind trying to help me."

"Well, now you can help *me*, if you wouldn't mind. I heard a very strange rumor and maybe you can tell me if there's any truth in it. A movement to see that I get retired, one way or another."

"Henry, this isn't the time to talk about that. It's way too early."

"Early? So there is something to it, then. My source was not misinformed."

"People talk all the time around here. You know that. Some of it's big talk, some of it's little talk. About ninety-five percent of it should be ignored."

"This is pretty big talk, wouldn't you say? Trying to push me out and make way for somebody's half-baked cronies?"

"Nobody's trying to push you out."

"Not yet, maybe. But they're talking about it. That's why you said it was 'early.'"

"Okay, there has been talk about what went on in the faculty meeting, the time you spoke up for Alicia. Some people were hurt by that and they had some bad feelings over that."

"I didn't mean to hurt anybody. I was just trying to keep her from being thrown out of here. Which, by the way, is just what happened."

"I know that. And I think most people feel you acted in good faith. But you said some things that were not really productive, in the long run. You said some things that made you a target."

"Okay, so I said some things. So I stepped on a few toes. I'm sorry. By the way, nobody around here seems to mind when my toes are being stepped on, but I'm still sorry. But that's not really what I'm talking about. From what I hear, there's someone who's been making some serious accusations against me. There's someone who seems to think I had some pretty bad motives for defending Alicia."

"Well, did you? I mean think about it. She's just an M.A. You're an M.A. Are you sure there wasn't anything personal about it? Because some people felt it sure sounded that way."

"Fine. Let's say even that's true. I don't happen to believe it, but let's say it's true. That's still not the specific accusation I had in mind. I'm thinking of something a lot more serious."

"All right. You tell me what you've heard, and I'll let you know if there's anything to it."

Henry decided to be forthright. "What I heard was that a certain friend of ours went to the dean and claimed I did it in return for 'favors' from a faculty member. Is that true? Did that happen?"

"From what I understand, there was a conversation with the dean. She has not contacted me directly, nor do I have any reason to think she will."

"But you do know what I'm talking about. You do know what I mean."

"I know what the accusation is," Bertram replied with a sigh. "The same person also talked to me."

"And you believe it?"

"I'm not in a position to believe or disbelieve anything. I'm trying to play the honest broker here. I have to listen to what everybody has to say and then try to sort it all out. And we haven't even begun that process yet."

"Process! So you are pursuing this. It isn't just a bizarre dream. It's happening."

"Henry, to tell you the truth I may not have any choice but to pursue it. I told you, the dean has not said anything to me yet. If I don't hear from her, as far as I'm concerned this is just a rumor and I'll leave it at that. I'm not interested in conducting any witch hunts. But if I do hear from her, that's a different story. If she tells me to look into it, then I have to do what I have to do."

"So basically what you're saying is you have no intention of sticking up for me, no intention of taking my side after all these years and everything I've done for you, after I mentored you through all those administrative and political minefields we used to talk about and helped you get tenure and even recommended you for the chairmanship. After all that, you're just going to hide behind this 'honest broker' crap and let them crucify me?"

"Henry, let me just ask you one question. Is it true?"

"No, it's not true. How could you even think that?"

"Well, there seems to be a lot of corroborating evidence."

"Corroborating evidence my—all right, Bertram. Have it your own way. I can see already how this is going to go. You've got your little group, your collaborators, and I'm going to be the sacrifice."

"It's not like that. First of all, we don't even know if anything will come of it. But even if it does, I promise you I will be fair. I'm not taking anybody's side in this thing."

"Yes, of course not. You're just an 'honest broker.' How could I forget."

Henry stood up.

"You're going now? You don't want to talk about this?"

"I think I've done enough talking. Go and do what you have to do. I guess I knew all along it would be something like this in the end."

NIGHT OF HORRORS

S O IT WAS TRUE. It really was true. They really were out to get him this time, just like Richie said. They were serious.

Bertram couldn't hide what was going on. Oh, Henry didn't believe his disavowal for a moment. He was too close to Malcolm. They were in this thing together. Bertram wasn't as bad as Malcolm but he was under Malcolm's spell. He wasn't going to stand by and let his beer-drinking buddy go it alone and possibly make a fool of himself. If Malcolm went after Henry, Bertram would be right there behind him. Maybe not on the front lines, but handling his communications. Neither one was going to step out on his own and expose himself. They were too cowardly for that.

It was clear to Henry that something had been set in motion. He wasn't sure exactly what, but something. He now had a vital confirmation—Malcolm had indeed gone to the dean, just as Richie said. Bertram didn't use his name, but they both knew who he meant. If Malcolm had gone to the dean, and Bertram knew it, then there could be no doubt that this was a coordinated, intentional effort. They were strategizing together. They had sensed their moment and were trying to figure out what to do with it.

"Is it true?" Bertram had asked him. To Henry, this was not an honest question. Bertram would not have even asked him if he did not believe it himself. He *wanted* to believe it. There was a difference between him and Richie, between a true and a fair-weather friend. Richie wanted to know if it was true because he did not want it to be true, because he wanted to make the rumors go away. This did not seem to be the case with Bertram. He wanted to know if it was true because he was looking for a conviction. "Honest broker." Who was he kidding? There was no honesty in any of this. Not right from the beginning was there even a stitch of honesty in the whole rotten fabric.

After all, what started the debacle in the first place? Henry's unfortunate outburst in the faculty meeting. But what had he said that was not perfectly true? What single word had he uttered that was not one hundred percent honest, if honesty means speaking the truth, if old Kent was honest? It was true that Credentialism had nothing to do with real music. It was true that having a Ph.D. meant absolutely nothing to real music-making. Mozart didn't have one. Beethoven didn't even dream of one. Music is a river that comes from mystic places. It cannot be diverted by the piling on of degrees. This was "honest"; this was real. The Credentialists tried to pretend it was not real, and therefore they were not being honest, as far as Henry was concerned. They were dissimulating to aggrandize themselves. They were using their fancy degrees and words to make themselves seem like something they were not.

It was also true and "honest" that Alicia was a talented conductor who had given a stunning concert; that Alicia was something they could never be—a natural musician. This was incontrovertible to anyone who had ears to hear and a sensibility for music. Malcolm's caviling about too much contrast or whatever was nothing but a smokescreen. That was how the rulemakers talked, the ones who tried to compensate for their lack of musicality by putting on guardrails. No portamento, the rulemakers said, no sentiment in music in the brave, new Modern age. Baloney! Portamento was the human voice, human emotion sighing for that which cannot be attained. Were we all supposed to be machines and pretenders now, like Malcolm, full of gobbledygook about metrics and metronomes and unable or unwilling to let our humanity show? Prisoners to the bars in the music, as if that was what Haydn or Beethoven intended? Was this the decadent state into which classical music had descended?

No portamento? Why? Because it took unusual skill and freedom to do it right? Because in order to do a portamento and have it be honestly expressive you also had to have a soul? Was this a war against the soul and people who believed in it? And if the soul was no longer admissible in classical music, then how could the genre survive? How can that which was written to be soulful lose its soulfulness without turning into museum music? The problem wasn't with Alicia or the lack of taste that was intimated.

Her portamentos would have been considered perfectly tasteful a hundred years ago, if not obligatory. The problem was the machine. The problem was people like Malcolm who were trying to drive the humanity out of music. Why? Because it made them look bad. Because they did not understand it. Because it did not show the will to power—which was what they were all about.

Honest? Really? For Malcolm to make a snide remark about Alicia putting a couple of little portamentos into a ninety minute concert—was that honest? Then honesty is a whore. And in a piece by Brahms, no less, the most expressive composer. No, there was no honesty in any of this. It was all about power. Bertram was no "honest broker." Not anymore. He had allowed himself to become one of them, drawn into their poisonous sphere of influence and their narrative. Henry could no more expect fair treatment from him than a Jew from a Nazi. He was on a campaign—they all were—a campaign to purge music of soulfulness and humanity and make themselves look more important than they really were. But none of it had anything to do with being "honest." Dear God, don't pretend this sordid little effort was "honest."

These were the kinds of bitter thoughts that dominated Henry's inner life for days. His enemies became hateful to him, inhuman, now that he knew they were his enemies, now that they had declared themselves and their intention to get rid of him. The charge against him was sordid, dehumanizing, made his indignation burn like fire. But it was Henry himself who was being incinerated. No one else knew about his fiery thoughts. His enemies were not hurt by them. If he expressed them out loud they would probably laugh at him, like they laughed at everything else. No, he was the only one who was suffering, and to a large extent it was his own anger that was making him suffer.

On some level he understood this but did not seem to be able to help himself. He was in hell and had no Beatrice to lead him out. No, he had driven his Beatrice away. All of those years he had been repressing his anger. He had been walking around with a smiling face and a kind word while they were all busy stabbing him in the back. It wasn't like he didn't know. The news always came back to him, one way or another. He'd gone around taking their hits and taking them again until he just did not feel like he could take any more—and then he snapped. Everything he had repressed rose up like a volcano. He was in a state of perpetual rage. His face was always red. He was clumsy, hurting himself. He tried to control it but he couldn't. He went to bed mad and woke up mad. He was turning into King Lear.

And to be frank he was a little scared. Richie wasn't exaggerating—they really were out to get him. For them to initiate a formal process and make such truly mean charges against him— not just false but dirty and malicious—was more than just a reversal. In Henry's eyes it was a personal repudiation of him and everything he had done at the university. It was a repudiation of his string program, of all the hard work and the suffering he had endured, of all the kindness and generosity he had shown toward students, of the high-minded vision he had consistently articulated and tried to bring to the school, of everything he believed in. They took that high-minded vision and turned it into something dirty. They were trying to make him look like a pervert and a clown.

Was he a clown with a sordid smile? Was that what he had become? To have gone from being one of the most honored professors at the college to this? He did not know if he could endure it. Maybe if he had Gabrielle, if he had her strength to lean on, her good counsel. But on top of the possibility of repudiation at the school there was repudiation from her. There was the immolation of his marriage. These two things flowing together made him feel desolate. He wanted to go out with the mad old king and tear his hair and stay in a shelter. Maybe in that shelter there would be a young Edgar who understood him better than he did himself, who would stand up for him in the end even when he could not stand, when he was too old and too tired to stand, when his world was overthrown. But who was he kidding? There were no wilds or wild shelters anymore. There were no Edgars. The age of poetry was dead.

No, there was no shelter for him, no place to go. He was completely exposed to the elements in his unfashionable nakedness. His shelter in the past had been his faith in music and in love, which had kept him from playing their game and getting involved in their brutal politics. He had broken this faith, however, and now it could not help him. Music and love could not come to his aid because he had been unfaithful to them. He still believed in music but he was a violinist with a sore left hand, a tired old man who never seemed to be able to find the time to practice. If he could not practice, where was his solace? How could he protect himself from the wolves? He had always had a sanctuary in the sheer excellence of his playing, a place where no one could touch him. He did not feel he could count on this any longer.

And what about love? Yes, he had betrayed this faith most of all. He betrayed it when he allowed himself to fall in love with Margie. He knew now it was not love—it was infatuation. He had betrayed love when he decided to strike out against his enemies. Love is a power that can protect you from harm if you believe in it and cling to it and refrain from acting like the world. But if you betray love and strike out at the world and its lovelessness—if you attempt to use love against the world—then you will no longer be protected by its hidden power. Henry had a choice to make between the world and love. He had always known on some level that for a lover like him to choose the world was disaster. What madness had come over him and caused him to let go of love?

On top of everything he was becoming increasingly concerned about his health. The unruly pounding in his chest, sometimes leading almost to paralysis, came on more and more often. He knew he should go to a doctor but he did not want to go. He did not want to be told that he had to go on five medications and stop concertizing, as had happened to one of his friends. He kept thinking the pounding was a passing thing. After all, it had started within the last year. It had come on suddenly, seemingly overnight; there was no reason why it couldn't go away just as suddenly. Maybe it was caused by some kind of persistent virus. Maybe it was allergies to what he was eating. He changed his diet, but the pounding still came.

The growing problem of his health led to one of the worst moments in his entire career as a musician. There was a concert at Swarthmore in late September. Henry arrived in the chains of anxiety. He tried to look like himself when he greeted the group but he was not himself. He was in a panic. His hand hurt. He felt he hadn't practiced enough. He had forgotten to have his tails dry cleaned and was forced to wear an old standby that was faded and didn't really fit him anymore. Karl sneered at him when he came barging in the door late, his hair uncombed. He tried to ignore it but couldn't. The open acrimony that had overtaken the group in recent months was killing him. It was the opposite of what he was and why he had gone into music in the first place.

Anyway, somehow he found himself sitting out in front of a large and enthusiastic crowd without really feeling like he belonged there or wanted to be there. He could not remember ever feeling that way before. For one thing, he was not optimistic about the program or their state of preparation. The recent rehearsals had not gone well. There was no unity of purpose, no sense of being on the same page. Most of all there was this damnable numbness in his left hand. Not good to have numbness when you're trying to play Beethoven. You have to be on top of your art.

Actually it was during the Beethoven that it happened. There was a difficult passage coming up for the first violin in the opening movement of the famous 131, and for the first time in his professional career Henry lost confidence in his ability to play it. He could see it coming from a long way off and he was intimidated by it because of his numb hand and because he hadn't practiced enough lately trying to rest it. His heart began to pound and it began all over again, including the nausea and everything, right there on the stage in front of a packed house, and the passage was still coming, it was getting closer.

Henry started to fudge his way through it—and then he just plain blacked out. He keeled over and would have fallen out of his chair if Jon, the second violinist, had not caught him. A collective gasp went up from the audience. It would have been better for him if he had gone all the way and lost consciousness. At least he would have been oblivious to the whole ridiculous scene. This was not what happened, however. He went into something like a trance. He was conscious and yet not conscious. He was awake but had no control over his body. His eyes were open but he could not speak and could not collect himself enough to sit in his chair on his own, without the assistance of Jon's steadying hand. He just hung there, in suspended animation, for what seemed like forever. He heard the gasps and the murmurs of the crowd. He saw the angry look on Karl's face. But there was nothing he could do.

Karl took charge of the situation and asked the audience to indulge them in an early intermission. They went backstage, and the chairwoman of the music department took Henry to the lounge and had him lie down on the couch; but he was already beginning to recover. The blood was beginning to flow normally again.

Karl came in and he was angry.

"What the hell happened out there?"

"I don't know. My heart started to pound and I just sort of blacked out."

"Your heart started to pound? You're saying you had a heart attack?"

"I don't know what it was. It's been going on a lot lately. But not like this."

"Have you seen a doctor?"

"Well, no. I don't have time."

"Nonsense! You have to make time. You can't show up at concerts like this. These people will eat us alive."

Henry did not bother to respond. He closed his eyes, and eventually Karl stormed back out, muttering to himself. Henry kept his eyes closed, and in a few minutes he began to feel better. Actually much better. He was almost embarrassed by how good he felt—almost wished he could get carted off by an ambulance to give him cover for the ridiculous scene that had just occurred. Instead he continued to improve. His color returned to normal, and within ten minutes he was ready to go out and play.

He wanted to go right back out on the stage. The group agreed with him—they seemed unhappy with him and this turn of events—but his hosts insisted that he rest at least a half hour, if for no other reason than to make sure he was all right. They brought him tea. They offered him aspirin, which he accepted. The chairwoman for the event tried to convince him to cancel and come back another day, but he would not hear of it. They had a room full of music lovers who had paid good money. He refused to disappoint them. He went back out on stage and waved at the audience as if to say all was well. Their relief was audible—they were on his side, and this gave him strength. This time he played the difficult passage flawlessly. After all, he had played it many, many times before.

The following Monday he gave in and actually went to see his doctor. He had high blood pressure and an arrhythmia. He tried to make a joke about the awkwardness of this latter condition, for a musician, but the doctor barely smiled. He seemed grave, and this scared Henry. There was a prescription for a water pill and for Cardizem for the blood pressure and arrhythmia and digitalis for emergency use, just in case he was planning on playing any more concerts. The doctor was being ironic—of course he was going to play concerts. But Henry was not so sure. Was his concert career over? The thought kept coming back to him. It was terrifying. He didn't bother saying anything about the pain in his hand. If there was more bad news he didn't want to hear it.

What Henry took away from this visit and from the doctor's grave behavior was that he was a very sick man. And lucky—to be alive. In fact those were the doctor's exact words. Up until then he had simply refused to believe that anything was seriously wrong with him. He could not afford to be sick—he had too much to do—he was under assault. And more than anything he did not want to have a sick heart. The sheer helplessness of having his heart rebel against him and his busy schedule was a terrible burden. He wanted to do, he wanted to go, but his heart was not willing. Henry found this depressing. It was the first time in his life he had come up against such an implacable obstacle. It was the first time he had given any serious thought to his own mortality.

Oh, he knew he was mortal, in an abstract way. He knew the years were flying by and his hair was turning gray and he couldn't do all the things he used to do. He knew he had aches and pains. He knew he had less energy. But this was different. This was playing chess with death. What was it like to die after a life of striving so hard to live? Henry was not used to having such thoughts; he was always too busy. He could not help having them now.

ODE TO A NIGHTINGALE

THE NEAR-DISASTER AT SWARTHMORE and the unsettling trip to the doctor made Henry yearn all the more for Gabrielle and her good company. If this had happened to him in the past, she would have been right there by his side. He knew it. She would have been taking care of him and loving him. Nobody was taking care of him or loving him now.

He came home from the doctor's office and sat in his empty condo and decided he had to see her. He had the perfect excuse—he could tell her he was sick. He could tell her what happened at the concert and what the doctor told him. She would want to know about that, wouldn't she? Even if she was still angry with him she would want to know if he was sick. But he was also secretly hoping for a softening of her heart toward him. He was different now. He knew how much she meant to him, how much he needed her. She would not listen to his apologies, but maybe she would listen to his sick heart. Maybe she would take pity on him and not be so cruel.

He looked up her classes on line and saw she had one that ended at four on Tuesday—tomorrow. Since she wouldn't answer his calls, his plan was to drive over to Dagny's condo in time to catch her as she arrived home. There wouldn't have to be any embarrassing knocking on the door or encounters with his sister-in-law, who, he assumed, was just as peeved with him as her brother. He couldn't take seeing Dagny. Not because he didn't like her, but because he liked her too much. He couldn't bear to discover that he was no longer in favor with her and was not permitted to josh with her in the old familiar way.

So this was best. He would simply go and sit in the parking lot in a convenient spot and wait for Gabrielle to come home. Which is what he did. It was a cloudy September afternoon, a little cool for the season, possible first frost predicted that night in low-lying valleys. Henry sat there in the Jeep shivering because he had underdressed. He wasn't expecting the cold and had simply worn his tweed jacket; and with the engine turned off it did not take long for him to feel the chill. He had calculated that Gabrielle would get there around five, so he came at half past four just to be safe. An hour went by without any sign of her. Dagny arrived home from work. She did not seem to notice the Jeep. Henry felt very strange sitting there watching her surreptitiously. They had been such good friends. What had life come to?

She went inside and a light went on in the living room. Every now and then he caught a glimpse of her in the windows. All of a sudden he was filled with sadness. He began to weep. He thought about all the fun they'd had over the years teasing Gabrielle for her primness. He thought about the vacations they used to take together, many years ago, and wept all over again. Then the tears blended in with the cold and made marks in the corners of his eyes and he began to shake. It was starting to get dark. How much longer could he stay there before someone called the police and reported him? He had no idea whether Gabrielle was expected home. She could be out with friends. She could have a concert that night. For all he knew, she may not have even been living with Dagny anymore. There had been no contact between them. She might have found a place of her own.

Then he saw some lights coming up the road—and sure enough, it was the familiar Corolla. He felt so glad to see it, his heart beat a little faster. He put his hand over it as if to slow it down. His hand felt cold. A dreadful thought came over him— what if she pulled into the garage and closed the automatic door behind her? But no, she parked behind the other door, where she had always parked. It was endearing. He knew she meant it as a sign of respect to her sister. Henry got out of the Jeep and walked slowly in the direction of her car. He was waiting for her to get out, and she was taking her time. Finally she did emerge, and he thought he saw a smile on her face, like she was laughing at some private joke. This made him smile.

"Hi there," he said, and she started. She turned and looked at him in surprise.

"What are you doing here?"

"That's funny. That's exactly what you said the last time."

"But why? What's the point?"

"Just to see you, that's all. I've missed you."

"Well, you shouldn't have come. You can't just keep showing up like this."

"I've got some news. I didn't know how else to tell you. You don't answer my emails."

"I really don't want to hear your news, Henry," she said, holding her hand to her head. "I want to be left alone. Can you leave me alone?"

"I just thought I'd give you a heads-up. There might be some changes coming. They're trying to get me to retire." He had planned to tell her about his health, but something stopped him.

"Haven't they been doing that for a long time?"

"Yes, but this is different. They're really serious. Formal 'process' and everything. Very exciting."

"Based on what? They can't just start the dismissal process for nothing. What happened?"

Henry was caught. He had not intended to go down this road, had not thought through the consequences, and now he was caught. "They've got this big trumped-up accusation against me."

"Oh—let me guess. It has something to do with that girl."

He stared at her. Did she know?

"Girl?" he said lamely.

"Henry, you're such a fool," she said laughing. "So now your little friend's gone and gotten you into trouble. And you come running to me? Why? Did you actually think I would help you?"

"No, it wasn't that at all. I just wanted to see you. I wasn't expecting anything."

"Sorry, you came to the wrong place. I can't give you what you want. I'm not even going to say I wish I could, because that would be a lie. You've gotten yourself into trouble. What did you do, go and make the three amigos mad at you?"

"Something like that."

"And let me guess—she put you up to it. Right?" She laughed again and shook her head. "No, you really shouldn't have come here. Did you think you would win my sympathy with a story like that? What kind of a fool do you think I am? I'm over you, Henry. You need to realize that. I'm not your lapdog anymore. You need to get yourself another slave and move on. Right now you're just making a fool of yourself. I'm sorry, but that's the truth."

"Thanks. That's very kind."

"Well? Look at you! You're a mess. You drive all the way over here to stalk me and you look like you've been sleeping in those clothes for weeks. How long have you been here? An hour? Two?"

"Closer to two."

"See? Pathetic. I'm not going to invite you in. Dagny's home, and I don't want to subject her to that. So basically you came all the way over here for nothing."

"I don't suppose I could interest you in a little drink."

"No, I don't want to go drinking with you, Henry. You don't even drink. Don't try to go all Humphrey Bogart on me now because you're not the type. Just go back where you came from and leave me alone."

She said this, but she did not turn and walk away. She stood there for a moment, almost as if waiting for him to say something.

"Come on. Just give me an hour. I want to try to explain myself."

"There's nothing to explain," she said annoyed. "It's called testosterone. At your age it should be under control."

This time she really did turn and walk. Henry just stood there and watched her go. He wanted to call out to her but he didn't want to make a spectacle of himself. He felt conspicuous enough as it was. He wanted her to stop because he wanted to tell her what he had come to tell her; about Swarthmore and the visit to the doctor and the somber reception he got. This was what he really wanted to say but he was stuck to the ground. He couldn't move and he couldn't get his mouth to move.

He had come down there to tell her about his health. He thought it would stir her sympathy, turn away some of her anger. But it seemed a little too manipulative. That was why he couldn't go through with it. He wanted to tell her about his health because he loved her and he wanted her to share his burden. He knew she was tenderhearted; he knew his best chance to break through her resistance was to get her to worry about him. And besides, he really was ill. He was not faking it. The doctor had left little doubt in his mind about the danger he was in with these episodes.

But the problem was he did not have any right to expect her to share his burden. He knew it. He had forfeited that right when he had broken his marriage vows. It was selfish to come to her and try to make her feel sorry for him, manipulate her by telling her how sick he was. He didn't look sick. He wasn't having an episode now. Would she even believe him? He could not blame her if she didn't. Besides, it was not love to come and ask her to help him. True love was to offer to help *her*. He wanted to help her. He longed to find some way to be of service to her. But how? She didn't need anything from him. No, he was the one who was needy.

Still, Henry didn't really feel crushed by the mixed results of this awkward meeting. He felt a little disappointed, of course, but he had not gone down there with the idea that he would tell her about his health and she would fall into his arms. It was more about having an opportunity to see her again. Even if she was still angry with him, even if she continued to reject him, it was wonderful to see her, just to stand there in the twilight and talk to her. True, her words were stinging, but he was not expecting anything else. Not really. He knew he didn't deserve it.

Actually he felt a little elated as he drove home. He had seen her! She had given him a good tongue-lashing, but even that made him smile, because it was so perfect, because everything she said was so true, because she had seen through him so clearly. He admired these things about her. Yes, they came at his expense, but he almost didn't mind. There was nothing she said that wasn't well-deserved. It was ridiculous to come to her whining about his predicament when the cause of his predicament was his weakness. The main thing was he had seen her and he was thrilled to see her. Even just for a few moments. Anything was better than nothing.

She laughed at him, but he considered his mission a success. Besides, he had been noble. He hadn't told her about his health.

A CHANCE ENCOUNTER

HENRY TOOK SICK DAYS on Monday and Tuesday. Monday was his visit to the doctor, and Tuesday his heart was still fluttery and he was feeling weak—although not enough to keep him from trying to see Gabrielle. Anyway, taking two sick days made it awkward to come in on Wednesday. He was worried about what had transpired in his absence, if anything; also the unscheduled time off would not be well-received.

The weak low-pressure system that had dominated the Northeast for several days continued to hold on. It was not exactly raining, but it was misting and clammy. Henry went in early—he had a lot to do. He made a visit to the copy room, and Bea walked in while he was trying to figure out the machine with its multitude of—to him—superfluous options.

"Oh!—hello," she said, looking a bit startled.

"Hate using this contraption. Much preferred it when monks did all the copying by hand."

She smiled. Henry's inaptitude for modern office machinery was legendary. "So how are you?"

"Doing as well as could be expected. I suppose you've heard."

"Yes—terrible. I've been meaning to come talk to you. Always so busy—you know."

"I know. There's always something, isn't there? Still, I'd love to hear what you have to say. I really could use some good advice right now."

She looked puzzled. "Well, you know I'm happy to talk to you. I'm not sure what advice I could give."

"You know the routine! You're a survivor. If you wouldn't have some good advice for me, I can't imagine who would." This flattery was deliberate. He was hoping to get her to open up a little, come out of that accustomed shell of abstraction that she always seemed to have when he was around her.

"I've never had to survive that sort of thing, thank God, so my advice would be purely speculative. I know it must be hard."

Henry looked at her. Were they talking about the same thing? "Harder than you can imagine. Can you believe it, after all these years? After all I've given to this department? It just seems incredible."

She paused. "All you've given to the department?"

"Well, I suppose if you put it that way. No, I guess I didn't actually 'give' anything. They were paying me. Still, I've tried hard to be a good team player all these years, in spite of all the stupidity and the insulting behavior. You would think it would count for something."

Bea still seemed a little disconcerted. Did she have a different take on what was going on? Was she siding with Malcolm? If so, he was doomed.

"It does count for something. I think you've been remarkably tolerant over the years. I don't know of anyone else who would put up with what you've put up with. But what exactly *is* going on?"

"You don't know?"

"I'm not sure. Not really."

Henry sighed. "Apparently now they're trying to get rid of me. Really. I'm not making this up. That's the plan. They have some kind of trumped-up charge they're using against me, and it sounds like they have the dean in on it. Which is just lovely, because you know what she's like. So this may be one of the last times we have one of these pleasant little chats around the copying machine."

"Get rid of you? Really?"

"Why? Wasn't that what you heard?"

"No. I know you've got some people upset with you. And I know they're not nice people. I also know they couldn't carry your shoes. But get rid of you? I find that hard to believe."

"That's what they're trying to do. I heard it from Bertram himself. Malcolm thinks he's uncovered some firing offense, and now they're looking at starting the official process for dismissal. Although I think the real end game is to get me to agree to retire."

"What is this charge?"

"Oh, it's too ridiculous to go into. I'm surprised you haven't heard about it."

"I haven't. Can you tell me?"

"Supposedly I'm a pervert now. I'm trading sexual favors for power. Can you believe it?"

Bea just looked at him for a moment. "But that's not true."

"Of course not! What do you take me for?" he said laughing. "But that won't stop them. They think they have the evidence and have every intention of using it. Even if I manage to survive, my reputation will be ruined. Nice way to end a career, isn't it?"

"They make me sick. I had no idea."

"Well, what did you think was going on?"

"I didn't know, exactly. I knew something was up, but not this. It's just jealousy. They never could stand the fact that you were better than they were. They were just waiting for a chance to take you down."

"And I very obligingly gave them one."

"Never. It will never happen. You have too many supporters in this department, too many people who love you with their whole hearts. They'll never get away with something like that."

"Bless you. Those are the kindest words I've heard in weeks."

This conversation, as awkward as it was, made Henry feel better, or at least a little less paranoid. Bea clearly did not know what the plotters had in mind—and if Bea didn't know, then there was a chance others might not know. Henry might not be quite the pariah he imagined; not yet, anyway. One of the hardest things about coming to work was the thought that everyone was eyeing him and whispering about him behind his back. It made him feel better to think this might not be the case.

He chuckled to himself when he thought about Bea. Had never been able to quite make her out. He liked her, in a way, or at least he wanted to like her. She was the only one left who had been there when he arrived, the only one who had gone through all the same nonsense and upheavals as himself. This in itself was a source of camaraderie. And he always felt over the years that they were in sync, if not entirely sympathetic. Although he did not discuss office politics with Bea—they did not socialize generally—he always felt she went out of her way to telegraph her support of the positions he took as well as the work he had done with the students. Bea always had a smile for him. It was a strange smile, perhaps, but the way he was feeling now any smile would do.

He often wondered about her, what her story was. She was stocky and somewhat odd-looking with some facial tics that made an amateur psychologist think of dyskinesia. He remembered there was something about a summer stay in some sort of facility about twenty years back. Never got all the details. Thought it might have something to do with alcohol, or maybe not. Maybe she was dealing with other demons. She seemed to keep to herself, which made her kind of fascinating. So much of what is called success in the modern university was based on politics and "networking." It was amazing that a true loner like her could survive.

Still, no matter how odd she may seem, Henry was glad for her unquestioning support. She said the words that were like honey to his ears. Not everyone believed he was licentious, apparently. Not everyone believed he had used power and influence in return for unspecified sexual favors from Margie. That was a relief. Until his talk with Bea, he did not know quite what to think about the mood of the department. Now he was inclined to be optimistic. Things might not be as bad as they seemed. And what she said made sense. He was not without supporters. It would not be easy for Malcolm and Jeff to do what they had apparently set out to do.

Buoyed somewhat by this chance encounter, Henry managed to glide through Wednesday and Thursday classes, his worst days of the week. He was not as prepared as he liked to be, he was not as patient with his private students as he wanted to be, but neither did work seem impossible, as it had at the beginning of the week when he was sitting in the doctor's waiting room and pondering his existence. He was not quite so afraid to greet his colleagues. Bea's kind words made him more trusting. He did not feel like such an alien walking the department hallways.

Then Thursday night came along. It was the new rehearsal night for Forum. Karl insisted on having it at his house. They had always rehearsed at Henry's house—he was central, plus he was the founder of the group—and then at his condo, which was not quite so central. But Karl did not want to rehearse there anymore. It was too small. He felt like he was right on top of the piano. He couldn't concentrate and was not getting anything accomplished. That was the reason they were quarreling—they needed more space.

Henry really did not want to go to Karl's house. It wasn't just the feeling of losing control and his privileged position in the hub; it was seeing Karl's family for the first time since the separation from Gabrielle. He suspected it would not be pleasant, and he was right. He was greeted coldly by Karl's wife, Judy. He caught a glimpse of the kids, Amy and Colbert, who were both home, but they seemed to be avoiding him. This change in their relations pained Henry more than he could say.

They were playing 131 again in three weeks and Karl wanted to practice. Henry thought they should work on the other things they were doing, but Karl was insistent. This clash broke into open warfare not ten minutes after they sat down in their usual circle.

"I don't see why you want to go over the first movement again right now," Henry was saying. "We all agree on how to play it. We just played it last weekend."

"Yeah, and that's the problem. We didn't play it very well," Karl said, flaring.

"On the contrary, I thought we played it quite well, once we got past the little problem."

"About that. Are you sure there was a problem? I noticed you hopped right back up and went back in there and played a full concert. That seemed a little strange."

"Of course there was a problem! I was sick. I thought I was having a heart attack."

"Yeah, well, maybe. I don't know. What I do know is this 'attack' seemed to happen when we were coming up on the passage you were having so much trouble with in rehearsal."

"What exactly are you implying, that I faked an attack so I wouldn't have to play it?"

"I don't know. You tell me."

"Obviously not. In that case I wouldn't have gotten up and gone back out there and played it later. You don't have any idea how sick I am."

"That's just it. You don't seem so sick. You played an entire concert. You stayed around afterward and chatted up the sponsors like nothing had happened. Just how 'sick' could you be?"

"I'll tell you how sick. I went to the doctor. He put me on medication."

"They put everybody on medication. That's nothing to brag about. But let's put all that aside. Let's say you were sick. We still need to practice this piece, in my opinion. Or at least you do."

"What's that supposed to mean?"

"I wouldn't say it was your best playing, would you? You seemed like you were only half there."

"I did all right. We got three ovations. The audience seemed pleased."

"That has more to do with reputation than with what actually happened in the concert. You're playing level has to come up. It hasn't been where it should be for some time. I'm sorry to be so blunt, but that's the truth. We all agree," he said, looking around at the group.

"Oh! So now you agree my playing isn't up to snuff. Who are you to agree? You've got a private agenda here."

"You mean I don't like the fact that you were unfaithful to my sister and ruined her life? No, I don't like that. But it doesn't have anything to do with what we're talking about now. This problem started long before that happened. It's been going on for years."

Henry's heart began to pound and his breathing became shallow. "You know what? I've just about had it. Maybe I'll disband the group."

"Disband!" Karl scoffed. "It's not yours to disband. You don't own Forum. You could leave and Frank could step right in, and nobody would know the difference. Except that we sound better."

"Boys, boys! Let's not fight. We have a concert to get ready for," said Jon.

They went back to work but Henry could hardly play. He was too sick. Several times during the evening he thought he was going to pass out. He kept going. He wasn't going to give Karl the satisfaction.

It was a long drive home. He honestly did not know if he was going to make it. When he finally did reach his dark condo it was all he could do to get through the door and throw himself on the couch. And then it started all over again—the pounding. He'd taken his medication but it didn't seem to make any difference. He could not stop the pounding and it was terrifying.

Henry did not know which was worse as he lay there in the dark by himself—the rough treatment he had received from Karl or the shunning by his wife and kids. They'd always had so much fun together. To Henry they were not just in-laws but family. Amy and Colbert were like his own kids. There had always been a special bond between them. It hurt him to think this all had been lost.

THE TURN OF THE SCREW

THINGS WERE TERRIBLE WITH FORUM, but the little spike he received from his encounter with Bea did not desert him. She did not know, which meant others did not know. It was a relief just to feel they weren't all talking about him. He had a couple of relatively good weeks at school. Things seemed normal in the classroom. If the students were aware of what was going on they didn't give any sign of it. He got some of his old energy back and began putting more effort into making his classes innovative and interesting. To tell the truth this was a good way to keep from thinking too much about other things. He even managed to walk past Malcolm in the parking lot without punching him.

The weather improved and there was the chill of fall in the air, his favorite season. The soreness in his left hand disappeared mysteriously as the low pressure system moved out to sea. His playing improved. He seemed to be able to do everything again. This gave him hope. He wasn't finished, as Karl intimated. It was just the darned hand. As long as he could find a way to keep the pain under control he would be all right. He made a promise to himself to see a good orthopedist, see if he could come up with a long-term solution that wasn't weather-dependent.

Then at the end of the month he received the news he'd been dreading. Bertram called him into his office.

"I promised you I would keep you apprised of what's going on," he said, after small talk and inquiring into Henry's health. "You remember I said I hadn't heard anything from the dean about

196

that little matter we talked about at the beginning of the semester. Well, she called me yesterday."

Henry froze. "They're actually going through with it."

"Now don't jump to any conclusions. This is just an inquiry, that's all. No one's brought any kind of formal charges. We just want to find out what the facts are and make sure we put this to rest once and for all."

"I don't even know how you can say that with a straight face. They're not interested in the facts. This is a lynch mob."

"*I'm* interested in them. There's no rush to judgment here. In fact that's just what the dean said to me, and I fully agree. You will have plenty of opportunity to tell your side of the story, believe me. We're just trying to determine what really happened."

"Don't condescend to me. You've already made up your minds about what happened—all of you. This is just a show trial to make believe you're being fair. There won't be anything fair about any of this. Malcolm will make sure of that."

"Well, I guess there's no harm in telling you it was Malcolm. You deserve to know that much, at least. Malcolm was the one who went to the dean."

"Yes, and charged me with sexual harassment. Isn't it rich? Malcolm, of all people. You could cut the irony with a knife."

"Look, maybe I could help here. Why don't I get you two together and see if we can't work this out among ourselves? I think he'd be willing to be reasonable."

"Oh, right. He's got me and he knows it. He's Javert now."

"He's really not that bad. He admires you. It's—complicated."

"How complicated is it that he wants to push me out of here? That doesn't seem very complicated at all. I hate him. Honestly, I could kill him right now."

"That wouldn't be very productive, would it?" Bertram said with a laugh. "Don't get yourself too worked up over this. It may not go the way you think."

"So I should just trust you, right?"

Bertram did not respond. Henry did not stay. He headed for his office but saw that Richie's door was open and went in.

"Well, it's official. It's started."

"What?"

"The inquiry you told me about. You weren't kidding. This time they really are out to get me."

"I was afraid of that. I'm so sorry. For this to happen to you."

"I brought it on myself. I broke my own rule. Malcolm's just doing what bloodhounds do."

"He's more like a junkyard dog. But what happens now?"

"I don't know. He didn't say—Bertram. He just informed me that an inquiry was underway. You know, 'getting the facts' and all that. As if they were really interested in the facts."

"I had a funny feeling about this going all the way back to last spring. Everybody was shocked when you spoke up—especially when you compared Malcolm to Alicia. I knew right then from the look on his face that this wasn't going to go well."

"I didn't compare them. I didn't say a word about Malcolm."

"But you might as well have. The one thing you have to remember about Malcolm is he's insecure. All this bravado is a show. He knows exactly what his weaknesses are and he hates it. He thinks they make him vulnerable, and this is what drives about eighty percent of his behavior."

"I don't know. Maybe. You could be right about that. But what does it have to do with me?"

"You struck at his vulnerability. You, Henry Larson, world-class violinist, called him on his musicianship. You did it in a very nice way, but the result was the same. To someone with no skin any little pinch is agony."

"But what can I do? You can't put someone's skin back on him. He should try putting up with the crap I have to put up with. He should try having a critic at the *Globe* pan your performance because your violin-playing was 'thin.'"

"I don't know what you can do. Honestly. I don't know what to tell you. I think it will probably blow over. I like to think he isn't a complete jerk and won't go too far with this. But I don't know."

"Well, I do know. This time they're going all the way. They want me out, and this is how they're going to do it."

"Well, look at it this way. You always said you wanted to retire."

"Not like this. On my own terms."

This conversation confirmed it. Henry was on a downward trajectory. Richie was always right about these things. It was one of reasons Henry liked him. He could always get a clear view of what was going on from his friend—but in this case he did not want the clear view. In this case he would have preferred a foggy view that gave him room to hope.

Henry went back into the unreal world. All of the gains, small as they were, that he had made in the last couple of weeks were gone. Any confidence he was trying to build up was utterly demolished. It wasn't just that they were out to get him. He'd been in that position before. It was the realization that there was nothing he could do to stop them. There was no way to fight. He couldn't use his power, his position, his place, his influence—he didn't seem to have any. He couldn't argue from reputation—it was reputation they had in their sights. Worst of all, they had the best of all arguments. Nothing was more likely to lead to your demise in the modern university than even the hint of sexual harassment. This was what they were charging. Henry could not see any way past it.

He was under siege. He went about his usual activities as if nothing were wrong, but inside he felt like he was dying. Everything he had worked for—all the years—all the relationships carefully built and nourished—this was all about to be exploded. The enemy had his artillery ready and pointed in Henry's direction. He could protest. He could try to stop them. But the end was inevitable. They would push him out and make him look like a dirty old man along the way. He taught his three classes, and it was a good thing he was well-prepared for them, because there were literally two streams of consciousness in his head. One was the lesson he was delivering, the other was his impending doom.

He went home exhausted and battered and sat in the afternoon light in his living area with its still-unpacked boxes and gazed out the window. Not at anything in particular—just gazing, like a prisoner from a cell. He made himself some supper, peas and a piece of salmon, but he wasn't hungry and basically just picked at it. The food turned cold so he left the plate at the counter and returned to his melancholy pose. He discovered how difficult it is to wait for the inevitable to happen, to extend yourself into the void. He thought of Marathon and the Spartans. What were they thinking as they watched the massive army advance? Were they thinking of death? Were they thinking of life? Was there any hope in their hearts—and if not, how had they fought so well? He thought of Pickett's charge. Did those poor boys know they were doomed before they even started up the hill? What kept them going under withering fire and against impossible odds? Courage? Honor? Groupthink? Resignation?

He was going into battle alone. No one would stand up for him, no one would fight for him. It was too dangerous in the current climate. The words "sexual harassment" were like a flesh-eating virus. They consumed everything they touched. He was living in a puritanical age that had no tolerance for foolish old men like himself, no tolerance for human weakness and no forgiveness. But hadn't Margie come to *him*? Hadn't she sought him out and, as he believed at the time, led him on? Wasn't she always careful to look a certain way, and wasn't the way she looked deliberately calculated to drive men crazy? Did she bear no part, no responsibility in this debacle, in Henry losing his way, in the destruction of his marriage, in the immolation of his academic career?

And what did the future hold for him? Where would he go when they threw him out of the university—er, let him retire? He wanted to immerse himself in his music, but would there even be a Forum to go to by then? If there was—would he be still be welcome? It did not sound like he was welcome. It sounded like Karl, at least, would have been happy to see him go. Suddenly he had a vision of himself sitting in that same lonely condo in the same chair twenty years on; twenty years of trying to fill up the void and stewing in regret and the unfulfilled desire for revenge. It was a lonely vision.

Family? There was none. He had given that up for his music. There was no son or daughter to call when he felt lonely, to see how they were doing or angle for consolation. There was no wife. There had been a wife, a very good wife, but he had taken care of that. Yes, he'd done a very good job of spoiling that connection. What was Gabrielle doing now, he wondered? It scared him to think of her seeing someone else. Nothing made him feel emptier than this hideous thought.

He tried calling her. This time he was going to do it—tell her about his heart problems. He wanted to do it. He wanted her to know—no, not because he was trying to manipulate her, but because she was the only person in the world who truly cared for him. And because he loved her. But she would not answer her phone. He let it ring until the message came on and then hung up and tried again. Same thing happened. This time he left a brief message. "Just calling to say hi. Hope you are well."

Night came, and midnight came, and Henry was exhausted but could not sleep. He dragged himself off to bed and managed to get out of his clothes but could not sleep. All he could think of was the barbarians agitating at the gates. Malcolm was in the midst of them with his usual snide smile. They would have no mercy. Why should they? Few understood him or what he was about. Few were able to appreciate the art that went into his music-making. What interested them was the cycle of life, the constant ebb and flow that raises up new generations and casts others down.

As far as they were concerned, Henry was just in the way.

NO EXIT

IT SEEMED LIKE HE HAD JUST DRIFTED OFF to sleep when he woke up again with a start. The alarm was blaring—it was time to go to work. His first thought was to call in sick, but he had already done too much of that for one semester. Besides, what was he going to do if he stayed home? Mope around all day feeling sorry for himself, wondering what new tricks his enemies were up to? No, better to be on the scene in case something could be done.

He managed to get to the university by around nine thirty, not long before his first class. The next thing he knew he found himself standing up in front of seventy students giving a lecture, but it was like being in a dream. He was so exhausted and had had so little sleep that there was a complete separation from himself. He could hear his voice droning on and on and he could see himself as if off to one side, observing. At the same time he could see the students, several of whom were on their cell phones. For a moment he became angry and thought about confronting them—but he kept on going like a train on its tracks and the anger passed.

He went to his next class, a theory class, only this time he was too tired to talk. He asked some leading questions, without worrying too much about their Socratic ingenuity, and let the talkative students take over while nodding sagely and occasionally interjecting a "well done," which he didn't really mean, since he wasn't really listening.

One of his favorite students, Todd, waited for the room to empty before approaching him.

"I heard about what's going on," he said with a mixture of bashfulness and concern. "I just want you to know we support you completely. I can't even believe someone's doing this to you."

Henry blinked. The words reached him through the gauze of weariness but it took him a moment to fully process them and realize they really did mean what he thought they meant. "How did you find out about that?" he said at last, too tired to even pretend he didn't understand.

"One of the professors told me. Everybody's upset about it. You're the best thing they have here. If they lose you, they won't have anything left."

"I'm not planning on going anywhere just yet. But what are they talking about, exactly?"

"Well, it's all kind of vague to me. Something about you and some girl?"

"Some professor," Henry corrected him—and then immediately regretted it.

"Well, whatever it is, I know you didn't do anything wrong. If there's anything I can do—"

"You've already done a great deal just by saying something. There are strange things going on in the world, my friend. But we'll get through it. We always do."

He was just babbling and didn't even know what he was saying. But it seemed to satisfy Todd, who toddled off into the hallway. Henry sat down. It might be more accurate to say he collapsed. The thing he feared the most had come upon him: the students knew. They were not all like Todd. Some of them would have been as happy to see him tripped up as Malcolm. There was the young lady who chalked up the "B" he had given her to "Eurocentrism." There was the handsome young violinist who thought he was a superstar and could not quite get over the fact that Henry did not agree with him on the basis of his actual playing. They were both vocal and they had both gone to Bertram to complain.

Henry felt powerless in the wake of this revelation, defeated. It was hard enough to keep students aligned and engaged, a constant battle, especially the wild ones in the gen ed courses. If they sensed blood in the water he was doomed. But it was more than that. Henry had always cherished his image as a good professor who cared about the students and was devoted to teaching. He cherished the generally good ratings he had received over the years, not because he catered to them but because he worked hard and his interest in them was genuine. But now he would just be a "harasser." This was especially difficult with all the indoctrination they were undergoing from the diversity juggernaut. Henry had walked right into the twenty-first century stereotype of devilry.

He needed some fresh air and went outside. He was too tired to walk or even stand, so he climbed into his car. He put his head back and drifted off and had a very strange dream about his mother. It was as if forty years ago were yesterday and she was still alive, and there was a girl in the room, and he realized he was connected to this girl in some way, at least in his mother's eyes, but he did not know why. Suddenly he woke himself up with a loud snort and realized he had been snoring with the window open. He looked around sheepishly just in time to see Malcolm and Camilla at the side door to the music building and looking very pleased with themselves. The young provocateur said something and she laughed; then he touched her arm and disappeared inside. She turned and walked toward the quad.

Henry felt his rage come all over him again. He looked down at the clock—two-thirty. He had a class to teach, but that wasn't what he was thinking about now. He was thinking about Malcolm and how much he detested him. Were they talking about him? Was that why they were laughing? He was tired of all the stuff going on behind his back. He got out of the car and slammed the door.

Henry rushed inside, stumbling as he climbed the stairs, not once but twice, the second time bloodying his shin on the metal tread and enraging himself all over again. He went directly to Malcolm's office and walked in without knocking.

Malcolm was hanging up his coat and turned around to face him. They were standing eye to eye.

"So I hear you went running to the dean."

"Say what?" Malcolm replied with a crooked smile.

"You and Jeff. You're going to try to take me down."

"What are you all excited about, Henry? No one's trying to 'take you down.'"

"Your little inquiry, or witch hunt, or whatever it is. Bertram told me yesterday. He also told me you went to Camilla with your ridiculous accusations."

"So did you," Malcolm retorted. "That's how this whole thing got started—remember? You went to the dean to accuse people of discrimination. Then you went even further and started accusing people of not being competent. Which wasn't very nice."

"A girl was being pushed out the door for nothing. I thought she had a right to know."

"Oh, so you're the noble one, are you? Too bad that isn't the way people see it. They think you did it because you had something else on your mind."

"You want to know why I did it? Because I finally reached my breaking point with people like you. It has to stop. Right now. You and Jeff and Bertram and all of your stupid little games. A lot of people have been hurt for nothing, and someone has to stop it."

"And would that someone be you, Henry?" Malcolm said with a smile. "You're not in a position to stop anything. If you can't keep your pants on that's one thing, but you might want to think about not running around pretending to be the protector of all that's right, good and true."

"You're the one who can't keep your pants on," Henry said, becoming even more enraged.

"What's that supposed to mean?"

He started to reply but realized things could get complicated and changed course. "The point is Alicia was treated unfairly. You went after her—you and Jeff—because she showed you up. There was no other reason and everybody knows it. She gave a great concert and you just couldn't tolerate that. It made you look bad, it exposed your pretensions, so you went after her."

"She gave a terrible concert, but that's beside the point. Alicia had to go because the budget was being cut. How many times do they have to tell you? But what's more interesting to me and a lot of people is why you're so darned hot on the subject. From what I hear you've been spending a lot of time with Margie. That's enough to send anybody over the edge."

"So this is your big ploy, huh? You've been wanting to get rid of me for years, and in your mind this is how you're going to do it. Pretend it had something to do with Margie."

"Well—does it? Tell the truth. Would you have gotten involved if she hadn't come to you?"

"So what if she did? She has a right to come to me if she sees something unsavory going on. This isn't a fascist state. Not yet."

"I would say that depends on the relationship. If it was just a casual conversation, then that's one thing. But my understanding is it went way beyond that. There were romantic moonlit dinners at the restaurant. There was a late night visit to her apartment."

"So it was you," Henry said, drawing closer, right in his face. "You were the one who sent the email."

"Here we go again with the email. I don't even know what email you're talking about. All I'm saying is you shouldn't be attacking people just because you're a little too friendly with other people in the department."

"And that's what I'm talking about, right there. The rush to judgment. People drawing conclusions. I saw you out there with the dean. Were you talking about me?"

"We're just trying to get the facts, Henry. Don't you think that's important? A very serious charge has been made. Do I believe it? Do I think you did it? I don't know. But I want to find out."

"So you're going to drag my name through the mud all over the university."

Malcolm laughed. "It's a little late for that, don't you think?"

Henry stumbled back. He felt ill. His heart was pounding like it never had before—he was afraid he might black out right there in Malcolm's office—but somehow he managed to find his way into the hallway. He went to his office and locked the door and lay down on the old couch, his heart pounding. He just lay there in a cold sweat and let it pound. There wasn't much he could do about it—he'd left the digitalis at home—so he just lay there. He wondered if he was going to die. He almost wished he could. He missed an appreciation class, but he didn't care. This was the first time he'd had an unscheduled absence for a class in all the years he had been at the university.

They really were doing it! This wasn't a dream anymore. They were going after him, and it was serious. A formal inquiry was underway, and who would be running it? Malcolm and his friends, directly or indirectly. Henry knew he didn't stand a chance. They would not have gone this far if they did not feel certain of success, if the path had not already been cleared. The "inquiry" would consist of the usual behind-doors discussions between people who did not wish him well. They would not bother to seek out opposing opinions. As far as they were concerned, there were no opposing opinions—no reasonable ones, anyway. Henry had been caught misbehaving, and something needed to be done.

The hardest thing for him as he lay there was the knowledge that he was the one who had handed them this opportunity. In a sense Malcolm was right. Without Margie, there would have been no outburst at the department meeting and therefore no inquiry. At his age, so stupid! There was no excuse. But it was too late now for regrets. Somehow they had seen the stain on him and they were not going to give up until it was made public, until he apologized for his sins against Malcolm and came crawling to them begging for forgiveness. That was what Bertram had in mind with his private meeting. But even then Henry did not believe they would relent. Malcolm had his golden opportunity at last. It was clear he had every intention of using it.

Henry went over the ten years of history he had with Malcolm. He thought about the time they were doing a concert together in a local church and Malcolm informed one of the paid soloists that he wanted to "do it with her right there on the altar." He said it in a joking way, but Henry was shocked and disgusted. He thought about the time he was in a workshop and Malcolm informed some students that anyone who wanted to be a section leader had to sleep with him—men excepted, of course. Again, all a big joke, but Henry could just imagine what the idealistic young women in the group were thinking when they heard such things coming from their award-winning teacher. There was the time Malcolm managed to find himself alone in a practice room with Jane Allston, a voice professor who was one of Henry's favorites on the staff. He tried to overpower her with his suave charm with a classroom full of students next door and people walking by in the halls, their silhouettes in clear view. Jane herself told Henry this. Soon after she accepted a position at Maryland. Said she couldn't take it anymore.

Jane was an outstanding professor and Maryland was an outstanding vocal school. But this was just the sort of thing that drove Henry crazy. Why couldn't they become an outstanding vocal school? Why couldn't they become outstanding in any area? All it took was the right kind professors and the right kind of students. But this was the very thing that Malcolm and his allies opposed. As far as they were concerned, this was "reaching." They didn't want to become like the state schools that had outstanding reputations, the Michigans and Indianas. Why? What possible reason could there be for such an attitude? It was because they wanted to ensure there was room for their own mediocrity. To Henry, this was the only possible explanation.

Henry thought about Malcolm's tone toward him, openly mocking. Here he was playing concerts all over the world, a well-known personality in chamber music circles, and this crafty Machiavelli, this politician, was triumphing over him, reducing him to a caricature and declaring his intention to take him down. Henry knew there was nothing he could do about it. He did not have the power to stop him. From their brief conversation it was clear that Malcolm was in classic form, twisting the truth in every way. It was what he excelled at. He was good at setting the narrative in such a way and giving it such momentum that it could not be turned. He was genuinely malicious, and this gave him power over Henry, who was unwilling to do certain things to fight back. The Malcolms of the world always won—because they had the will to win.

Henry lay there for hours, heart periodically pounding, not moving, unable to move. The phone rang and people knocked on the door, but he didn't respond. He just lay there in the gathering gloom staring listlessly up at the ceiling. Then he fell into a deep sleep, filled with gargoyles and bizarre dreams. When he awoke, it was pitch black outside. He looked at his watch. It was seven.

He tried to get up. It was difficult. He managed to roll off the couch onto his hands and knees. He put his forehead on the cool floor and just stayed there in that supplicating pose for a few minutes. The cold marble tile felt good on his head, soothing. Finally he managed to stand. He was dizzy and steadied himself by putting his hand on his desk. He put on his fall jacket and picked up his violin and walked out to his car. There was no one around.

It was dark, so dark, one of those pitch-dark nights with no moon. He climbed into the Jeep, still feeling quite listless, and started the engine. For a few moments he just sat there listening to it. His heart started pounding again, and he was afraid. Was he going to die, right there in the parking lot? Would they find him in the morning slumped over in his seat? Then the pounding stopped and he was able to breathe. But could he make it all the way home? What if he had another attack?

He sat there for quite a long time, thinking about it, convincing himself that he could make the ten mile drive to his condo. Finally he put the car in gear and started to go. He turned the corner at the south end of the music building listlessly. It was a long, sweeping turn, almost as if the car were driving itself.

Then he saw him in his headlights—Malcolm. He was stepping off the sidewalk and onto the road. Henry's heart began to pound. He saw the usual sneer on that handsome face, and his heart started pounding some more. He felt like he was going to be sick. He fumbled unsuccessfully with the window button, gasping for air. Then it was like the concert. Everything started to go dark.

Somehow in turning to the left to finagle the window Henry seemed to lose control of the rest of his body. He could sense his right foot pressing on the accelerator as if it had a mind of its own. He looked up and saw Malcolm's now terrified face coming closer, closer, but there was nothing he could do. He felt like he was frozen in time. The last thing he remembered was Malcolm disappearing under the car. He ran right over him. Then he stopped and turned off the engine. He did not turn off the lights. He just sat there in a trance.

DE PROFUNDIS

MALCOLM WAS QUITE DEAD. If Henry had been driving the Corolla it might have been different. After all, he wasn't going that fast. Malcolm might have been thrown onto the hood and had some minor injuries. But the Jeep was built high, which was why the smirking one wound up underneath it. Henry swerved instinctively, trying to avoid him, and wound up running over his handsome head with the left rear wheel.

Some students were coming out of the music building when it happened and one of them saw the whole thing. They called 911 in a panic but there was nothing the paramedics could do. Malcolm was already gone when they arrived. His head was crushed—it was obvious even in the bad light. There was blood everywhere. They pronounced him dead on the scene and didn't bother rushing to the hospital.

Henry stood off to the side while all this was going on staring uncomprehendingly at the limp twisted body in the road. He could not believe what had just happened. What exactly *had* happened? He wasn't sure. He felt like he was blacking out and the next thing he knew he felt a sickening bump. The bump was still there in his mind and it was horrifying, playing over and over again. Some students tried to talk to him, see if he was all right, but it was like he was comatose. He heard their questions but could not answer them or even look at them. He just stood there in the dark, his hands in his pockets, not even shivering, although it was a chilly night and headed for frost.

The limp body lying there in the road stole his being. It was as if it sucked his soul right out of him. Henry Larson, the biggest pacifist on the face of the earth, had just killed a man. He was a killer and the limp body forced him to see that he could never go back—he would never undo what he had done. He blinked but the body did not go away. It was still there. He could see the dark matter flowing out of Malcolm's head and was horrified all over again. What should he do? What could he do? He felt completely helpless. In a few minutes the campus police arrived and then the ambulance. Henry was not going to get in the way. He just stood there with his hands in his pockets, in shock.

He knew how it looked. He had run over his arch-enemy. Of course he didn't do it on purpose. He simply blacked out. His foot pressed against the pedal involuntarily. Sudden acceleration—wasn't that what they called it? People had been going along, minding their own business, and their cars had started accelerating on their own and gone out of control, often ending in a crash, sometimes fatal. Could this be what had happened to him? He tried to convince himself it was. But then he realized it was no good. Only certain models were said to have this problem and his wasn't among them. Also he could remember his foot pressing on the gas pedal. He still had the sensation of it in his mind.

A crowd gathered and it was a wild scene. A couple of female students who knew Malcolm were wailing and out of control. Everyone was buzzing. Henry stood there immobile as this great drama swirled around him. Only a few of the students knew about his role in the accident. The rest assumed he was like one of them, a curiosity seeker. They jostled him and pushed by him and didn't pay any attention to him. A couple recognized him and said his name but he did not respond.

He thought of Malcolm's wife. He thought of his three daughters. What heartbreaking horror were they about to endure? He remembered when his mother died in that terrible accident, hit by a drunk driver. He remembered his sister calling him and giving him the news. "Mother?" he kept saying over and over again. It would be the same for Malcolm's family. They would be in shock. There would be crying and a sleepless night. Henry was in shock. He could only imagine how they would feel.

The campus police were now looking at his car and trying to find a driver. One of the students led them to Henry. He nodded blankly when they asked him if he had been driving. Then the town police arrived, and they were a little rougher. They talked like cops and they had a lot of questions. They wanted him to come down to the station, which he was glad to do. They asked more questions and then they let him go. It was obvious to them it was just an accident. There was no reason to detain him. One of the officers drove him back to campus and his car. Henry climbed in and drove home—in the car that had run over Malcolm Faust. It seemed in perfect condition, as if nothing had happened.

When he got home, Henry called Gabrielle. He did not know what else to do. She did not answer, of course, but he left a message—"Please call me. I have to talk to you." There must have been something in his tone of voice because she did call. Almost right away.

"Something terrible has happened."

"What is it? What's wrong?"

"There's been an accident. Someone was killed."

"Oh my goodness, Henry. Are you all right? Were you involved?"

"I was driving."

There was a pause. "I'm so sorry. Did someone run into you?"

"No, it wasn't like that. I—ran over someone."

"You ran over someone?"

"Yes. It was horrible."

"You said someone was killed..."

"Yes—they were. At least it was quick. Head trauma." He did not know what he was saying. He didn't realize how hard it would be to tell her.

"Oh, Henry. I'm so sorry. Do they know who it was?"

Now he paused. "Well—yes, they do. It was Malcolm."

"Malcolm Faust?"

"Yes."

"Oh my God. How did that happen?"

"I don't know. It was dark. I was in the school parking lot. I was having one of my episodes—and I just don't know what happened after that."

"'Episodes?' What are you talking about?"

"Oh, I've been having these cardiac episodes—heart goes out of control and I sort of black out. It's been going on for a couple of months now."

"Why didn't you tell me?"

"I didn't want to bother you."

"You wouldn't 'bother' me. I'm so sorry. This must be terrible for you."

He was glad to hear her voice, this time without the anger, her old voice. He wanted to stay on the phone with her forever, but that was selfish. He forced himself to say goodbye. After they hung up he went to his bed and lay down. He just lay there for a long time thinking about the sound of her voice, the tenderness in her tone. Then he thought about the tone that crept in when she realized what happened and who was involved. This was his future. This was the tone he would have to deal with from now on. From everyone. Forever.

But then he could not think about her or her voice anymore, even though he wanted to. His mind was pulled inevitably back to the place where he did not want it to go. He had just killed a man. It was not like he could ignore it. He did not want to ignore it. He wanted to condemn himself and mete out full punishment in the hope that some of the terrible pain he was now experiencing might go away. It did not. It would never go away. He knew it would never go away. All Henry could see was the ruined image of himself in that smashed twisted body, the turning of the bloom of identity into something rancid and gross. Malcolm was dead and he was the one who had done it. Like the boy who accidentally shoots his brother playing with his father's rifle, Henry had killed his brother in music.

All of the nasty things about Malcolm were forgotten now and forgiven. He, Henry Larson, outspoken proponent of "love, love, love," was the killer of a magnificent young man.

SCANDAL

ENRY DID SLEEP THAT NIGHT with the help of a couple of shots of expensive brandy that someone had given him many years ago which had never been opened. It was a night of crazy dreams. When he awoke he did not feel at all refreshed. The sun was shining—it was half past nine—time to get out of bed. But it took him a good hour to get moving.

In the end he had to get moving because to lie there any longer was intolerable. All he could think of when he closed his eyes and tried to sleep was Malcolm and his face looking at him in the last moment before it happened. Was it all a dream? He kept asking himself. You know how when you have a horrible dream sometimes it takes a while to wake up—to convince yourself it was just a dreadful dream. Henry tried to wake himself out of the dream but it was real. In his half-sleep, half-waking state the thought kept nagging him—This is not a dream. This is real. It was unbelievable but he knew he had to believe it.

His thoughts turned again to Malcolm's family. He would have to go see them. It was his duty. It got him out of bed and showered and shaved. He even managed to drum up a clean suit. He stepped out into the bright morning light and it was just oppressive. It felt like it was jabbing his eyes. When he reached his car he stopped and stood there for a while staring at it like a stranger. It was a car that had killed someone. He glanced at the right front fender and was relieved to see there was no blood. He didn't care if there was damage but blood he could not endure.

Henry got into it and drove in the direction of Malcolm's house. There were a lot of cars in the driveway and on the street when he arrived. He should have known. It made things more challenging, but he was determined. He walked up the manicured front steps feeling like a character in a movie—the steps that Malcolm himself had manicured and took such pride in—rang the bell and was let in by someone he did not know. It was crowded inside. Henry started to lose heart—but then he saw her, Madeline, or Maddie, as her friends called her. He had never dared to call her Maddie himself. He found her too intimidating. He saw her, and then she turned and she saw him. She just looked at him.

He couldn't stop now. He walked in her direction at a gracious pace and greeted her kindly. He did not try to reach out for her—they did not have that kind of relationship.

"Maddie—Madeline—I am so sorry," he said softly. "So horrifying. Such a fine young man."

"Yes—not real somehow."

"Are you—all right?"

"I don't know. Guess I'm kind of in shock."

"Perfectly understandable. I am so sorry. If there is anything I can do—anything."

"Well—thank you."

Someone else greeted her and she turned away, and Henry knew it was time to go. He could not be welcome there. When he felt it was safe he began to quietly drift through the crowd to the door, greeting people he knew with a somber unsmiling face. In this way he passed through the house where he had been a guest so many times; through Malcolm's house. Only Malcolm was not there. And Malcolm would not be coming home. He saw the three girls on the couch. A woman was bending over them, consoling them. He saw their red eyes and pale faces and was sick. Should he say something to them? No, it was too much. It was an intrusion.

The uproar that ensued in town and in the whole region was entirely predictable. Professors don't get run over in the college parking lot every day, especially by other professors. The sensational story had already become the lead on the New York City stations by 10:00 PM on the night of the accident and was on all the major news outlets the next day. From then on the coverage was non-stop. There were news crews all over the place sniffing out a fresh angle. A lot of them were looking for Henry—and he was not always able to avoid being found. He was under siege in his own condo.

The school was completely traumatized. Malcolm suddenly became the most wonderful professor and humanitarian in the history of the university as emotional tributes poured forth from the hearts of stricken students and colleagues. There was to be a spectacular funeral with incredible music and an expected throng of at least a thousand. Henry was conflicted about going. He wanted to go, as painful as he knew it would be; he felt it was his duty to go and show support for the family, but he did not want to be disruptive. He did not know if the family wanted him there. He knew of a few of Malcolm's friends who definitely would *not* want him. And what about the press? They might see him and cause a commotion.

He called Gabrielle to ask what he should do. This was what he had always done in the past when facing a difficult situation—ask Gabrielle. She actually answered the phone, which was thrilling. She agreed with him that he needed to be there. It would be disrespectful to Maddie not to go. But she also offered to call and make sure. The next day she called back with the news that Maddie wanted him to come. She was not angry with him. It was an accident. So Henry went, and tried to sit out of the way, in a corner of the balcony. This corner afforded him a good view of the nave. He saw Gabrielle come in. He started to cry. He couldn't help himself—the tears just streamed down his face.

The funeral was indescribably strange for Henry. After all, put yourself in his position. He found it easy to let go of his former animosity toward Malcolm as he listened to the encomiums, some emotional, some humorous, some biographical, all powerful. Actually it struck him that there was a surprising amount of balance on display. Malcolm's seamier side did not make an appearance in any of the testimonies, of course, but on the whole there seemed to be less lying than is typical on such occasions and even some effort to show him as a normal human being with human foibles. Henry found himself feeling a new appreciation for his former antagonist as he looked at him through the eyes of others; but of course this just made the whole experience more horrible.

Maddie did not speak. He could not help looking in her direction. She was a mess. He felt her grief like physical pain and was oppressed with a feeling of dread. He was the killer of this fine flower of academia. He could not keep his mind from going to his foot on the gas pedal. He did not push down intentionally; and anyway, it was not much of a push. He blacked out for a moment and lost control of his body. It was an accident. He kept reassuring himself it was nothing more than that.

That's the way everyone else saw it, too—at first. Henry had come around the corner and not seen Malcolm, and Malcolm wasn't watching where he was going and froze when he saw the car. There was an uproar about the lack of streetlamps on that part of campus. It quickly became a meme and even made it into the press reports. But bad lighting was the only culprit in the collective consciousness. Henry even enjoyed a good deal of sympathy. It was terrible for someone so venerated to be involved in such an accident and to have killed his own friend. Then it came out that he was sick and on heart medications. The episode at Swarthmore was talked about. A rumor went around that he'd had a heart attack just before the accident and almost died himself. This was shocking. They felt sorry for him.

Then the funeral was over and the media crews went back to chasing three-alarm fires and all the shock and commotion and excitement gradually subsided. Which was when things began to unravel for Henry. He had given his account of events both to the campus police and the town police. They'd questioned a few students who were on the scene and who corroborated his story. Henry turned the corner and Malcolm stumbled out onto the road and there was a bump! and the next thing they knew he was lying in the road and Henry was sitting in the car with his forehead on the wheel.

But the police had not talked to all of the witnesses, not right away. By the time they arrived there was a large crowd milling about, so they had grabbed whomever they could find. Later on they began to look into the case a little more carefully. It seems they received an anonymous tip that there had been bad blood between Henry and Malcolm. Something about an investigation into sexual harassment. People overheard them arguing in Malcolm's office that very day. Now if the police had known Henry and his reputation, they might not have paid much attention to this report, especially since the caller refused to identify himself. They might even have dismissed it as a prank. But they had no notion of Henry's notoriety. Their idea of the classics was the Beatles.

There was one young, freshly-minted detective sergeant whose interest was particularly piqued by the case. He went back and talked to a couple of the witnesses and soon found that there was a witness who had not been heard from, the only witness who had actually seen what happened. Our intrepid investigator tracked down this elusive young man and found him to be suspiciously persistent in his elusiveness. At first he claimed he didn't see much of anything at all. He was walking with his friends and glanced over at the headlights coming around the corner and just caught the end of what happened. It was just like everyone said. Malcolm was in the wrong place at the wrong time.

But Detective Sergeant Martin had a keen eye and thought he saw some reluctance in the part of the young man, whose name was Daryl, to say more. With friendly prodding he uncovered some interesting information. The witness had the impression of the car accelerating at the time of impact. Not a lot, but noticeable. In any case it was not slowing down. What made it even more striking was that he himself clearly did not want to believe it. After all, it was dark—it was late—he must have been mistaken. But at the same time it also bothered him or he would not have wanted to keep it to himself. Detective Sergeant Martin found this interesting. It was his "Ah ha!" moment.

He'd never had anything like this case before in his short and successful career—a potential murder in their upscale university town—and he was excited. He wanted to know more about that argument between Henry and Malcolm and the sexual harassment thing. The first person he went to see was Bertram, chairperson of the department. This professor also seemed a little reluctant to talk. In fact his reluctance reminded Detective Sergeant Martin of Darryl's. What was going on here? What did all these people know about the situation that he did not know? Whom were they trying to protect? He wanted to find out. It was a national case. The person who cracked it would have a reputation.

It didn't take long to figure out that there had been a long-standing animosity between Henry and Malcolm. He heard about Henry attacking Malcolm in the faculty meeting (this was how it was perceived by Malcolm's friends—as an "attack"). He heard about Henry and Margie and Malcolm's belief that there had been sexual harassment, under the broad university definition. He heard about the dean's intended inquiry into this charge and Henry's reaction to it. Armed with all this information, he went back to the reluctant chairman to see if there wasn't something more he could tell him, something he had neglected to tell him the first go-round. That was when Bertram gave up the surprising words Henry had used just the day before the accident: "I could kill him right now."

This was all Detective Sergeant Martin needed to hear. He wanted Henry to "go down," as he colorfully phrased it with his colleagues back at the station. In his mind it had turned into a full-blown murder investigation, and he was DB. This one professor had wanted to murder the other professor to keep him from exposing him as a letch and ruining his reputation. He had a motive and he had a weapon and he was caught red-handed. What else could you want? Detective Sergeant Martin was all for taking a closer look at Henry's Jeep. How hard was it to press the accelerator, and what would acceleration have looked like in that particular make over a short distance?

Fortunately cooler heads prevailed. The general consensus, after much discussion, was, first of all, that it was probably just a tragic freak accident; the classy old professor with the international reputation (as they now understood it) just did not strike them as a cold-blooded killer. But if it was something more than that, then everyone except Detective Sergeant Martin agreed they were looking at voluntary manslaughter, at the most. There were at least two mitigating factors. They all agreed that Malcolm had provoked Henry by trying to get him pushed out of the university. And there was Henry's health. There was a well-documented prior incident at a concert at Swarthmore. There was confirmation from his doctor about crippling arrhythmia. There was his self-report of an incident just before and during the accident.

So it was voluntary manslaughter in the end. The charge was brought because Detective Sergeant Martin insisted on it and they were afraid of what he might do if they refused. Henry's lawyer wanted him to fight it. As far as he was concerned, it was nothing more than an accident. Henry wasn't driving around looking for Malcolm that night and he certainly had no intention of running him over. Malcolm had simply appeared in front of him as he turned a corner in an empty parking lot. He didn't have time to react. Malcolm was there and he couldn't stop the car. Besides, he was having a heart attack. He could not control his body.

All the fight had gone out of Henry with this investigation, however. He had become the silent man with sad eyes. After all, he had killed a man—he for whom love and compassion and kindness were everything. As far as he was concerned, he deserved to be punished. Actually he wanted to die. When the prosecutor offered a sentence of three years, he told his lawyer to take it. He didn't want a trial. He didn't mind going to jail. His life was over anyway. He accepted the plea bargain and was sentenced by an openly reluctant judge who kept giving his lawyer dirty looks.

The last person who came to see him before they carted him off to the penitentiary was Gabrielle.

"I'm surprised you came," he said.

"How could I not come? I wanted to see you."

"Are you sure? I was under the impression you hated me."

"Hated you! Never. Why would you think that?"

"Oh, I don't know—because you refused to have anything to do with me? Because you wouldn't answer my calls? Because of those divorce papers you sent me?"

"Henry, if you only knew," she said, shaking her head.

"Knew what? Tell me. You better get it out now, before they toss me in jail. Who knows if I'll ever get out of there again."

"Don't be so morbid. It's only three years. They're sending you to the country club in Danbury. You'll still be a young man when you get out."

"Young! I'll be an old man of sixty-five who has lost everything. Including you."

"You can't lose me Henry," she said quietly. "You can never lose me."

Henry was shocked. This was the last thing he expected her to say. "I don't understand. "

"Don't you, after all these years? No, I guess you don't. You really don't understand me at all."

There was a long silence. Henry genuinely did not know what to say. Gabrielle seemed to be waiting for a reply, and when one did not seem forthcoming she sighed. "Well, I guess I should go."

Henry sat with his head down, looking at nothing in particular, bowed down and subdued, a wreck of his former self, a violinist in ruins. Then he looked up at her. "Would you mind very much if I told you something?"

"Of course not. What do you want to tell me?"

"I don't know quite how to say this, it's been so many years. I'm afraid you're going to think I'm taking advantage of the situation—or of you. I swear, that's not it at all."

"You know perfectly well I'm not going to think any such thing. What is it?"

"I just wanted to say—I love you. So much. I can't even tell you how much. I realize I'm just a wreck of an old man and you definitely don't need to hear this from me right now. You need to get on with your life. But it's how I feel. I just wanted to say it before I go and you never see me again."

Gabrielle got a look on her face and he did not know how to read that look. He had seen a lot of looks on her face in their thirty-five years together but never one quite like this. It looked like a mixture of anger and incredulity and something else, he wasn't sure what. He braced himself for what was coming—but then she began to sob.

"Do you really mean it?"

"Of course I mean it! Why would I say it if I didn't mean it?"

"I don't know—to make me feel better. Because you think I'm angry with you. To make me feel sorry for you."

"That's not it. That has nothing to do with it. I've been wanting to say this to you for a long time. I was just afraid to."

"Afraid! Why?"

"It just didn't seem right. It wasn't the kind of relationship we had. I didn't know. I'm so mixed up."

She shook her head. "Well, I'm going to let you in on a little secret, since you started it. I've loved you ever since the first time I saw you. I've loved you so much, I can't say—"

Henry was stunned. "Why didn't you ever tell me?"

"You said so yourself. It wasn't part of the bargain. I was afraid of scaring you away."

"Oh my God, after all these years. You really do love me?"

"Yes, Henry, I really do. Madly, deeply, and everything else. I just didn't know that you loved me."

"Amazing. Why couldn't we have said this before?"

"Well, we said it now. We said it now."

Their time was up. Henry looked at her again before they took him away. The expression on her face had changed. Gabrielle looked happy in spite of her tears. She was beautiful.

FINALE

IT WAS HALLOWEEN IN COLLEGE TOWN and fairly balmy for the last day in October under a huge orange harvest moon to boot and you know what that means—party!

There was quite a show going on and it was right there in the streets. There was President Obama and there was Lady Gaga and—we're just guessing—but it seemed there was a Julius Caesar and a Mark Twain and even Marcel Proust, who was asked a question in French but politely declined to answer.

On the corner of 3rd and Main there were three witches stirring a copper cauldron. "Double, double toil and trouble"—yes, they did the whole scene, on a loop, as it were, with occasional interpolations. Harry Potter stopped by to express his solidarity. "Go fly away," one of the witches told him, perhaps feeling that Harry was a bit of a hogger, or maybe just an arriviste.

It was early, so spirits were still high and students were not stumbling around yet or puking in the alleys but were either on their way to parties or on their way to Trick or Treat or to the most promising venues. There was the thump, thump of hip-hop in the air and there were crowds moving hither and fro and some were not even waiting to get inside but dancing in the streets.

Meanwhile off in a somewhat quieter corner of town a different kind of celebration was going on. Margie was eating dinner with Bea at a cozy restaurant. Margie had a salad and Bea had "broiled scrod" and they were working on a bottle of soft chardonnay.

"I still can't believe it happened," Margie was saying. "I mean, when does something like that ever happen at a place like this? A professor getting killed at the university? I know there was the shooting at Va Tech and all that, but this was professor-on-professor. So weird."

"Frankly, I have a hard time believing any of it," Bea said, pushing the fish around on her plate. "And this wasn't 'professor on professor.' It was just Malcolm acting stupid."

"I don't know—that's not what they're saying. I mean, they did convict him. So they must have thought something was going on."

"Of course something was going on. Something's always going on in this crazy department. But if any of what they're saying is true—and I don't believe anything I see in the press—then Malcolm must have pushed him into it. They're not telling the whole story. It's just not like him."

"I hope I didn't have something to do with it," Margie said with a self-conscious little laugh.

"What do you mean?"

"Well—I told him Malcolm got me pregnant."

"Malcolm got you pregnant?" Bea said wide-eyed.

"No, of course not! I've been on the pill since I was fifteen. No, I was just improvising. I didn't know what else to say, it just sort of popped out of my mouth. Actually I still can't believe I said it."

"Are you saying you think he deliberately ran over Malcolm because of that?"

"I don't know. I hope not! Anyway, you have no idea what that bastard did to me. Malcolm, I mean. He just about ruined my life. He made it sound like he was madly in love with me and we were going to be the greatest thing ever. You wouldn't believe some of the things he said to me. And then I came in one day and it was like I never existed. Wouldn't return my calls. Wouldn't even look at me."

"Poor Marianne. But I still don't understood why you had to drag Henry into it. He never did anything to hurt anybody."

"Well, I wouldn't have—not if I had known it would lead to this. Believe me, I'm just as shocked as you are. All I can think about is Malcolm's wife and kids. It's terrible."

"But then why did you go to him? Why Henry? Why couldn't you just leave him alone?"

"I heard he didn't like Malcolm. Actually I kind of did it on a whim. I was walking by his office one day and saw him in there and just waltzed right in. I figured he would just pat me on the head and send me on my way."

"But he didn't."

"No. We seemed to hit it off, strangely enough. I didn't even think he knew I existed. But to tell you the truth I think he had a kind of a thing for me."

"I know—you told me all about it. The park."

"Oh—that," Margie said with a laugh. "That was one weird day, let me tell you. I guess I felt kind of sorry for him. He was all emotional and everything. I didn't know whether to hug him or what to do. I think he wanted to hug *me*, but that wasn't really what I had in mind."

"Well, you know, even great men stumble," Bea said, trying to control her anger.

"Hey, speaking of which—what about that email?"

"What email?"

"Did you send an email to his wife—what's her name?"

"Gabrielle? No, I didn't send her any email."

"That's really weird. You didn't happen to tell anyone else about the park thing, did you? I mean about what he said to me?"

"Of course not!" Bea said turning red. "I would never do that."

"Well, the thing is somehow somebody found out about it. It was in the email. His actual words. I just can't imagine how they would have known."

"You were probably at a party drinking wine and let it slip and forgot about it."

Margie looked at her and laughed. "You know, you're probably right. That's probably exactly what happened. He confronted me about it, and I didn't know what to say."

"I hope you didn't tell him about me."

"No, he was pretty angry so I thought I better keep it to myself."

"Well, thank you very much. And I would appreciate it if you could continue keeping it to yourself."

"I would never tell him that. Besides, it's not like I'm ever going to see him again. What is it, ten years or something? He'll be lucky to get out of there alive."

Bea looked at her for a moment. "First of all, it's three years. And I very much doubt he'll even be in there that long. They don't keep people like Henry in prison."

For all the contempt Bea felt for her little friend at that moment, she was being very careful not to antagonize her. Margie scared her when she asked about the email. Yes, she was the one who sent it. Of course she sent it. She had been in love with Henry for thirty long years, madly in love, Adele H. in love. She went to all of his concerts she could get to, not just down in Manhattan but as far away as Newport and Boston. There was no other man for her, in fact no other man in the whole world, in her mind.

Then she heard a strange rumor. It seems Margie had been seen coming out of Henry's office. Bea knew her very well. Margie had attached herself to her when she first arrived at the school, dropping by on a regular basis or asking her to go out for a cup of coffee or a drink. Bea did not particularly care for Margie, but neither did she have the energy to resist these friendly overtures. She did not have many friends. Besides, it was flattering. Margie would sit there and listen to her talk about department history for hours on end with a rapt look on her face. Nobody else listened to her like that. And Margie was entertaining. She could be funny in a wicked way and had an inexhaustible store of gossip.

Margie did not attempt to conceal her sordid little fling with Malcolm. No, she bragged about it. As her confidante, Bea was disgusted and fascinated at the same time. She hated Malcolm because of the disrespectful way he treated her Henry. The thought of him falling for someone like Margie justified her low opinion of him. Then the perfectly predictable happened—he dumped her. Margie was crushed. Bea didn't think Margie had deep enough feelings to be crushed, but there were tears and more tears and they seemed real enough. The holidays came and Margie didn't even bother going home. She just stayed in her apartment and cried.

A distinct change came over her with the new year, a new resolve; and then she became a little scary. Sure, it was natural for grief to turn to anger, but anger revealed a side of Margie that Bea had neither seen nor suspected. There was no word for it, not in English anyway. People can be angry and still be integrated into the whole of society in the deepest parts of their being; still be trustworthy or predictable because of their allegiances. But this was not like that. Margie in her anger was someone without allegiances. She was not like Hotspur. There was no sense of kinship. There was just irrational anger and something like strangeness. It was uncomfortable to be around.

That's why Bea turned stone cold when she heard the rumor about Margie and Henry. What was the little psycho up to? There could be a perfectly innocent explanation for why she was seen coming out of Henry's office, but the smirking smile on the face of the person who shared this news suggested otherwise, and something in Bea concurred. Margie had a mystical power over men. It had been amusing to watch her use this power on Malcolm, the handsome clown—they deserved each other. But her power seemed considerably less amusing when it came to Henry. In a panic, Bea confronted him. Well, all right; it wasn't really a confrontation. But considering how much she was in love with him and how much she wanted to avoid offending him it was pretty close. She told herself it was for his own good. He did not know what he was getting into with that girl.

She thought Henry looked self-conscious during the brief conversation. Then he shocked her by telling her he was having dinner with Margie. That was how she found herself in a darkened window on the third floor. She felt compelled to watch them and see if it was true. Sure enough, they met in the parking lot, got into their cars, and drove off in the same direction. Bea felt so lonely standing there, never lonelier in her life. What was Henry thinking? After all these years of knowing her as a friend and seeing how she supported him and practically worshipped him—after all this to fall for a little upstart who had quite the reputation for sleeping around?

After that she started watching them more closely. A few weeks went by and nothing happened. She did not see any interaction between them in spite of practically attaching herself to Margie like Jimmy Stewart in *Vertigo*. She began to wonder if it was all her imagination, a bad dream. Henry could not possibly be interested in a little trollop like Margie. He was way above her. But then another Thursday night came and she found herself irresistibly drawn to the dark window again; where she saw the very thing she did not want to see. There they were, walking out of the building together just like the last time, getting into separate cars but driving off together.

They were headed toward the lake. Bea knew about a restaurant down there that Henry liked. It was on her way home, more or less, so she decided to drive by. She immediately spotted their two cars together in the sparse driveway and was filled with fury. She went in with half a mind to confront them but could not see them from the entryway and did not have the courage to go looking. She darted into the bar and found a corner booth to hide in. Four large glasses of wine later she was beginning to feel quite drunk and was startled to see them appear at the doorway. She knew she was in no condition to be seen by them. She would never be able to explain what she was doing there. She waited a couple of minutes to give them a chance to get away and then rushed to her car in the frigid winter night.

Bea became obsessive. A couple of weeks later she was sitting in the same spot on Thursday night when the whole thing repeated itself, almost as if they were trying to get caught. Again she went to the restaurant and again she saw their cars. She found another inconspicuous booth, this time in the dining area. She ordered some dinner in addition to her usual glass of wine but couldn't eat it; wasn't hungry. Henry and Margie were in the next room, at an open table near the window. She had seen them when she came in, and now she could hear their raised voices from time to time. They certainly seemed to be enjoying each other. It didn't sound like it was just about Alicia.

Finally she saw them heading out. She went to the vestibule to watch them through the frosty glass. Margie was doing a lot of hand signaling toward the road, pointing in the direction of her apartment. Was that where they were going? Bea couldn't believe it. She drove over there with her heart in her mouth and saw Henry's car parked in front. She found a spot with a good view. Henry did not come out right away. After a while she pulled out her smart phone and checked her messages. She texted some friends and family members, and they texted back; she checked Facebook; this was how she occupied herself while she waited, shivering in the cold. It was also how she got the infamous photo. Suddenly the two of them appeared at the door and walked out onto the stoop together. It was almost instinctive on Bea's part. She already had the phone in her hand; all she had to do was point and click.

She was surprised at the result. The image was dark but clear. There was enough light to see them. "Got you," she said in a state of heightened agitation. For several days she gloated over this electronic image and thought about ways she could use it to inflict pain on Margie, whom she had come to regard as a hated rival. Nothing came to mind, however. And then she began to feel rather ashamed of herself. What in the world was she doing, running around and spying on people? Especially Henry and her own "friend"? Besides, she didn't have any way of knowing what actually went on in the apartment. He'd only been in there an hour. Maybe it wasn't as bad as it looked.

She started to feel downright sheepish about the picture she had taken and deleted it from her phone. She had downloaded it to her iMac and had every intention of deleting it there too, but she never got around to it. Seemed like she was never at the computer when she had this thought. Then everything changed on the fateful April day when Margie delivered her news. Apparently Henry had told her that he loved her. And she laughed about it! Bea could have killed her. These were the words she had coveted from Henry all of her adult life, the words she had imagined him saying to her over and over again in various romantic settings. And here he was saying them to this worthless little vixen who didn't even care about him. She couldn't stand it!

Now she remembered the picture on her computer. She hadn't thought of it for a long time, but there it was, just waiting to be put to good use. She would send Gabrielle a little poison email and cause some mayhem on the home front. She never liked Gabrielle. She never felt she was good enough for Henry, with her haughty, cold demeanor. Gabrielle didn't love Henry the way she did. She could see it when they were together. Also Gabrielle had said some things about her in the past that she didn't appreciate. She had never forgotten and never been able to forgive her, or even tried very hard.

The other one she had in her sights was Margie, who didn't love her beloved Henry by her own account. The fact that he thought he was in love with her was astonishing, but Bea had the perfect remedy. She would free him from his mad delusion. With one little email she would not only chase Gabrielle away but also put an end to Henry's unseasonable infatuation. Originally she planned on sending it to Henry himself, but she realized this was not likely to be very effective. He would simply delete it. Also the idea of sending such a missive directly to him made her nervous, even though she was planning on using a library computer.

She realized she needed to send it to Gabrielle. She had never sent Gabrielle an email directly before, but she had her address on many messages from Henry and other friends. Bea wrote it down and went to the library and sent her poison email and settled down to watch the fireworks. It worked remarkably well. In the summer there was a rumor about Henry and Gabrielle—they were separated. As soon as she heard it she knew it was because of the email. She felt a twinge of guilt, but her overpowering feeling was giddiness. After all, Henry did not love Gabrielle anymore—if he had ever loved her. Not if he was chasing after Margie.

In any case it looked like he was finally going to be free. Gabrielle was out of the picture, and Margie was out of the picture too, having ruined his marriage and also having no interest in him. The blinders were off. Bea began to hope again. Her time would come. Henry wouldn't be in prison forever. Three years is not long. She would be there to pick up the pieces when he came home. It would give her a chance to show her devotion.

Margie laughed and Bea laughed and they had another glass of wine while costumed students danced outside in the streets. Margie had her revenge and Bea had her Henry, at least in her own mind.

They were both rather happy in their own way.

THE END

ABOUT THE AUTHOR

Jay Trott is an author of essays and fiction who lives in sunny Connecticut with his wife Beth. They have four children and love long walks and good company.

Made in the USA
Middletown, DE
23 June 2015